REAL DEAL

PIPER RAYNE

Cover design: MadHat Covers

Model: Marcus J.

Photographer: Wander Aguilar

Line Editor: Love N Books

Proof Reader: Shawna Gavas, Behind The Writer

About Real Deal

Red Flags...

Too loud.
Too clingy.
Too much make-up.

I could go on and on. The other guys in the Single Dad's Club would say I'm obsessed with finding them. But none of their kid's mothers is the epic fail that my daughter's is, so their opinions mean shit.

Caterina Santora has her own list of red flags...

She's too young.
She's my client's daughter.
She's my five-year old's camp counselor.

The fact that she doesn't remember me from six years before grates on me until I don't have it in me to leave her alone any longer. I *have* to have her. But our lives are opposites in every way. In no way compatible.

When we're together all the complications fade away and I have to keep reminding myself, even if I can *have* her— I can't *keep* her.

Real
DEAL

DEDICATION

To all the women that bring control freaks to their knees.

1

MARCUS

"**D**addy!" Lily screams from the top of the stairs. "I can't find my bracelet!"

I lay the knife down next to the butter, walk into the foyer and look up to the top of the stairs where my five-year-old daughter stands, practically in tears.

"It's on the bathroom counter, and if you'd brushed your teeth already, you would have seen it." I eye her with a skeptical smirk.

The little devil is going to have twenty cavities her next trip to the dentist.

Her face lights up with a 'you're the best daddy ever smile' and my heart melts, as it always does. And she knows it. She runs away from the banister and into the bathroom.

"Brush your teeth, Lily!" I call out after her.

I shake my head to myself as I head back to the kitchen. She's the only kid I know that insists on brushing her teeth before she eats. After years of arguing with her every morning, I decided it wasn't a battle worth fighting. If she wants to do it before breakfast, who am I to argue. But honestly, have you ever tasted fruit right after brushing your teeth? It's fucking nasty.

As I finish buttering her toast and placing it next to her eggs and fruit, she runs into the room and hops up onto the breakfast stool.

"Eggs." She sticks out her tongue.

"We're out of waffles," I say, moving from the fridge to the counter to pour her a glass of milk.

"Lily?" I question, inspecting her. "What is on your face?"

She looks up from sliding her fork around the eggs, the devil's gleam in her eyes. "Mallory's sister gave us some."

There's purple eyeshadow arched well over her eyebrows mixed with lines of hot pink. I mean, I'm not RuPaul, but I'm pretty sure lipstick isn't supposed to be on your eyelids.

"You aren't allowed to wear make-up." I take a sip of my coffee and set the mug back down on the counter. Moving to the sink, I wet a paper towel and round the counter toward Lily.

"No Daddy, I'm pretty," she whines swiveling her head to the side to dodge me.

"Lily, this is your first day of camp. How about we save this for Halloween?" I try again to clean her off, but she won't stop wiggling. "Or wait until you're at least twenty-one before you start wearing this crap," I add under my breath.

"Halloween!" she screeches like a thirteen-year-old teenager.

"How about we'll do dress-up this weekend?"

I glance at the clock. Five minutes before we need to leave if I'm going to be on time.

"Daddy, Mallory is wearing hers."

The whine that always seems to work on me seals the

deal. My little girl will attend her first day of camp looking like a clown. Wonderful.

Remember—pick your battles.

I release a breath and grab the brush off the counter. "Hair time and eat your eggs." I use the brush to point down at her plate.

She positions herself on the chair, familiar with the drill.

"Braids, pigtails or ponytail?"

Please no braids. Please no braids.

"Braids."

Of course. On an already stressful morning where we're running behind, she picks the one hairstyle that's the equivalent of asking me to crochet a blanket.

I split her long blonde hair into two and run the brush through each side. "Are you excited for camp?" I ask her, pleased to see that she's at least eating her fruit.

"I'm kinda scared."

I secure one side of her hair in a ponytail so I can concentrate on the braid for the other side. "Why are you nervous?" I peer over her shoulder to see her chomping on a piece of cantaloupe she's stabbed with her fork.

Lily is one of those happy children who's usually bouncing around in some joyful manner like in the Disney movies. That princess that lived up in a tower with long hair always reminds me of her. I forget her name. I've been forced to sit through so many princess movies that they all sort of run together in my mind.

"What if I don't know anyone?" Her voice is small and scared and it tugs at the heartstrings I didn't know I had until the first time I looked upon her angelic face when she was born.

"Don't be. You make friends easily." I stretch my fingers a

few times after finishing one braid and squeeze her shoulder before moving to the other side.

"Mallory will be there." Her voice doesn't hold the excitement it once did.

"That's good," I say absently as I struggle to secure the second braid in place. "Sometimes I wish I didn't give you my thick hair." With my hands on her shoulders now I lean over and kiss her cheek.

She turns her head and smiles at me. I return her smile and round the counter to pour my coffee in a travel mug since the time to get the caffeine flowing through my veins has passed.

"Daddy?" Lily says from behind me.

I peek over my shoulder so she knows I'm listening even as I pack her bag and get my own shit together.

"I got my thick hair from you?" she asks.

"Yeah," I say absent-mindedly, glancing at my phone on the counter to see we're now running three minutes late.

"What did I get from my mommy?" Her voice is low and unsure and despite my best efforts over the past few years I know she's worried about my reaction to her question.

I've always tried to instill a certain trust between Lily and me. We're all we have, and she needs to be secure with me, so, our conversations have always been open and honest, except for one topic—her mother.

My hands freeze on the zipper of her backpack. She's quiet and my assumption is her eyes are on me. Waiting for an answer.

I turn around and lean against the counter. I force my lips into a smile to let her know this is a topic we can discuss. Certain information will surely be off-limits, but if she wants to discuss her mom, I can toe the line.

"I would say you got her wild streak." I lean forward and squeeze her waist.

She giggles and her blue eyes light up for a moment before she pushes my hand away. "Wild streak?" she asks.

I rack my brain for the kid-friendly definition to clarify.

"Tell you what...I'll explain it in the car. We've gotta get going. You don't want to be late on your first day."

I let the make-up thing go, along with the fact she didn't touch her eggs—anything to escape this conversation.

She quickly secures her bracelet to her wrist. A bracelet that is more like a security blanket than a fashion symbol. Eventually, we're going to have to discuss her getting rid of it.

"Camp!" she yells, jumping from the stool and hoping over to me.

There's my Rapunzel.

See? I knew the name would come to me.

Leaving my driveway, I turn my pickup truck down Greyfalls Hill and head into downtown Climax Cove. I use the word downtown lightly.

Once known for being a small fishing town, it's grown into a heavily traveled destination during the summer. Our downtown shops and restaurants mixed with the harbor and marina is appealing to most city folk coming in from either Portland or San Francisco because they can make the trip here in less than a day. During the winter months, it's mostly just the townies, but it's a nice place for Lily to grow up and I like the feeling of safety and security a small town like this provides. Most of the people in Climax Cove know and love, Lily and I both.

"Hey, it's Miss Betty," Lily says excitedly from the back seat.

I glance to the side and see our town librarian walking along Main Street.

"Can I roll down the window?" Lily asks.

We're stopped at a streetlight, so I hit the button and the glass retreats into the door with a mechanical whir.

"Hi, Miss Betty. I'm going to camp!" Lily yells.

Betty stops at the corner and looks over. When she sees it's us, she steps a little closer and peeks into the truck.

"How fun! I do hope you'll find time to stop by the library this summer." She glances over at me with a reproachful expression.

So, I'm not much of a reader.

"I will," Lily says.

I glance in the rearview mirror to see Lily with a huge smile on her face, practically bouncing out of her booster seat with excitement.

"I sure hope so." Betty side eyes me again.

I get the point and make a mental note to get Lily in there at least once over the summer months.

"We have a summer reading incentive. Maybe you'd both like to be involved?" Betty asks.

"Oh yeah!" Lily exclaims.

Betty, who was my deceased dad's old girlfriend, smiles at me now. She knows she's got me.

"Bye, Betty," I say, the light turning green and giving me an out.

"Have fun at camp, Lily," she says and waves goodbye.

I roll up Lily's window as we pass through downtown before someone wrangles me into hosting the fish derby this fall.

"Can we go to the library tonight?" Lily asks.

"We'll see." My usual answer when I'm putting off something I don't want to commit to earns me a huff from the backseat.

Main Street is soon in my rearview mirror and I drive up into the hills. Fifteen minutes later, I turn my truck into the Camp Tall Pines entrance and we're swallowed up by rows of trees that shoot high in the sky.

We follow a line of pickup trucks down the dirt road, but I spot my friend's Mustang up ahead when we round a curve. Dane's the only moron that would buy a sports car to drive around the hills of Oregon. I've had to pull him out of a ditch more than twenty times since I moved here six years ago.

"Daddy!" Lily screeches and rolls down her window. "Look at all the kids." I glance in my mirror to see her gaze focused on the clusters of children and parents trying to find their way as I park the truck.

Camp Tall Pines is a camp for single parents. Lily will only attend during the day, but there is an overnight camp for kids coming from farther away. It was an option for Lily this year, but I'm not ready for that. Even if it's only fifteen minutes away.

I open my door to get Lily out and take in the scene.

Shit, there are a lot of kids, and I have no idea where the hell Lily is supposed to go.

My hand is on the handle of Lily's door when a fancy sports car grabs my attention. It's red and shiny and sticks out in this small town just like the blonde currently bent over digging through the trunk.

Damn, that ass. I shift my stance and wonder how one glimpse has made my dick jolt for the first time in a month. Well, without the help of Pornhub.

Climax Cove isn't exactly known for its beautiful single

women. Not to say there aren't any—there are—but they're all looking for something I can't give them. Marriage. My last serious relationship didn't work out so well after Lily's mother decided she'd rather party than be a mother and I'm not willing to jeopardize my little girl's heart again.

I can't pull my gaze from this woman's long legs. Or maybe it's the short shorts she's wearing. She shouldn't be able to wear those scraps of material around all the single dads. There's going to be a pissing match at our next meeting over who gets to ask out the new girl in town.

A bang on the truck window pulls me from my trance of imagining those long legs wrapped around my head and I look over to find Lily's shoulders slumped and her mouth hung open.

"Sorry," I say and open her door.

She jumps out of the truck and turns her attention to where I was looking. I take the opportunity to adjust myself.

The woman is now standing up, thank God, and she's propped a box on her hip as she shuts the trunk.

My gaze roams from her sneaker covered feet, up her long and tanned legs, past the too-short shorts, noticing the way her Camp Tall Pines blue t-shirt hugs her breasts and lastly, lands on her face.

"Shit," I murmur.

"Daddy!" Lily holds her hand out in the air. "That's a dollar."

My eyes focus in on the woman across the parking lot and I'd bet my house it's her.

Caterina Santora.

My client, Bill Santora's daughter. I haven't seen her in six years. Not since the time she hit on me. I wince remembering how harsh I was to her, but she was young, barely legal and 'no' wasn't in her vocabulary at the time. Still, I've remembered my cruel words more than once since then and regretted them. Especially after I had a daughter of my own.

"Daddy," Lily's voice pulls my focus back to her.

I dig my wallet out of my back pocket, finding a dollar and shoving it into her hand.

"Nice doing business with ya," she says and slides by me to the curb. "Let's go! I don't want to be the last one."

My eyes refuse to look away from the woman. If it is Caterina, she's definitely *all* woman now. A smile teases her lips as she passes a camper and his dad. Concentrating ahead, she rounds a car and she scans her surroundings. There. That dimple in her left cheek. It's her. It has to be her.

Her eyes find me and I smile, moving my hand up in a small wave, but she only returns the gesture with a polite smile. One that says, *I have no idea who the hell you are, but just in case I'm wrong, I'll smile.* Then she turns on her heel and heads in the other direction. Great, I probably freaked her out. I'm sure she thinks I'm some pervy stalker-type guy.

"Daddy!" Lily screams and my head snaps back to her.

"Sorry," I murmur, still processing what I think I saw.

"I don't want to be late," she says, walking ahead of me.

I look at the signs, trying to figure out which direction I'm supposed to go in, but I haven't a clue. There are parents wandering around everywhere with similar looks of bewildered frustration.

"Toby, get out of the car!" I hear to my right. My buddy, Dane is standing next to his Mustang trying to coax his son out into the sunshine. I turn Lily in that direction. If I'm going to be lost, might as well be with Dane. At least he'll keep things interesting.

2

"Put the iPad down!" Dane's voice booms through the dirt parking lot and the serene woods.

Not like he gives a shit. The word conformist is an antonym next to the word Dane.

He's dressed in athletic pants and a white t-shirt. I'm not sure the man owns anything other than jeans and workout gear and his stash of white t-shirts must overfill his drawers. He was my first friend in Climax Cove and he's a true good-time-guy. Hence why when he's behind the bar he owns—Happy Daze—he's in his element.

"Why is Uncle Dane so loud?" Lily places her fingers in her ears and shakes her head back and forth.

"Because he likes to be the center of attention," I say, watching him take the iPad from Toby's hands and toss it in the front seat. Then he proceeds to unbuckle his eight-year-old and hold the door open.

"Jeez, Dad, I was in the last two seconds of the game." Toby files out of the car and sends a death glare Dane's way.

"I asked you ten times." Dane slams the car door, and

Toby secures his backpack and walks through the small space between Dane's Mustang and an SUV.

"Hey, Uncle Marcus. Lily." He keeps his head down but is polite nonetheless.

"At least you haven't lost your manners," Dane says, stepping up onto the curb.

Lily follows Toby down the dirt path toward two guys with Camp Tall Pines t-shirts who are directing everyone to the path that takes them where they're supposed to be.

"Shitty ass morning." Dane rubs his temples. "Late night closing."

He snaps his fingers and points to me. "What about Dirty Harry?"

I stare over at him with an are-you-fucking-kidding-me look. Dane's been trying to change his bar name since I met him.

It's one of the many things we have in common—both our father's left us their business. Difference is, Dane's dad is still alive and is usually saddled to a bar stool Monday through Friday from open to six at night, telling Dane how to run the business.

"I like Happy Daze," I say, walking behind Lily and Toby.

"I like Happy Daze," he repeats, mimicking my tone.

I hit him in the shoulder and he pretends to lose balance.

"Want to talk about a shitty morning? Lily asked about her mom," I say, still trying to figure out how to get that line of questioning out of my daughter's inquisitive mind. I've dodged this bullet for years and I know this morning isn't the last of the questions to come from her.

"Did you tell her that you pray every night she doesn't turn bat shit crazy like her mom did?"

I glance over at Dane and find him smirking. I can't even

argue the point. My ex, Lily's mom has issues, but worse than that is the fact that she effectively abandoned Lily.

We stop near the benches of the outside auditorium and he shoves his hands in his pockets. All the parents and kids are filling into the bleacher-style sitting arrangement.

Looking at my watch, I wonder how much longer until I can start my day at the shop.

"Garrett!" Dane screams to our other friend who's perched in the top row closest to the edge like he can't wait to make his escape.

Garrett has an eleven-year-old daughter. All his complaining about his adolescent daughter makes me feel like Lily is perfect, but his situation also reminds me that the nightmare of adolescence isn't too far away. Sydney, his daughter, isn't even sitting near him.

"What's up Sexy Beast?" Dane asks, fist bumping him.

Garrett's blank stare says he's not amused with Dane's new nickname. I bump fists with Garrett and sit down. Lily and Toby sit in front of us, but soon, Toby's friends come by and he's chatting with them.

"Mallory!" Lily screeches and a bunch of parents turn their heads in our direction. Mallory and her mom turn around and smile. I give the obligatory wave. "Can I go down there?" Lily's up off her seat now, jumping up and down, braids bouncing around everywhere.

I check to see that Mallory's mom is still looking so I non-verbally ask her and she waves Lily down.

"Stop flirtin'," Dane says and elbows me.

I'm not sure I've ever met someone as cheerful in the morning as Dane.

"I'm not flirting," I deadpan.

He laughs and then elbows Garrett who shifts to the

side. "Yeah, Marcus and flirting can't be strung in the same sentence. Am I right?"

A few people look back at us as he peels with laughter at his own joke.

"How long is this going to take?" I ask Garrett, who's been sending his daughter here forever.

"Not long. Just an introduction and then they're off to the groups." Garrett's all business all the time. "I need it over with now though. My foreman just called and that log cabin on Cedar Circle is due for inspection."

I smile over at my friend. "That's fantastic, man. What is that, four this year?"

His lips turn up slightly, but never a full-on grin. Never from Garrett. "Yeah." He shrugs.

Garrett owns a small but successful company that builds log cabins. Some he's built especially for the families, others he owns and rents out to tourists during summers.

"You still workin' on the same boat?" Dane peers past Garrett, shooting me that annoying smirk.

"Boats and houses are two different things," I remind him for the millionth time since we met.

"Boats have to float, but houses have to stay upright. Same difference if you ask me." Dane runs his mouth, always happy to bust my balls.

I'm happy to return the favor. "Keep serving those shots of whiskey." I raise my eyebrows in challenge.

For once I shut him up, but only because a familiar deep voice is now talking over the intercom.

"I'm Victor Pearson, the Camp Tall Pines owner." Vic is a fellow member of the Single Dads Club and though we're friendly, I've never seen him in this environment. "Thank you all for joining us this year." All the kids cheer with their arms raised. Lily looks over her shoulder to me and I plaster on an excited smile for her benefit.

Her fingers run over her bead and thread bracelet. She's nervous.

Vic continues talking about how he started this camp as a single dad himself seventeen years ago and how his own daughter now works here as a camp counselor. He apologizes that she's not there for us to meet at the moment and explains that she's off seeing to a couple of final details before the campers split up into their groups. A few other employees walk up on the makeshift stage. All of them are new camp counselors and they're all young and appear eager to be here. They all seem cool, but I'm only concerned about one. The blonde from the parking lot that I now know for certain is Caterina Santora since Vic just introduced her.

So, she's *pretending* not to know who I am? Interesting.

A HALF HOUR LATER, Lily and I are following the directions to the group Lily has been assigned to.

"See you tonight?" Garrett asks, doing the man handshake thing we do.

"Yeah." I run my fingers through my hair, remembering that the library won't happen for Lily since I have the Single Dads Club meeting tonight.

"See you guys." Garrett turns and follows Sydney and her beehive of friends to the overnight camping area.

"Now don't go getting confused. You might have as much facial hair and be as big as them but the Grizzlies are not your family," Dane calls out, again, laughing at his own joke.

Garrett shakes his head and I'm sure that middle finger would be raised if there weren't so many kids around.

"I love poking the giant," he continues the jokes about Garrett's size.

He's big, that's irrefutable, but Dane acts like he's the comedian up on stage with how many Bigfoot jokes he tells at Garrett's expense.

We come to a fork in the road—literally—I don't mean that in a metaphorical sense. Toby's green group heads to the right and Lily's orange group veers left.

"I guess this is where we part." Dane places his hand over his heart. "Call me." He feigns sadness, clutching his white t-shirt, but as soon as we're a distance away, his contagious laugh bounces off the trees.

"Uncle Dane is funny," Lily says, clasping her small hand in mine.

"Yes, he is." I agree and squeeze her hand.

We walk a few steps in silence and I know she's nervous, but after her first day she'll have made a ton of friends and be fine.

"Daddy?" she asks.

"Yeah," I say, continuing down the path surrounded by large earthy green trees that block out the sunlight.

"What if no one likes me?"

Realizing that this is going to be a heavier talk than I anticipated, I stop us on the path.

Bending down, my gaze reaches hers and I can see how worried she is. I wonder why she's so self-conscious? Lily has always been eager to meet new kids and make new friends. She's never feared the unknown, which is something I'm sure she inherited from her mom. This side of Lily, the tentative side, is me.

"Everyone will love you," I assure her.

Her eyes cast down to that bracelet. When Lily was three, she had a blanket that she never went anywhere without. On the advice of some other dads in the Single Dads Club, I tried swapping it out with something else. I chose a bracelet. The ratty and worn bracelet now tied around her wrist, hanging on, literally, by a thread. Mistake number one thousand and thirteen I've made with Lily.

Her small head nods and she's still not looking at me.

"Hey now." I tilt her chin up with my finger. Usually my smile alone makes Lily giddy.

"Excuse me," a voice sounds from next to us.

Lily and I both look up and I can't stop my gaze from running over her body. Caterina is like a mirage that keeps appearing.

"Lily?" she asks and bends down to Lily's level. "I have a cool bird feeder craft for us to do. Do you want to join us?"

Lily inches closer and her hand stays securely fastened to mine.

"I'm sorry, she's not usually shy," I comment.

Cat barely grants me a fleeting look before concentrating back on Lily.

"Come on. I promise we'll have fun." She holds her hand out, but Lily doesn't take it.

"Can my dad come?" Lily asks and this time Cat's gaze meets my eyes.

Only for a brief second and then she turns away. I know I'm a little older than the guys she usually dates, but I've been told I'm easy on the eyes. This girl was shoving her naked breasts in my face six years ago and now she's acting like she doesn't have a clue who I am.

Something primal unleashes inside me, roaring to life. Maybe it's ego or maybe it has more to do with the spectacular woman Caterina has grown into, but I'm suddenly really fucking perturbed that she doesn't seem to remember me.

"Sure," Cat says in a small voice.

Her blonde hair is short and sassy now, unlike the long braid she had the first time I met her. I thought all girls hit puberty by eighteen, but she's developed more curves—her breasts straining her t-shirt and her shorts hugging the swell of her ass. As I'm busy checking Cat out, Lily takes her hand and the two stroll down the path toward a log cabin.

There's a few other counselors in the room with kids mostly Lily's age. I don't see Mallory anywhere and the thought that perhaps I should try to switch her into her group comes to mind. Maybe it would set her at ease.

But after a minute Cat gets her started on the craft and Lily is busy chatting with the boy across from her. She hasn't sought me out, so, I walk over to say good-bye.

"I'm going to go to work. I'll be back for you at the end of the day," I whisper in her ear.

"Bye, Daddy." She kisses my cheek and quickly turns to tell her new friend about her Uncle Dane and all the bad words he says.

Great. She'll teach all the kids the bad words during camp.

Unable to let the need to make Cat acknowledge our shared history go, I decide to approach her before I leave.

Her back is to me and she's talking to another one of the counselors. The redhead she's talking to notices me and her gaze flicks from Cat to me. Finally, Cat looks over her shoulder and turns to face me, though she takes a step back. She probably thinks I'm some pervert dad who keeps eye fucking her.

"Can I talk to you a sec?" I ask and she dries her hands with the paper towel she's holding and heads out the door, not bothering to wait for me.

"Caterina Santora?" I ask and she nods, her expression blank without an ounce of acknowledgment in them.

"Yes, you're Lily's dad." She places her hand out in front of me. "Nice to meet you. So she's not normally this shy?"

She really doesn't seem to recognize me at all. It's probably better that way anyway. At least I know she won't be taking my bad behavior out on my kid.

"No, that's rare. I'm guessing first-day jitters maybe."

She nods. "Well, she's adjusting well now. The camp has your number so I'll call you if there are any problems." She moves to step away and I know she probably has a million things to do, but I can't help trying to figure out if she really doesn't recognize me.

"Yeah, okay."

She smiles and starts walking back to the cabin.

"It's Marcus," I call out and her footsteps stop.

She slowly turns around and a small smile graces her lips.

"Marcus Kent," I give her my full name, waiting for some form of recognition.

"Nice to meet you, Mr. Kent. Don't worry. We'll take good care of Lily."

Then she disappears inside the cabin.

I get nothing more from her. Zip. Zilch. Nada. No hint of remembering who I am at all.

"Marcus!" Dane yells and I look up the hill to find him staring down at me, his phone in his hand.

I trudge back up the hill, my mind a jumbled mess. Dane's watching some video when I get up there.

"See these Ninja Warriors? I'm thinking of building Toby one."

"One what?" I ask while we make our way to the parking

lot. "An obstacle course?" Seriously, where does he come up with this shit?

"Yeah, to get him away from the electronics."

"A broken arm is a better option?" I shake my head to myself.

"Come on. My kid's more coordinated than that."

"Why don't you just have designated electronic time?" I ask, digging in my pocket for my keys.

As we approach the parking lot, I see that most of the moms are standing in clusters chatting. Garrett gave me a heads up about this. They're here for one of two reasons. They're gossiping or they're waiting for the single dads.

"You know I hate rules," Dane comments.

My eyes zoom in on a mom who definitely knows me, Krystal. She's a single mom of three boys. She's nice and all, but too up in everyone's business for me. Plus, Krystal's assertive and I'm not big on a woman who goes after what she wants like she's a lion hunting her dinner.

"Huh?" I ask, not remembering what we were talking about.

"Electronics. Forget it, I'll ask the group tonight." He waves me off.

The two of us pass by Krystal and her gang of other moms.

"Hey, Marcus," she coos. "Dane."

Dane stops and I want to grab his arm to keep him moving.

"Krystal, lookin' good." He steps closer to her and she narrows her eyes. "Oh, I'm sorry, you want Marcus, right?" He chuckles. "Marcus buddy, Krystal likes you," he pretends to whisper and the other moms all laugh. I've been warped back to the halls of junior high with his little display.

"I gotta get to the shop," I say. "Nice to see you all again."

I nod and walk off, Dane following behind me. I'm polite and courteous, but I'm sure they all think I'm an asshole because I'm not interested.

"Later!" Dane calls out, folding himself into his car.

As I put my key into the ignition, the red flashy sports car across the lot catches my eye. There's a Berkeley sticker in the back windshield.

She has to be messing with me. I can't possibly be that forgettable, can I?

3

CATERINA

As I hoisted a box to my hip and walked through the parking lot, I swore I saw Marcus Kent standing by a pickup truck, slack-jawed and staring. A frisson of embarrassment, anger and I'll begrudgingly admit, heat, zipped through my body.

It wasn't until after I decided to take the job at Camp Tall Pines and was searching for an apartment that I realized the nearest small town was Climax Cove. I knew then that there was a slight chance I might run into the man I had titled "biggest douchebag ever" in my mind. His shop is still the place to go and my dad still makes an annual trip up here to have Marcus check out his yacht.

After he humiliated me six years ago, I never much cared to see him again. Okay, that's a lie. The man had made a lasting impression on me that few since have been able to. But after I threw myself at him and he not only shut me down but did it in front of a kitchen full of people? There was a fat chance you'd find me pining away for him.

I didn't think he'd remember me. I'm more woman than girl now and I'm not that innocent adolescent who wanted him to take her virginity. That said virginity is long gone now. I can confidently say that I know what I want in a man and what I need in the bedroom. Six years is a long time and I've had enough experience to know.

"Marcus Kent," I say to myself, watching him trek up the hill.

Camp Tall Pines is for single parents only, hence another reason I thought I'd be safe from seeing him this summer. But he has a daughter.

Where is the mother?

My gaze shoots over to where the cutest little blonde haired girl chats it up with the other kids. I walk around the cabin to make sure my assistants aren't having any trouble helping the kids make their bird feeders. My eyes focus in on Lily who's doing more talking than working on her project.

"You doing okay, Lily?" I ask.

She looks over at me and smiles. "Yep," she says, turning to Ben across from her while at the same time her small fingers brush the bracelet on her right wrist.

The two continue talking about sports and I lean against the counter, listening to her go on and on about the Giants and how much better they are than the Dodgers. Being that I'm from San Francisco and my dad has box seats at AT&T Park I agree with her, but I can't help but wonder what this little girl knows about baseball.

Lily and Ben continue to argue as Marcus' eyes swim in my mind. They're still that sparkling blue—as bright and sparkling as the Mediterranean Sea with the sun glistening above. And it seems, they still bear the capacity to make me lose my train of thought for a second or two.

He's grown his hair out a little longer on top and I wonder what it would feel like to have my hands thread through the silky dark brown strands. To grip it, as his head's buried between my legs.

Shit. No. Nope. I'm not going there again.

You can humiliate me once, but not twice. Marcus Kent might be as appealing as a Popsicle on a scorching hot day, but he's on my shit list, if not at the very top. If only my va-jay-jay would get the message my mind is trying to send it.

"Cat," a small voice says next to me.

I bend down to meet Lily's gaze. Who of course, shares her daddy's blue eyes, just to make this summer even tougher.

"Yes, Lily," I say.

"I'm done," she says proudly, lifting her paper plate with the birdseed attached to all the Crisco.

"Oh, great. Let's lay it over here to dry and you can take it home tonight."

She follows me over to the table I placed in the corner for all the art projects to dry.

"Where do you think you'll hang it?" I ask her, and tap on the table where she should lay it out.

"In a tree." She lays it down gently and then arranges the plate exactly how she wants it.

I chuckle. "Yeah, is there a special tree you have in mind?"

She shrugs her shoulders. "My dad let me put up a bird feeder last year and then too many birds came and daddy said they were pooping too much. So, I'm gonna sneak it in the small one outside my bedroom window." She whispers the last part as though Marcus is right next to us.

"So, you live with your dad?" I ask, knowing I'm a terrible person for trying to dig information out of a five-year-old.

Her small eyes crinkle, contemplating my question. "I

can't live by myself," she says in a tone that implies 'duh' and walks away.

So, she does live with him. He's not just playing summer time dad. The question remains, where is the mother?

The bigger question is why do I care?

4

I park my truck next to my boat shop, Kent's Restoration. Originality was never my dad's strong suit, and the name of the shop I inherited shows that. My stomach growls so I head across the street to Double D's Diner, owned by Don and Debbie Verner.

They're lifers. Grew-up here, married right out of high school, and if I do the math I'm pretty sure their son, Don Jr., was the perfect wedding gift for Don. All in all, they're good people, even if their diner sounds like a strip joint.

The door chimes when I walk in. I glance around at the booths and the stools at the counter and sure enough, it's the same crew that's here every day. All the retirees in town sit around drinking their coffee and talking about the good ol' days.

"Marcus," Debbie says, grabbing a to-go cup and pouring coffee. She slides it across the worn counter to me.

"Thanks, Debbie."

"Running late again this morning?" she asks, placing a menu down in front of me.

I chuckle lightly. Is my daily struggle that noticeable to everyone around me?

"Yeah, first day of camp." I give a cursory glance to the menu and place my order with Debbie.

Don peeks his head out from the cut out in the wall behind the counter, where I'm hoping he's starting to cook my breakfast. I give a friendly wave to him and shoot the shit with Debbie for a few.

A short time later Don comes strolling over from the back, my breakfast in hand. "Tell Lily, to stop by, I have a sundae I need her to try out." He winks and hands my take-out container to his wife.

I pull out my wallet and pay Debbie. She looks down at the money, scoops it up and smiles.

"See you tomorrow," she says as I'm leaving.

"Probably," I remark.

When I duck into my shop, I place my food and coffee on my desk and stare at the boat I'm refinishing for a client out of Portland. He's expecting it in a few weeks and I'll be hard-pressed to finish on time.

I inhale my breakfast, then turn my attention to the boat again, sipping my coffee as I appraise what still needs doing in order for it to be perfect. My thoughts drift away from the boat in seconds.

Caterina Santora.

She's gorgeous and sexy and I want her underneath me for an hour or two so I can make sure she'll never forget me again.

Shit. I should be thankful she doesn't remember me because I was a Grade A asshole to her.

My phone rings on the table, but I've programmed a special ring for the camp into it and since that's not it, I ignore it, returning my thoughts back to the boat where they should be.

Where was I? I stand and walk over to my project, my hand trailing along the hardwood that still needs sanding, but my mind once again floats to Cat and I wonder how soft her skin is.

I think of the way her blonde hair swishes around when she turns her head. The way her crystal blue eyes looked down on Lily and appeared so caring. The contrary nature of her hips that are somehow slim, but still curvy.

Stop it. You're such a pervert. She's ten years younger than you.

My phone rings again, so, I walk through the shop and pick it up off my desk.

Dane.

I swipe the screen with my thumb. "Yeah."

"Who pissed in your oatmeal?"

"It's Cheerios," I say, unenthused.

"Like I don't know that. It's called being original."

"Not exactly original. You just changed the breakfast—"

"I used oatmeal because you're like an old man."

I plop down on the office chair. "Why'd you call?" I ask, taking a sip of my coffee.

"Any of your shows on tomorrow night? Family Feud? Jeopardy? Wheel of Fortune?" I blow out a large breath and he chuckles. "I thought maybe we could have dinner later than four o'clock."

"You have ten seconds to make your point or I'm hanging up."

I'm half-listening to the conversation because my gaze veers to the boat again. Something's just not right. Something's missing. I stand, still holding the phone to my ear.

"I'm serious about the dinner thing. How about six

thirty? That won't upset your REM sleep, right?" The clanking of glasses in the background tells me he's probably getting the bar ready to open for lunch.

"I'll make dinner. You and Toby come over. I can call Garrett," I say, inspecting the boat further, seeing the problem that needs immediate attention.

"How about just me, you and Nina and Polly?" he asks.

The line goes silent and we both know why.

Most people would say, "You should really start dating" or "I have this woman and I need a wingman for her friend." But Dane's making a point. A point he's been hellbent on needling me with for the past month. He thinks I need female companionship.

Well, I had female companionship when I was in Seattle for business a few months ago. It was easy and uncomplicated and we parted ways the next morning without exchanging phone numbers.

"What did I get from Mommy?" Lily's sweet voice from this morning echoes in my head. My little girl is too inquisitive to not keep asking about her mom now that it's on her mind. She needs security in her life and as she gets older, I know she'll need a female role model.

"So, whaddya say?"

"Okay."

"Okay?" His voice moves up an octave like he's an adolescent boy.

"Don't make a big deal about it," I grumble.

"Sweet. Let's meet here at six thirty. I'll take care of all the details. You just get yourself all pretty."

"Bye, Dane." I click the phone off and stuff it in my pocket.

"Jack!" I yell for my right-hand man.

He walks in from the side entrance to the second shop,

his coveralls dirty with grease from using his hands and not a rag.

Jack handles the mechanic area of the boats. I brought him on a few years ago when I realized Lily needed more stability—a set bedtime and bath time. After Jack came Clive and Wes. Between the four of us, I can usually get home at a decent hour every night and have dinner with my favorite girl.

"What?" As usual, his snippy attitude is present.

"Check out this right here," I point to the issue that's bothering me. "It's gotta be fixed before we can move on."

He nods, bending over to get a better look. "I'll take care of it once I finish with the Roberts boat."

He heads back to the other shop and I sit down at my computer. I swear I was going to pull up the schematics for a boat sitting in my shop, but somehow Caterina's Facebook page pops up on my screen.

Fuck if I know how that happened.

5

MARCUS

The next evening I'm sitting on top of the picnic table, my elbows resting on my knees, pretending to watch children wade in the shallow end of the lake. I'm definitely not staring at Lily's camp counselor's ass in a blue bikini that should be forbidden in front of children. Maybe it should be outlawed in front of virile, healthy males over the age of thirty like myself.

My phone rings in my pocket and surprise, surprise, it's Dane.

"Where are you?" I ask.

Camp was over ten minutes ago, but I guess the counselors got delayed, or maybe they wanted to torture the single dads by forcing us to witness fit, wet twenty-somethings play in the water.

Vic should be assigning them generic black one-piece swimsuits.

"I'm almost there. Can you grab Toby? You're on the emergency list." The roar of his muffler sounds through the phone.

"You're missing out." I chuckle.

Toby and all his friends start splashing all the camp counselors and suddenly it's my lucky day. I take back my earlier stance. White generic swimsuits would be much better than black.

"What's all that girly screaming?" he asks.

"It's swim day. And no prob. I'll grab Toby."

"Swim day? As in, counselors in swimsuits?"

"Maybe. Gotta go. There's a water fight." I chuckle, hanging up the phone.

I bet he'll be here in five minutes and if I'm lucky he'll miss all the action so I can razz him about it.

There are at least ten camp counselors currently standing in the water watching the children, and six of them are female. Victor doesn't understand the epidemic he's going to have on his hands. The longer I sit there, the more dads find their way down to the lake, thinking it's an everyday Thursday pickup. To their surprise, it's a teenage boy's wet dream. And maybe that teenage boy's dad's, too.

Caterina is laughing with another female counselor. I never noticed how her cheeks rise into two small apples when she smiles. Nor did I notice the way her hands cover her mouth to stifle a laugh or how she briefly touches the other person's arm when she's amused. Damn, I want to pull that reaction out of her.

But all I've gotten this week since camp started is a few polite smiles and 'hello Mr. Kent.' She hasn't acted as though I've seen more of her than what that bikini she's wearing reveals.

"What did I miss?" Dane sits down next to me, trying to catch his breath.

"What the hell do you do all day that you can't be here on time?"

He glances over to me and then concentrates ahead of

him. I can't blame him, we don't get views like this in Climax Cove very often.

"Does Victor realize he's giving every dad here beat off material for tonight?" Dane asks. A few of the dads milling about laugh, knowing it's true.

A small ball of anger begins brewing in my center. The idea of these dickheads thinking about what's under the blue bikini hugging Cat's tits gets under my skin. That beat off material is for me and only me.

"And to answer your question, I had to go down to the county for some paperwork."

Dane's been doing some heavy renovations to Happy Daze the last few years, expanding and making it a more family-friendly bar and grill during the day.

"Sorry, that sucks."

Both of us continue our conversation as we pretend to watch our children. I can multitask though. My gaze veers to Lily to make sure she's not drowning, but she's taken swimming lessons since she was one, so I don't have to worry too much.

"We can talk about that shit later." Dane waves me off. "Fuck, this is so not fair. How is my kid getting more action than I've seen this week?" He bites his fist, watching Toby and his friends pour a bucket of water over his camp counselor's head. Her yellow bikini doesn't exactly hide the fact the water might have been slightly chilly.

Lily looks away from the action in the lake, finds me sitting there, and smiles. "Why do I suddenly feel dirty?" I mumble to myself.

Lily runs from the lake and Caterina says something to one of the other counselors and follows Lily's path. Our eyes lock, but Cat is quick to shift her focus elsewhere.

"Daddy!" Lily screams and jumps into my arms, soaking me in the process.

"Hi, sweetie." I prop her on my knee.

"Hi, Uncle Dane," her sweet voice says.

I clear my throat so he'll turn his attention from the lake to my daughter. Dane turns to me, back to the lake, and then realizes why I'm clearing my throat.

"Hey, kiddo. Swim day, huh?" He leans back on his hands, focusing his attention on her.

"Come," she jumps down from my lap and grabs my hand.

"No, sweetie. I'll wait until you're done. Go have fun with your friends."

She smiles and runs off.

"Damn, a little warning, huh? I'm practically tucking my dick between my legs," Dane says and shifts in his seat.

"Um, how do you think I feel?"

"Who's the dickhead?" Dane asks, head nodding to the lake.

One of the male camp counselors approaches Cat. She laughs at his joke and shakes her head. I don't miss the way his eyes light up when she puts her hand on his forearm.

"Who?" I pretend my heart isn't skipping beats from the adrenaline coursing through my system. Just call me a fucking caveman.

"Yeah, okay. Your eyes have been glued to one counselor, in particular, this whole week."

"I have no idea what you're talking about." I glance around to make sure no other parents overheard us.

"Is that how you're gonna play it?" he asks, turning toward me and raising his eyebrows in question.

I say nothing, watching the dickhead pick up Caterina by

the waist, her squealing and him dropping her in the deeper part of the lake. She stands up and now she's dripping wet in her blue bikini that probably matches the color of my balls.

Once again, I swear her gaze veers over to me as she pushes her hands through her drenched hair. Before I can be certain, she's concentrating on the kids again. She claps her hands and announces swim time is over for her group.

"Man, your chick is a fun sponge," Dane says because Toby's camp counselor is still in a water battle with her kids.

I push off the picnic table to head over to pick up Lily and gather her things.

"Just makes your blue balls a helluva lot more painful than mine." I clap him on the shoulder and walk away.

"Don't forget, six thirty," he calls out.

I forgot about the date I agreed to for a second. With a sigh, I wave my hand up in the air to him.

"Good practice if you ever want to go after what you really want."

I shake my head and suppress the urge to give him the finger as I continue walking toward the lake.

While all the other parents make their way over to their kids, Cat approaches with a towel wrapped around her waist. Her shoulder length hair has a slight wave to it that I never noticed before.

"I'm so sorry we're running late," she apologizes. "They all did a great job listening today and deserved an award for their hard work. I'll walk them back to the cabin, they'll change and then be ready for pick up."

The group starts walking toward the cabin, and I pull out my phone to look like I have something to do since I just noticed Krystal heading toward the lake.

"Mr. Kent." Cat's voice sounds from nearby in that professional tone she uses with me.

I look up to find her at my side and the smell of coconut fills my nostrils. This must be some kind of test from up above I swear to God. There's not much more that could make Caterina Santora more tempting right now.

"What's up?" I ask trying to appear as nonchalant as possible and not at all like the guy in his mid-thirties checking her out.

"Do you mind walking with me for a moment?" she asks.

"Sure."

Is she going to fess up that she remembers me? Maybe she's going to ask me to keep it quiet. Like I would tell anyone.

She nods her head indicating the path that leads to the cabin.

I fall into step beside her, stuffing my hands in my pockets to try and stop the urge to pull that string around her neck.

"We had an assembly today," she says.

Obviously, she's all about business talk. "Oh, okay."

I glance to my side and see her twist her lips for second before continuing. "It was about family dynamics. The different types of families."

"Okaaay..."

"I don't want to overstep, but Lily started crying afterward." She meets my gaze for the first time.

"Crying?"

She nods. "Yes. She has a lot of questions concerning her mom."

I blow out a breath and rub the back of my neck as we walk. Other than the first day of camp, Lily hasn't asked me anything else about her mom. And like hell I'm going to bring up the topic of her mother when she's in prison.

"Her mother isn't in the picture," I comment, hoping to keep this conversation brief.

"I got that much from the talk I had with her, but Lily's pushing for more information."

I can't help but wonder who wants it—Lily or Caterina?

"She's not old enough to understand. Thanks for your concern, but I'll handle it."

She huffs and stops in the middle of the path before we catch up to some of the other parents. "By ignoring it?" Her tone is judgmental and she almost seems angry. I'm wondering why she thinks this is her business at all.

"Excuse me?" My own tone is firm and I'm trying to make it clear that she should back off, but I see the gleam in her eyes. She's going to push this issue.

"You can't just act like nothing is happening when a little girl wants to know if she has a mother or not." She plants her hands on her hips and glares at me.

I take a step back a little stunned and a whole lot pissed off at her reaction. That she thinks she knows anything about me and my daughter. "Maybe you should stick to popsicle sticks and glitter, Miss Santora."

Her chest heaves with a deep breath and her eyes widen. "I think you should be honest with your daughter, Mr. Kent."

My fist clenches in my pocket. "With all due respect, you're what twenty-four? What do you know about raising a child and more specifically about raising my daughter?"

Her gaze darts to a set of dads walking by us before she pins those fiery blue eyes back on me. It's as if she's a storm front and the energy in our little five-by-five area shifts. Gone are the summer skies and humidity and I prepare myself for an ice storm.

"I'm old enough to know that you're fooling yourself. If you continue lying to her, it'll only be harder when she's older."

I cross my arms over my chest. "Do you know this from personal experience?" I tilt my head in a condescending way as if I'm talking to a child myself.

Her parents are married. She was raised with the luxury of money, country clubs, opportunities and two parents who loved one another.

I step closer and she draws back, her back hitting the tree at the edge of the path.

When I glance both ways I see no one coming, so I inch forward until I can whisper in her ear. "Let's stick to things we know, all right, Miss Santora? You stick to art when it comes to my daughter and I'll worry about the stuff that matters."

The scent of coconut drifts my way again and with her body so close, even as pissed as I am, my dick twitches. Stepping back, I see that her face is flushed.

"We'll have to agree to disagree, Mr. Kent."

"I suppose we will."

A couple of kids run up the path from the cabin with their parents following behind, their curious gazes on us.

"Thank you for raising the issue, Miss Santora. I'll make sure to handle it," I say congenially, smiling to one of the mothers walking past.

Caterina quickly pulls herself together and nods. "Thank you, Mr. Kent."

I continue down the path to get my daughter, realizing that Cat is just as headstrong and temperamental as she was all those years ago. The only difference is that now those qualities make me want to pull her closer instead of pushing her away.

H e is such an asshole.
Asshole with a capital fucking A.
A Fucking Asshole.

An FA.

Stick to your popsicle sticks and glitter. Little does he know, I have five New York galleries inquiring about my work. Five. Mr. Fix it thinks I'm beneath him, but why should I be surprised? That's classic coming from him.

"Cat?" a voice pulls me from the vulgar rant on Marcus Kent in my head.

I look up from straightening up today's activities to find my roommates, Ava and Charlie, waiting by the cabin door. We carpool to work together and my gaze slips to the wall clock.

"Oh, I'm sorry, girls." I rush to finish so we can get home.

"We'll help." Charlie digs in right away, helping me place the crayons in the canisters while Ava closes the glue bottles and places them by the sink.

"Thanks. The swimming delayed us." I push Marcus Kent out of my head, but as usual, Charlie lets very little go.

"So, who's the fucking asshole?" she asks, scooping up crayon bins in her arms and meeting Ava over by the table.

"What?" I told the other two assistants no scissors and here I am picking up little pieces of paper some five-year-old found amusement in cutting for ten minutes.

"You were mumbling about some asshole," Ava says and plops down on a table.

"Ugh, just some dad who thinks he knows everything and I'm some little young girl he can push around."

They both still, Charlie pausing mid-step to look over at me.

I could be truthful with my roommates. Fill them in on what happened six years ago, but I've known them for a week and I don't really feel comfortable telling them about the most mortifying thing ever to happen to me. A moment I never even wrote in my journal in case my big sister, Tahlia, ever decided to be nosy. Plus, that way it was like it never happened. At least in my mind it didn't.

"Why are you guys staring at me?" I ask.

Charlie looks at Ava and a slow smile turns up the corner of her lips. "You just seem worked up."

The two of them go about putting the stuff away again.

"You'd be mad too if some dad told you to stick to Popsicle sticks and glitter."

Ava laughs, but Charlie elbows her in the ribs. "He said that?" Ava asks. "Who is it?"

I point to her. "Nope. I'm not saying. You guys know way too many people in this town."

She laughs. "You do realize most of the campers are from all over Oregon and California, not just Climax Cove. Plus, I only spent summers here with my dad and rarely went into town." We're finishing up so she sits on one of the shorter tables, examining some string she's holding in her hand with a look of disgust.

Ava's dad owns Camp Tall Pines, but it's a summer thing for them both. Victor just moved to Climax Cove after Ava started college, so she's rarely here now.

"Still. I'll probably say his name and then one of you'll tell me something about him."

"What are you scared we'll say?" Charlie asks. I'm most worried about what she'll have to say since she grew up in Climax Cove.

"Something nice that will make me second guess hating him and I need all my energy to loathe this man."

Ava drops what's in her hand and my eyes widen. I rush over to make sure it really is what I think it is.

Lily's bracelet. Shit. She left it.

If I were as stupid as Marcus Kent believes I am, I wouldn't know how important that bracelet is. How Lily rubs it occasionally, mostly when she's unsure or nervous about something. I tuck it into my pocket.

"Do you have a fondness for old string?" Ava's perfectly arched eyebrows scrunch together.

"It belongs to one of the girls in my group."

Ava hops off the table. "Well, someone should make her a new one. That thing probably has more germs than a rest area's bathroom floor." She shakes her head.

"I think it's really important to her," I say. But one thing I've figured out in the short time I've lived with her is that she's very blunt.

"Well, sanitize your hands before you come in the house. I'm not catching some petri dish disgusto disease." Her eyes roll to the back of her head and she does a full body shiver.

"You aren't the one who has it tucked in their pocket."

"Yeah, relax germaphobe." Charlie steps in, another girl

who isn't afraid to share her opinions. Truth be told, it's one of the things I like most about them.

Ava sticks her tongue out a Charlie and she laughs. "Anyway. He can't be as bad as some of the dads in my group." She frowns for a second before she continues. "One actually stripped off his t-shirt this afternoon and asked if I'd like to go for a dip with him."

I laugh and Charlie looks at her as though she has three heads. "Seriously?" Charlie asks.

Ava nods. "Yep."

"What did you say?" I ask, flipping the lights off in the cabin and shutting the door.

"I said that camp policy says I'm not allowed to be alone with little boys." She fans herself. "But he does have a nice set of abs. He had that whole V thing going on."

The three of us let out a tortured moan in unison because, hello—the V. Every girl knows the V is panty-scorching material. It makes smart girls do stupid things.

"And then he left?" Charlie asks.

She stares at me unblinking. "No. Then he played with his son and his friends. Then when I rounded all the boys up, he tried to sneak in as a camper." She shakes her head and rolls her eyes as the three of us continue along the path through the woods. "I feel bad for his son. I don't think he has a serious bone in his muscled, rock hard body." She hip checks me. "But enough about my annoying single daddy. Who's yours?"

"It doesn't really matter. My anger is dwindling." I shrug.

"Interesting," Charlie says and waggles her brows.

Surprisingly, they both let the topic go and we all climb into Charlie's Jeep. It's lime green and kind of obnoxious, but more comfortable for the three of us than my car.

She speeds out of the parking lot and Ava grabs the roll

bar in front of her. "How many times have I told you, this is not the Indy 500!" she screams at her, but Charlie shrugs her shoulders.

In the ten-minute trip from Camp Tall Pines to Climax Cove, Marcus Kent highjacks all my thoughts. As pissed off as he made me today, it seems I can't *not* want him. When he was only inches from pressing into my body, I was hyper-aware of the way his breath tickled my neck and the scent of cedar wafting off him from his work earlier in the day. I wanted his arms to cage me into the tree, his fingers to brush along my neck and pull the string of my bikini top so I'd be exposed to him.

But his words were like venom in my ear, poisoning all my lustful thoughts. I have to face the facts...Marcus still sees me as nothing but an annoying child.

7

I'd hoped swimming would tire Lily out, but she's bouncing around the bathroom while I shave talking about the kids in her camp group. How she was talking to someone and then met someone new and then someone else got upset. I'm not following because I'm barely listening. I'm still preoccupied and seething from Cat's earlier comments.

"Daddy?" she questions and I meet her gaze in the mirror.

Her eyes are wide and focused in on me, so I'm guessing I missed a question.

"Sorry, sweetheart, what did you say?" I ask.

"Do I have a mommy?" she asks.

I clench the shaving cream in my hand, forcing it out between my fingers. "Of course, you have a mommy."

"Then where is she? Beth said that her mommy lives across the world, but she FaceTimes her anytime she wants."

Well, FaceTime with your mom isn't so easy, sweetie.

I pat the shaving cream onto my face and rinse my hand

off before I reach for the razor on the counter. "Can we talk about this another time?"

I glance at her reflection in the mirror as I take my first swipe with the razor up my cheek. I watch the way her lips droop and how her gaze veers to the tiled bathroom floor and it feels like a fist just wrapped itself around my heart and squeezed.

Lily and I have always had an open relationship. I'm truthful about everything with her to the point that we've even had the conversation about how she should call her private area a vagina instead of a hoo-haw. Do you know how horribly painful it is to hear your sweet, innocent daughter say her vagina hurts? But when it comes to her mom, someone has to protect her and that's my job.

She's quiet for a while and the guilt burrows even further under my skin. I know it can't stay this way forever— me trying to protect her from the truth. Truth is, I understand Caterina's point even if it really is none of her concern. She's a camp counselor, not a child psychologist.

"So, guess what?" I try to lighten the mood a bit.

Lily doesn't answer.

"Ashley is coming over tonight," I say, knowing she enjoys playing with Ashley while she's watching her.

"Where are you going?"

Instead of the excitement I assumed I'd get, I get a snappish question with narrowed eyes. Women. Even at five, they're all the same.

"I'm going out with Uncle Dane."

"On a date?" she asks and I wonder how she even knows what that is. Lily has never seen me with a woman and any extracurriculars I did have over the years were done well away from my everyday life with her.

"Where did you learn that word?" I ask.

A small smile graces her lips. "Toby told me Uncle Dane goes on a lot of dates."

That man could use a lesson or two in discretion.

"What does Toby think about that?" I ask, running the razor down my other cheek.

She shrugs. "He just asked if you went on dates."

"And what did you say?" I turn on the faucet to rinse the razor.

"I asked what a date was."

Good girl.

I glance at her as I bring the razor to my chin. She's looking at me waiting for an answer. "Oh...a date is when two people go to dinner or a movie."

"So, are you going on a date with Uncle Dane?" Her big blue eyes stare up at me innocently waiting for an answer.

I let the sound of the tap fill the room for a moment while I contemplate my options.

I nod. "Yes, I'm going on a date with Uncle Dane."

"Can I go on a date with Toby?" She jumps up and down clapping her hands. "We can double date," she squeals.

"You know what double date means?"

She giggles at my furrowed brow. "Toby says that's when four people are there. Come on, Dad."

I chuckle. "I promise another time." I ruffle her blonde locks, but again her eyes focus on the floor and her bottom lip droops.

No one can make you feel like a bigger failure than your own children.

My phone rings from where it sits on the counter and I see Dane's name flashing on the screen. My thumb hovers over the accept button. Lily's already asking way too many questions. I click ignore.

While I finish up shaving, Lily leaves the bathroom, her

feet dragging, her chin to her chest, arms swinging side to side in a dramatic fashion.

As I finish up, I replay the conversation with Caterina through my head. Maybe I shouldn't have come down so hard on her, but damn. Lily's mother is none of her business.

My phone rings again and I press the button on speaker now that Lily isn't here. "You're becoming like a nagging wife."

Dane's deep chuckle rings over the line. "Don't be wearing jeans and a baggy shirt tonight. You need to show off those guns if you wanna get some."

I roll my eyes. "Thanks for the tip but I can dress myself."

"Well, I know it's been awhile. Figured you could use my help."

"I don't."

I'm starting to regret saying yes to this already.

"Hey now, don't show up tonight with this pissy attitude. You'll never get laid." I hear the clinking of glasses behind me.

I should tell him that I have no plans on getting laid, but I have a feeling that would only make this phone call more painful.

"Dane. You're toeing the line between annoying and asshole. Tread carefully."

He laughs again. "Okay, okay, but get all prettied up will ya?"

"Bye, Dane."

"Six thirty at Breakers."

"I'm hanging up now." I hit the little red button that delivers blissful silence once again.

As soon as I've wiped my face with a towel, the doorbell

rings. Lily's footsteps barrel to the door, but I run out and catch her before she gets there.

"Dad, I can answer the door." She turns the knob, but I place my hand on the wood door to stop her.

"Lily, you never open this door without me, do you understand?" I stare down at her.

She sighs and nods. "Okay."

"I'm serious. Never by yourself."

She nods again. "Okay, Daddy." She opens the door and there's Ashley with a bag packed full of stuff to keep Lily busy.

"Hi, Mr. Kent," she says, her cheeks flushing pink.

It's then that I realize, I'm shirtless. Great.

"I'm going to go finish getting ready, Lily," I say, focusing my attention on her. "Listen to Ashley, okay?"

She doesn't bother answering, instead grabbing Ashley's hand, pulling her into the family room.

"I should be out of here in about a half hour. I left some money for pizza on the kitchen counter," I call after them.

"Thank you, Mr. Kent." The two of them disappear around the corner.

I shake my head and head into my bedroom to decide what I'm wearing. I pull a few shirts out one at a time, decide they're not right and put them back. Eventually my mind drifts to how appealing Cat looked in that scrap of fabric she calls a swimsuit. Despite my best efforts, I can't get the image from my mind and my cock twitches in my pants.

Damn it. I'm going to need to take care of this if I stand any chance of not being distracted tonight. I lock the door of my bedroom and quickly head to the ensuite and run the shower for the second time this evening.

Once I'm under the cascade of water in the shower,

visions of Caterina float into my mind and my fist wraps around my cock. I pump, thinking about that blue bikini. The way her tits look fuller than they did when she was younger, how they strained against the thin fabric, begging for attention.

While I imagine exactly what I would've done to her if we were alone and she wasn't a decade younger *and* my daughter's camp counselor, I squeeze the head of my cock and groan.

I cage her up against a tree and the way her breath hitches tells me she wants this as much as I do. As I inch closer to her, goose bumps prick her skin and her chest heaves as if she can't take in enough air.

"Mr. Kent," she's trying to use that proper tone she always does with me, but instead it comes out breathy and wanting. It practically begs for me to do what I want to her, to control both her actions and her reactions, and for a man like me, there is no bigger turn-on.

I continue pumping my stiff dick and use my other hand to cup my balls and squeeze, eliciting another low groan from my throat.

"Call me, Marcus," I tell her. I eye the string of the bikini dangling from where it's tied at her neck and twirl it around my finger, letting her know that I'm going to give her exactly what she wants. Eventually.

I take a moment to let her feel the need she has for me. Let it settle in until she's standing there with eyes full of lust, squirming and pressing her thighs together to try and relieve the pressure building in her center. Her breasts rise and fall with her heavy breaths, the stiff rigid peaks begging for attention.

There's no nasty words now. No professional barrier separating the two of us.

"You do remember me, don't you?" I ask and her teeth bite down on her plump lower lip.

She nods, admitting the truth without words.

"Do you want me to pull this string, Caterina?" My voice is low and seductive.

She inhales sharply. "Yes," she practically whispers.

I tug on the string, and it loosens just a bit.

"Please," she begs.

My fist tightens around my dick and I pump and pump, twisting my palm at the head the way I like it.

"What do you want me to do to you, Caterina?" I ask.

Her head falls back against the tree and her eyes drift closed. I slide my hand down past the curve of her waist until it lands on her hip. My thumb dips under the edge of her bikini bottom and she sucks in another breath, her stomach indenting. I want to know what she tastes like and have her begging for release under my tongue.

My hand plants on the tile wall of my shower and my head hangs down as the water pelts my back and my fist pumps harder.

"I want you, Marcus," she practically moans and I lick up her neck as my finger tugs on the string again. A reward for her calling me by my name.

The fabric falls away from her tits and she's bared to me. My mouth waters at the thought of taking her nipples into my mouth and finding out what I need to do to make her breathless.

"Let's take this inside the cabin."

I reach down under her ass and pick her up. She wraps her legs around my torso and I swear I can feel the heat between her legs as her center presses against me. Once inside the cabin, I lay her down on the first table I see, pushing her legs apart.

"I'm going to make you come with my tongue," I say. She

arches her back as though the idea alone makes her squirm. "And then I'm going to come when I taste your release."

Hooking my fingers on either side of her bottoms, I drag them down her legs and drop them to the floor. Her blue eyes lock with mine as I grab her by the hips and drag her ass to the edge of the table then drop to my knees.

"Please...now."

My head nestles between her legs and I unbutton and unzip my pants, pulling out and fisting my cock as I enjoy my first taste of Caterina Santora. She's unbelievably sweet. I could stay here for hours especially if she continues whimpering those fuck-me noises.

I suck her clit into my mouth and fist my dick tighter and faster. Alternating between fucking her with my tongue and sucking on her clit it's only minutes until she's a panting, needy mess.

She tries to press her thighs together and I know she's close. Her responsiveness makes my rock-hard cock even stiffer to the point that it's almost painful.

I pin her with a stare and shake my head between her legs, my teeth lightly scraping her clit. She takes the order as it was intended and lets her legs drop back to the side.

I'd remove my hand from my dick and force her to stay open to me, but the pressure in my dick is building to heights I'm not sure even I can hold off.

Her fingers weave through my hair, and she pulls my head into her sweet pussy. Her taste and scent intoxicate me, and as her fingernails scrape through my hair and her hips rise off the table I know I could never get enough of this.

"Marcus," she sighs, "I'm going to come."

And it's enough. A hot stream of cum shoots from my dick.

Caterina's pussy pulses against my mouth a few times before her hand disappears from my head and her hips fall to the table.

The hot water chills to a lukewarm and I'm back in my shower. The realization that it was all a daydream leaving me feeling disappointed and slightly depraved.

No, she's not an eighteen-year-old girl anymore—she's all woman. Still, Cat equals complications, and I've strived to give Lily a secure, stable, drama-free life because at some point when she finds out about her mother, she's going to need that to be the foundation holding her up.

Regardless, just the thought of Cat does something to me even if it shouldn't. Even if I'm hell bent on stopping it, it's starting to feel like I don't have any say in the matter.

8

I walk into Breakers twenty-five minutes after exploding into my hand from visualizing a woman that is *not* the one I'm about to have dinner with. I haven't come like that in months, maybe years.

Damn it. Caterina Santora is the last person I should be thinking of sprawled on a craft table in my own daughter's camp, spread-eagle waiting for my mouth. If her father, Bill, ever found out I had one sexual thought about his daughter, he'd do more than pull his business from me. He seems like the kind of man who has Italian connections he keeps only for the people that really screw him over. Fucking around with his youngest daughter for the summer would be at the top of the list of ways to piss him off. I'm sure of it.

Breakers is on the water right next to the marina. It's decorated like a typical seafood restaurant, with caught fish mounted on wooden planks hung from the ceiling in fisherman nets. It's a popular place because of their sea to table fare. What's caught that day is what they serve. There's other fish they get from suppliers, but every day you can find at least one dish that is freshly caught and in limited supply.

"Hey, Marcus," the hostess, Tammi, greets me. She doesn't bother grabbing the crayons and children's menu, which means Dane beat me here.

Of course, he beat me—I trolled the apartment complexes of Climax Cove looking for a red sports car. Why? I still don't know. Not like I was about to go up and ring the doorbell of the devil in a blue bikini.

Tammi smiles, sliding her red hair off her shoulder. She's the owner's daughter and she's a nice woman, but her father threatens to castrate any male that tries anything with her with his meat cleaver. Don't need that drama in my life, that's for sure.

She isn't my type anyways. She's attractive, yes, but she does this thing when she tells a story and constantly repeats the word 'like'. We aren't in Los Angeles nor are we in the nineteen eighties during the valley girl era.

Yeah, my buddies at the Single Dads Club say I find asinine stuff wrong with women. So, what? I don't need to settle for someone who is going to annoy me every day of my life and any decisions I make affect my daughter.

"Dane here?" I ask.

Her lips spread into a bigger smile and she nods. "He's in the back room." She points to the room that has fewer tables but windows on three sides so you can view the sunset. Dane's laying it on thick tonight. He must really want in this girl's pants.

"Thanks, Tammi."

I wind my way through the tables, waving hello to the townies who have become mine and Lily's family. My feet stop when I'm in the archway to the back room. Dane sits at the table beside a brunette while a woman with darker hair sits across from them. Each of them have their phones out and they're showing each other their screens, laughing.

Fucking great. The faster I sit down, the faster it's over.

Dane catches me approaching the table and stands up. He does the whole raising of eyebrows discreetly side-glancing to my date. My eyes veer to her overly toothy smile and back to him. Even if she were the latest Victoria Secret model, I wouldn't be smiling like the goon he is. She doesn't have shiny blonde hair, or eyes as blue as the ocean, or perfectly molded hips I know are made for my hands.

Jesus. Get her out of your head.

Dane stands alongside me and both women's eyes are open wide, their over-whitened teeth gleaming. I wonder if they could be our flashlights if we lost power?

He pats me on the back. "This is Marcus." Dane slaps me again and I look at him from the corner of my eye. "This is Nina." He points to his date who smiles, never holding her hand out to me. Then he puts both of his hands on my shoulders turning me to face my date, as though he has some sort of surprise waiting for me. "This is Polly."

She holds her hand out to me, but when I take it and start shaking, she pulls my arm toward her and I stumble into the chair. Once I'm in the chair still trying to figure out what just happened, she kisses both my cheeks.

"Sorry, I just came back from Paris. Have you ever been? Oh my gosh, I could go on and on about the Louvre or the Eiffel Tower. After Paris, we took the train down to Italy. Oh, don't go getting all jealous, I went with a friend of mine from high school. Another woman, not a man." Her brown eyes flare for a moment as she gives me the once over. "I took Italian in college, but I never really used it, so I was a little rusty, but I surprised the waiters and waitresses by doing my best with their language."

Good God, Dane has set me up on a date with himself.

"Hey, are you on Snapchat? We should totally be friends

on there." She grabs her phone from the table and I glance at Dane, my one eyebrow cocked.

He's laughing to himself while he swings his arm around his date's shoulders. His *quiet* date. I think there was a mix-up in the who-is-whose type department.

"Pull out your phone, silly." Polly sets her phone back on the table and proceeds to lean overtop of me, patting my pockets for it.

I slide the chair back, part panic, part horror, at the same time as the waitress, Heather, comes over. She's Tammi's youngest sister and up until now, I didn't realize she'd started working here.

She takes in the scene in front of her. "Mr. Kent. Mr. Murray." She greets both of us, and her presence at least slows Polly's hands before she starts cupping my balls. I was not expecting a random prison pat down with dinner.

"Hey, Heather." I fidget to push my chair out and stand. Thankfully, Polly straightens up and sits back in her chair. "I'll have a Rusty Nail." I look to the table, where Dane's choking back a laugh. I'm glad one of us finds this so fucking amusing. "I'll be right back," I say to Polly, who looks like she wants me to be on the menu after feeling me up.

"Don't be too long, we were just getting to know one another," she responds in a syrupy sweet voice.

I smile politely and then lean into Heather. "Make it a double."

She nods, biting her lip to keep from laughing. "Sure thing, Mr. Kent."

I leave the back room, figuring I'll use my escape to call Ashley and make sure everything with Lily is good. Tonight, was a horrible idea. Why did I agree to this damn date? It's a waste of time. Time that I should be spending with Lily.

I pull my phone out of my pocket and catch a glimpse of Garrett sitting at the bar, drinking a beer. Maybe he can trade places with me. He could use some female companionship just as much as I could.

I walk over to where he sits. "Trade places with me," I beg, sitting down on a stool next to him.

"Tonight's the date thing?" he asks, sipping his beer.

"Yeah, and she practically makes Dane look like a mute. Oh, and she felt my dick up looking for my phone so we could be Snapchat friends."

"Snapchat?" Garrett asks, his forehead creasing.

"Yeah, you know that app?"

"You really have that shit on your phone?" The judgment in his voice is clear. Garrett doesn't have any use for frivolous things including the latest social media apps. If it weren't for his business, I bet he wouldn't even have a cell phone.

"Hell no. Dane does though."

He chuckles. "Of course, he does." He lets a deep sigh escape and his shoulders sag. "Sydney wants to get it on her phone, but I told her no until I screw around with it and see what it's all about. Make sure it's safe and all that shit, but I don't even know where to start." This might be the first time Garrett doesn't seem completely sure of himself. Christ. Tween girl shit is real and I'm terrified for myself just seeing him navigate this foreign world that will be my life in a short number of years.

"Yeah, I should probably check it out too, but who wants me to Snapchat how I design and build a fucking boat?"

Tammi brings over his bag of food, placing it on the bar top and Garrett tosses back the last of his beer. "That's nineteen, twenty-three," she says and Garrett pulls money from his pocket.

"That's all for you?" I ask.

He nods. "With Syd at camp, I'm not into the whole cooking for one thing. Not that I was some gourmet chef when she was home." He takes the bag and tucks his wallet back in his pocket.

"Seriously, man. I'll buy your dinner, plus I'll offer up my kidney should anything ever happen on those tall ladders you're climbing all the time."

The thought of going back into that room is as terrifying as if I were in an episode of one of those paranormal haunted house shows I watch alone at night. The reminder of how I'm always alone at night surfing channels after Lily is asleep brings to the forefront why I agreed to go on this date tonight. Maybe I do need this date. Maybe Dane is right. The problem is Dane and right aren't usually in a sentence together.

"You know I don't date." He pats me on the shoulder and I think I glimpse a teasing smile underneath his beard. I'm sure he's enjoying seeing me squirming.

"Yeah, yeah. One day you will, but go have a lonely dinner by yourself. The least you could do is call me in ten minutes and pretend you're the babysitter." I take a step backward to head back to the table.

"I'm sure there's an app to do that, right?" He raises both his eyebrows in a smug way then he's out the door and Tammi shifts her gaze to the back room before returning to me.

I hold my hand up in the air. "I'm going, I'm going."

She laughs.

Polly's laugh is about as loud as her make-up and hair. I hear her cackle before I enter the room. There's Dane, Nina and Polly all with their phones out again. Someone needs to mention that they're not thirteen and should be capable of having a conversation that doesn't have to be posted on social media.

"Finally," Dane whines and I want to take the napkin I'm placing over my lap and throw it at his face.

He got me into this mess and he needs to get me out.

"We missed you," Polly coos next to me, swinging her arm through mine. If she ever asks me why she's still single, I'm sure I can give her a few ideas.

I give her a polite smile, biting back the harsh words that burn like venom on my lips.

"Did you guys order?" I ask.

"Just appetizers," Nina comments. Her voice is soft and sweet, so unlike her obnoxious friend.

"I saw on the board when I got here that oysters are the special tonight," I say.

My right hand goes to my drink, which means Polly's arm falls off and lays limp on the arm of my chair. Bringing my drink to my mouth, the ice clinks to the glass and I swallow down a hefty amount.

"Oysters," Polly raises her eyebrows a few times.

Dane points to her. "I know what you're thinking."

Polly licks her lips and Dane laughs. Nina's busy fiddling with her phone.

"I love this unspoken connection between us," Polly says to Dane. "It's like we're one and the same." Her eyes light up with a flirtatious gleam and this time Nina rolls her eyes. I'm guessing this must happen a lot.

Heather comes back over and places the appetizers down on the table and asks us if we're ready to order. Each of us orders a meal and I'm the only one who gets the oysters. I contemplated not getting them because I don't want to throw a wrong signal Polly's way, but if I have to endure this horrific evening, I'm at least eating what I want.

"So, you said your Snapchat username is Pollyanna?" Dane asks with his thumbs poised overtop of his phone.

Nina busies herself eating a salad and Polly nods enthusiastically while chewing on a coconut shrimp.

"Okay, I found you." Dane clicks a few buttons and places his phone down, granting some attention to his lonesome date.

"Do you have Snapchat?" Polly directs the question to me again and not for the first time I'm wondering why I'm even here.

"I don't have much time, what with my five-year-old daughter."

Did Dane tell her about Lily or not?

She leans back for a second and I get my answer. Dane told her nothing about Lily. If I'm lucky she's one of those women who doesn't want to deal with the drama of a baby daddy.

"Oh, you're a weekend dad?" she asks, picking up her fork.

Sweet, for once the kid thing worked the way I wanted it to.

"No, I'm a full-time dad."

My gaze catches Dane's across the table and a sly smile crosses his lips, knowing why I just let the single dad tidbit out of the bag.

At our single dads' meetings, it's a consensus never to tell a woman until you're serious. A single dad gets one of two reactions to the news. There's the gushing and asking for pictures because they think we're looking for a mother for our child. Or there's the reaction like Polly's. She doesn't really know what to do, how to react. I've thrown her off kilter, which means she's not ready for a kid.

"Can I see a picture?" She leans closer and it feels like a

knife jabbing my stomach. I thought for sure I pegged her right.

I glance across the table and there's Dane's sly grin spreading wider.

Fuck him.

"Heather," I announce a little too eagerly and she eyes me while placing the tray of food next to the table.

Thank God for the distraction.

We each eat our meal, the conversation moving to Nina and Polly's nearby town of Wet Rock and how most of the downtown is starting to close. The town's been on a decline the last few years and they haven't gotten a lot of younger people to take over the businesses. So, as the older generation retires, there's no one to keep the businesses going. As much as Polly annoys the shit out of me, I can't help feeling for them. It's something that could've happened to Climax Cove if I hadn't have taken over my dad's company and if Dane didn't take over Happy Daze.

My stomach growls as I look down at the slippery oysters sitting on their shells. I plop some cocktail sauce and horseradish on top and my fingers are around the rough shell bringing it to my lips. At least I'll enjoy this tonight.

Flash.

My eyes blink a few times and then Polly's phone is in my face.

"Our first meeting," she's practically bouncing up and down on the chair like an overexcited toddler who got to skip dinner and move straight to the ice cream.

My hands leave the shell and I wipe them on the napkin that rests on my lap as I take the phone from her. It's us. Well, her smiling face but me on the other hand, I have one of my eyes closed and my lips are pressed in a tight line. I look like an asshole in the picture, but that's not what bothers me.

What has me wanting to make like a banana and split is the fact that there are stickers or some shit over our faces. On the bottom of the picture it says, 'Just Married' with a bouquet of flowers. She's got some veil on top of her head and I have a bow tie.

"We can show this on the big day to prove that we knew immediately where this was leading," she whispers in my ear.

My hand moves for my Rusty Nail, finding the glass empty except for a few waterlogged drops mixed in with the ice cubes. I grab Dane's beer and he tilts his head but asks no questions.

He should be lucky I'm still here. If this was his date and she was about to post some picture of them getting married, he'd have jumped off the balcony and into the Pacific never to be heard from again.

I cough, and chug down the rest of his beer, saying nothing and making a mental note to find a way to return the favor back to Dane. My revenge will be sweet.

I unbutton my shorts and strip down to take a shower after the long day at camp. One thing about being outside all day is the amount of dirt embedded into your skin when you leave. My mom thought I was crazy when I told her I was going to be a camp counselor for the summer.

"Oh, Cat, you'll be outside all day. If you want to be around kids why don't you be a nanny?"

A nanny.

So, I could transport kids to tennis, swim, horseback riding and any other extracurricular activity? No thanks. If that were the case, I'd be the nanny for my older sister, Tahlia.

No, I wanted to come to the camp to teach kids about art. To watch them fall in love with exploring your feelings and emotions with crayons, paint and whatever their little imaginations can conjure up. I saw it as a way to pay back my mentor, Mrs. Quinton. Surely, one summer spent without progressing my career isn't horrible. The studios will still be there this fall, looking for new talent.

I turn the shower on, but I catch sight of some string on the tiled bathroom floor.

The bracelet.

Lily's bracelet.

After we got home from camp, Charlie went to the Happy Daze to work her shift and Ava's been baking up a storm in the kitchen. I immediately went where I always go.

The balcony outside my room where my easel and canvases are. As the sun fell from the sky and disappeared behind the edge of the ocean, my hands frantically tried to capture the magic in that moment.

I was never a sunset or sunrise type of girl. My pieces are usually more abstract and up for interpretation, but there's something about Climax Cove. I haven't been able to stop painting the town and the landscapes since I arrived.

With my view from my small corner balcony, I see the friendly people and small children running along the edge of the water fountain in the middle of town, the boats that come in for daily shipments, and the tourists who park their boats in the marina and stay for a few days. The fisherman with their waterlogged pants and gruff beards are a daily occurrence as they step on dry land after a day spent at sea, catching the best seafood this side of the Pacific. It's all been an inspiration of new material that I can't seem to get my fill of.

I'm a little fearful that coming to Climax Cove ruined me. I've done nothing but hotel art for the past two weeks. And hotel art isn't going to sell in New York. My edge is disappearing to be replaced by a dime a dozen starving artist pieces. Not good for an up-and-coming artist.

I pick up the bracelet and weave it through my fingers remembering how Lily would run her little fingertips along it and check periodically to make sure it was there. It's obvious that the few frayed strands of yarn and beads are something she holds dear.

Without thinking much about it, I turn off the water, step into my shorts and camp t-shirt once again. Checking my cell phone, I find it's just before eight. My fingers move across my screen, googling the name Marcus Kent and Climax Cove, but nothing comes up.

Maybe Lily can go without the bracelet for one night. I mean, it's only a bracelet, right? A bracelet I noticed her touch several times throughout the day whenever she seemed shy or uncomfortable.

My teeth clench and my jaw tightens. Damn it to hell. Why does it have to be Marcus Kent's daughter?

Screw him, I can face his smug know-it-all hot as fuck face. After all, he thinks I don't remember him and that case of instant amnesia I gave myself has worked swimmingly so far.

I open the bathroom door and the steam from my hot shower follows me into the hallway. The aroma of something sweet grows in intensity the closer I get to the kitchen. Once I enter, I smile, watching Ava bent over the oven, taking out a tray of cupcakes. There are bowls and spatulas, flour, sugar, eggs and butter on every surface of the counter and you'd think *Pillsbury* just invaded our house.

Her finger presses one of the cupcakes and a giddiness rings from her throat before she pulls them out completely.

"So delicious," she says to herself and with the tray in her hand, she turns from the oven and looks up. "Fuck!" she screams, dropping the tray. It lands half on the counter, starts to slide and then slips off and onto the floor.

"I'm so sorry, Ava!" I run over to help her.

She's already picking them up and placing them back in

the tray. "You scared the shit out of me. Do you enjoy sneaking up on people?" she asks, her voice a little bitter.

I pick up the cupcakes and place them in the pan. I'm sure they are fine to eat. I mean Ava is a germaphobe to the max and she probably Mr. Clean'd the entire kitchen before she even started baking.

"I was just going to ask you something," I say, embarrassed that when I ask the question, she'll know who I was talking about earlier today.

She puts the tray on the counter, away from the other cupcakes she's already baked.

"What?" she asks, obviously frustrated.

"Never mind. Do you want me to help you make more?" I offer.

She tosses the potholder onto the counter, rounds the island and sits down on a stool. "No. I'm not sure why I even do a whole recipe. I mean no one eats them." She almost seems down. I wonder why. Usually Ava is the happiest roomie of the bunch.

"I'll eat them," I walk over to take one. "What kind are they?"

"Don't eat the ones from the floor. And you have to wait until I frost them." She stands from the stool and moves back behind the counter. "They're cookies and cream."

I spot the pieces of Oreos in the white cake batter. "Yum," I say, unwrapping the cupcake I picked up.

Ava takes it from my hands and throws it in the trash.

"Um?"

"I told you, no to the ones that fell."

"It was less than ten seconds."

"That is the stupidest rule ever." She shakes her head. "I'll frost these and then you can have a cupcake."

I shrug, knowing my hips don't necessarily need another

sweet. If Ava keeps spending all her free time in the kitchen, I'll be heading to New York three sizes bigger.

"What did you need?" she asks and I tilt my head not remembering what we were talking about.

"Oh, I need to know where someone lives, but I don't want to hear anything about it." I pin her with a warning glare.

She laughs, moving to her teal *Kitchen Aid* mixer. "Okay."

Her back is turned to me and the mixer is going, so I step closer. "I need Marcus Kent's address."

The spatula keeps scraping the sides as the mixer goes through her frosting and she doesn't answer me.

"Ava?" I question and she turns my way.

"Marcus Kent," I say his name again.

A slow smirk slinks across her lips. "I'm sorry who?" She acts like she can't hear me over the mixer, which is bullshit.

"Marcus Kent," I say a little louder.

Her smirk turns into a full smile. "Is this the dad who was giving you grief?" she asks.

I blow out a breath. She's never going to let this go.

"Maybe."

"And now you want to go to his house?" She turns down the speed of the mixer and walks over to a cabinet on the other side of the kitchen.

"That bracelet we found is his daughter's."

She nods nice and slow, pulling out a plastic bag in the shape of a triangle.

"And that's the only reason? I mean, you *are* going there at close to nine o'clock at night."

I say nothing, jut my hip out and wait for her to grant me her undivided attention.

She peers up from placing the frosting tip in the bag and

cracks up laughing. Bent over, she hits the counter a few times, obviously finding herself funny.

She's the only one in this room who does.

"Okay, okay. Man, you are no fun. I do know who he is. He was building a new house when I was here a few summers back. It's on Greyfalls Hill. If you go through downtown, it's like the fourth streetlight. He's the only house on the Hill, so it should be easy to find." She smiles overly sweetly as though she didn't drill me. "Don't go getting lost and find yourself in say...his bedroom accidentally."

I roll my eyes. "I'm going to drop it off and I'll be back for those cupcakes in fifteen minutes tops."

"Well, he looks like a man that probably rocks some serious groin cleavage. Like I said before, anything can happen when there's groin cleavage involved."

"Groin cleavage?" I question.

She looks at me over her shoulder. "You know that V thing we were talking about before. Take it from me, groin cleavage can make you do some pretty stupid shit." Her back is turned to me once again as she scoops the frosting into the bag.

"I've never heard it called that before." I chuckle.

She shrugs. "Meh. Got it from some jerkoff who landed me in bed once. I just remembered it. What can I say? He used the power of his groin cleavage against me." She gives a wry laugh.

I grab my keys and walk over to the screen door. "Nothing to worry about here. I'm impervious to the power of groin cleavage *and* sex packs."

"Sex packs?" she turns and asks me.

"Yeah, you know like a six pack or an eight pack. They've

been known to have the same effect as groin cleavage." I wink and then head out the screen door.

"I'm going to use that lingo," Ava calls out after me.

The night is warm and the few lightening bugs flitting around makes the feeling of summer that much more prevalent.

The town is empty at this time of the night. A few lingering couples walking in the marina, but all the families must have retired for the night.

As I'm stopped at the red light outside Breakers, one of the only places that make this town look like it entertains living people this time of night, I spot it. The truck. The gray pickup truck that belongs to Marcus. It looks freshly washed, and there isn't any lumber coming off the back like there usually is. If I didn't know better, I wouldn't guess it belonged to a man that does physical labor every day.

My eyes are so transfixed on the truck, that I don't notice a couple approaching it at first. My heart skips a beat when he comes into view under the street light he's parked near. I can't get a good look at the woman he's with, but Marcus' hands are stuffed in his pockets like they seem to be a lot. He's wearing a pair of slacks and a button-down that doesn't scream small town father of a five-year-old who likes to spend his nights watching CSI. I made that last part up. Not that I've given any thought to what Marcus might do with his evenings when he's alone.

The slacks mold to his ass, his shirt fits snug around his broad shoulders, tapering into his taut waist, his hair is gelled and perfectly placed. His look screams city man, single, rich, and promises nights filled with satisfied screams and multiple orgasms.

A horn honks behind me and I snap to attention, glancing in my rearview mirror. It's another sports car with classic rock blaring from it. I press the gas immediately, not slowing down until I'm through downtown.

This is a good thing, I tell myself. I can drop the bracelet off and get the hell out of here . He isn't home, so maybe there's a babysitter, or I can leave it by the door.

A minute or so passes after I turn onto Greyfalls Hill before a lighted house comes into view. It's gorgeous, dark, and more contemporary than I was expecting. I park in front of the garage, and light pours from every window.

Grabbing the bracelet, I hop out of the car, knowing I have limited time before Marcus returns. If I'm lucky, he's going to drive his date home. Oh, God. What if he planned to bring her home to...

My hand moves up and massages the knife-like feeling in my heart as I bound up the cement steps and press the doorbell. Lily comes into view from the side window. She's barreling down the hall in her nightgown, her hair wet.

Another girl, a teenager follows behind, telling her not to open the door.

"Miss Cat!" Lily screams, jumping up and down as the girl struggles with the lock.

I glance behind me, swearing I heard something, but we're high in the hills of this town surrounded by forest so I'm sure there's a bunch of furry animals nearby. Fingers crossed they're of the fuzzy cute variety.

The teenager opens the door and Lily squeezes between her and the door until she's on the porch with me.

"Hi, Miss Cat," she says with a huge smile on her face.

I glance from Lily to the girl. "Sorry, I'm Lily's camp counselor, Caterina." I give the young girl a wave.

"I'm Ashley, the babysitter," she smiles and stays in the doorframe, letting Lily stay out on the porch with me.

"I found something when I was cleaning up in the cabin," I say.

Her clear blue eyes light up. "Today was so fun! Are we doing more crafts tomorrow?" The excitement is reverberating from Lily and I'm wondering if it's ridiculous that I drove up here to return her bracelet. She's obviously fine without it.

"We'll see. Listen, I stopped by because I have your bracelet." I open my hand to reveal the worn piece of string.

Lily's shoulders fall. "I almost forgot," she says, her voice as small as a mouse. Her finger runs over the heart beads and she looks up at me. "Thank you."

I smile. "I'm glad I made the trip."

Ashley steps out and looks over Lily's shoulder. Her eyes widen and she nods.

"Thank you." Her voice is one of relief.

"Sure." I pat Lily's wet hair and those eyes just like her dad's stare up at me like I'm her very own fairy godmother.

"Can Miss Cat come in?" Lily asks and turns her attention to Ashley.

"Lily you're already up *way* past your bedtime."

I need to get out of here before Marcus returns so I wouldn't be staying even if I was welcome. "I have to get back home, but I'll see you in the morning."

I step back, waving my hand, but Lily runs into me, her small arms wrapping around my legs. I pat her back and she only grips me tighter.

"Thank you," she murmurs and then steps back, turns around and skips into the house. "Bye, Miss Cat."

"Thanks again," Ashley says. "That was going to be an issue when I tried to put her to bed."

"You're welcome." The door shuts and I turn around and take the steps two at a time to try and make my escape.

My hand is on my door handle and I'm breathing a sigh of relief that I was able to get Lily her bracelet without seeing Marcus when the garage door opens. I close my eyes, hoping to hell, Lily or Ashley opened it from the inside, but headlights light up the driveway and I slowly turn to find his grey truck pulling up the driveway.

Seriously, can't I catch one break when it comes to this asshole?

Am I delusional? Because the red sports car in my driveway looks an awful lot like Cat's. And then I see the woman herself as if my imagination conjured her up for my viewing pleasure.

My gaze remains on her as I pass by, pulling my truck into the garage. She's a mix of cute and sexy in her jean shorts and tight t-shirt, her short hair pulled back in a small ponytail. But it's her eyes that intrigue me, filled with fear and a touch of indignation. All because I'm here presumably. What does she expect? I live here.

I climb out of my truck and approach her and her sweet scent floats on the warm summer breeze to greet me. My dick twitches in my pants and I'm half thankful it's still alive and well after an evening with Polly. I was beginning to worry it had shriveled up and died in an act of self-preservation.

"Hey," I say, approaching her.

She stuffs her hands in her back pockets, effectively pushing her tits out to me. I can't help but glance down and she immediately removes her hands and clasps them in front of her.

"I had Lily's bracelet, so I returned it to her." Her gaze never fully reaches mine, which is different than any other time we've spoken.

"Thank you. She sleeps with it. It's like her security blanket," I say and she smiles.

"I thought it might be important to her." She shifts her weight and chews the inside of her lip as if she's uncomfortable talking to me.

"How did you know?" I can't help but wonder how she's noticed my daughter's obsession with a bracelet that was made years prior in such a short time.

Her fidgeting stops and she finally meets my gaze and something sparks in her eyes. "I'm her counselor. I would hope I'd notice when a girl touches a bracelet every time she's worried or nervous. That's my job."

Snarky and snippy, that's Caterina and it only makes me want to push her down on the hood of her flashy car, spread her legs and make her scream.

I don't say that though. "Well, then you're good at your job." I twirl my keys around my finger as we stand there in awkward silence before I tuck them into my pocket.

Her eyes follow my movements and then trace up my muscled arm to meet my gaze again. Seems Cat might enjoy the view as much as I am right now.

"I should get going." She steps back and for a moment, my throat closes as panic flares in my chest. I don't want her to leave.

"Do you want to come in for a drink?" I ask, though I shouldn't.

She shakes her head and crosses her arms in front of her. "Lily's up," she says.

"If she was asleep would you come in?" I ask, taking a step forward.

She takes another step back but runs into the bumper of her car. Her hand slides out reaching for the hood of her car.

"No, I just meant—"

"Meant what?" My footsteps halt. I've pressed far enough and I don't want to scare her too much since she's about a second from bolting.

"I need to go." She turns around and steps around the hood until she's holding the door handle.

"I had a date tonight." It's a stupid thing to say. I don't know why I said it. But this is the first opportunity we've had alone together and I want to try and have a normal conversation with this woman.

My admission halts her escape. She turns her head toward me, the light from the porch letting me get a good look at her eyes. Eyes that are narrowed in my direction.

"That's nice," she says in a voice that tells me she doesn't think it's nice at all.

"Not really." I shrug. "It was a bust. Apparently, while I was busy raising Lily, SnapChat was invented and all people do is look at their phones during dinner and take pictures of what they're doing to let the world at large know, all while they ignore the people they're actually with. I think there's a picture of me somewhere in cyberspace announcing that I'm getting married."

The corner of her lip tilts up and she raises a brow, so I continue.

"Something about filters. She took my picture and made me look like a groom." Her smile continues to grow and there's a possibility it will turn into a laugh. As much as I want her to scream underneath me, I want to hear her laugh from something I said.

"Really?" she asks in astonishment, the hand poised on the door handle dropping to her side.

"Dead serious. Bow tie and 'just married' written at the bottom. I've been out of the game for a while, but tell me—is this modern-day dating?"

Then it happens, she giggles. An affectionate laugh rolls out of her and makes a direct hit to my dick.

"Maybe you should get someone to give you SnapChat lessons?" she says with a smile. She's facing me now, the idea of taking off no longer at the forefront of her mind.

"Maybe I should. You know, so that I'm not suddenly married and Lily has fictional siblings."

She laughs again and I swear it's a sound I could become addicted to.

"I'm sorry, Caterina," I say.

Her body freezes mid laugh and she holds my gaze, swallowing deeply.

"What I said, was wrong. Lily loves having you as a counselor, it's just when the subject of her mom comes up, I tend to go on the defense." I step forward and she doesn't move. One hand presses on the roof of her car and my other reaches to grab the free hand hanging at her side. She doesn't pull back when I entwine our fingers.

"I shouldn't have overstepped," she says softly.

True, but this is not the time to discuss that.

I shake my head. "You were trying to help and I appreciate it."

I squeeze her hand. Is she uncomfortable or unsure what to do? She wanted me a long time ago, and from the way her eyes still burn with desire, she still does. The question remains, do I want her? She still has a lot of red flags, but when I'm in her presence, the reasons to stay away don't seem so important.

"Cat," I say, inching closer, wanting to feel her body pressed to mine, wanting to know how sweet she tastes.

"Marcus," her voice is shallow and the fight that's usually there is absent. "We—"

"What? We what? Tell me Cat, if I kissed you right now, what would you do?" I inhale her scent and one hand leaves the roof of the car, grazing down the side of her forehead.

"Marcus," she gives a small shake of her head, but her eyes fall closed when I brush my fingers to her temple.

"Answer me."

Our breathing is the only sound I hear, drowning out the rustling of the forest around us.

"I'd...kiss you back."

Pushing my body against hers, a small growl escapes my throat at the way she fits perfectly against me. I let go of her hand and wrap my arm around her small waist.

Swallowing down all the confusion and hesitancy I've had toward her, I decide to show her exactly what I've been imagining doing to her since she showed up in Climax Cove.

I lean in, our lips only a few inches apart and I can practically taste the sweetness of her. Cat sucks in a shallow breath and I close my eyes, preparing for the moment I'm sure to beat off to later.

Squeal.

A car barrels into my driveway, screeching its brakes when it comes to an abrupt stop. I know who it is before he climbs out of his stupid ass car.

"What the—" Dane stops, taking in the scene in front of him.

Cat tries to squirm out of my hold, but my hand tightens along her side to keep her pressed against me.

Dane stares at us, confusion wrinkling his face. I've never seen him speechless, and I must admit, I'm enjoying it. Especially after the nightmare date he hooked me up with earlier tonight.

"Leave."

Finding his voice, his annoying laugh echoes through the air. "Well, I think I should apologize." He rounds the back of Cat's car.

Her gaze darts between me and him. She wiggles her body and this time I let her go because Dane is about to make a jackass out of himself, but in the end, it'll be me who cares, not him.

"Apologize?" I ask.

Dane winks at me and holds his hand out to Cat.

"I'm Dane Murray, this guy's best friend." He nods his head in my direction.

Her hand smoothly slides into his and he shakes it once. I'm happy to see that his eyes remain fixed on her face instead of dipping to those curves of hers that beg for attention.

"Caterina Santora," she introduces herself.

"If I'd known that our Marcus was already taken, I wouldn't have tried to hook him up tonight."

He lets her hand go and she tucks both her hands behind her back, leaning back onto the car.

"He's not, I mean, we're not..." she stumbles over her words and I don't bother trying to help her out for a minute.

"She's Lily's counselor," I finally say and her head whips in my direction. I cock my eyebrow. Wasn't she the one who was just insisting that nothing was going on between us?

He winks and Cat's cheeks pink. "Counselor. Right. Got

it." He takes his fingers and runs them along his lips in a zipper motion. "My lips are sealed."

"Now that you've met, you can leave." I direct my words to Dane.

"Oh, no, I should get going." Cat opens her car door and before either of us can argue, she's in her seat with the door closed.

"I can skedaddle so you two can...you know...continue doing whatever it is single dads do with camp counselors." Dane laughs and I control the urge to wipe that smirk off his face with my fist.

I shake my head at him and then peer into the car. Her hands are on the steering wheel and her eyes focused on the back of my truck in the garage.

"Thank you for the bracelet, you saved me from one hell of a night."

She turns her head in my direction. Her eyes are so blue...I'd love to stare into them as I'm drilling in and out of her.

Fuck. Stop thinking, you asshole.

She must catch Dane still behind me because that lust filled look in her eyes moments before he barreled in has disappeared. Whatever moment we shared is now over.

"You're welcome. See you tomorrow."

She reverses the car and I barely have time to get out of the way so she doesn't run over my feet.

I watch her car leave my driveway and I wish it were turning in. Six years ago, I may not have wanted anything to do with Caterina Santora, but she's all grown up now and I want to feel my way around exactly how grown up she's become.

"The camp counselor?" Dane's hand plants on my shoulder.

"Leave it alone, Dane."

"I didn't think you had it in yah."

I turn to go into my house, but he's on my heels.

"I don't remember inviting you in," I say, never turning around.

"I'm practically family. I don't need an invite. Plus, I want to hear all about how you started hittin' it with the camp counselor. You bend her over a tree stump yet?"

I shake my head, walking into my house through the garage and making my way to the kitchen. "It's none of your business."

"Everything is my business."

"Daddy!" Lily runs up to me in the princess nightgown Santa brought her last Christmas.

Ashley's not far behind her and she glances at Dane, her gaze remaining fixed there.

"Why are you up?" I ask Lily, placing her on the counter.

"Lily, you're a party girl." Dane walks up to give her a high five.

"Hi, Uncle Dane." She smacks his hand.

I walk toward Ashley, who's gaze still hasn't moved off Dane. Pulling out my wallet, I grab the cash to pay her. "Ashley?" I ask, waving my hand in front of her face.

She snaps out of the trance she's in and smiles, the apples of her cheeks now flushed.

"Thank you, Mr. Kent." She takes the money and shoves it into her pocket.

"I'll walk you out." I wait for her to go first, but she's not moving. Once again, her eyes are zeroed in on Dane.

"Want some ice cream?" Dane asks Lily, opening the freezer.

"Yeah!"

"No, she doesn't." I shoot a warning glare to Dane.

He rolls his eyes and holds his hands up in the air. "Papa Bear says no." He hops on the counter beside Lily and plasters on a matching gloomy face. He's like a child himself half the time.

"He always says no," Lily says and the words cut me.

I never wanted to be the strict father. Not that I gave it much thought before Gretchen told me she was pregnant. But before Lily was born, I didn't see this being my role. I wanted to have pillow fights, build forts, let her eat crappy food until late at night. But that scenario evaporates into the ether when you're the sole parent. I have to be the mom *and* the dad. It sucks, but Lily needs stability and rules if she's going to grow up to be a responsible adult.

Dane's lips purse and he nods, his eyes finding mine across the room. We couldn't be more opposite in our parenting tactics.

"Bye, Lily." Ashley waves.

"Bye, Ashley." She waves back and then Dane jumps off the counter, taking her into his arms and dancing around the kitchen.

Lily laughs and Dane pulls out his phone for music. With Lily secure in his arms, the two of them circle the island and the kitchen table. I'm not a jealous person, but at this moment, the fact that Dane gets to be the fun one hurts.

11

MARCUS

I had hoped to run home and shower before heading to pick up Lily. I doubt you have to ask why. Cat doesn't need to see me in my jeans and boots covered in sawdust. Not that I was going to put on cologne and a fucking tuxedo, but a clean pair of jeans or shorts would've been better than this. As usual though, time wasn't on my side.

I run my hands through my hair and little chunks of wood fall to the gravel path below.

Story of my life. Running from one place to the other.

When I arrive, all the kids are outside the cabin playing a game of hide and seek. My footsteps slow when I see Cat sitting down on a bench, placing a Band-Aid on one of the kids. She blows some loose blonde strands of hair blocking her vision out of her face only to have them fly up and fall right where they were a second ago.

The little boy sits, tears staining his cheeks as she says something I can't hear, but the small smile that emerges when she's done tells me she has the trust of these kids. After only a few weeks, that's impressive.

The boy runs away and Cat searches the group of adults until she spots what must be his parent. It's another dad who appears to be high on the white-collar spectrum. He's in a pair of khaki's and polo, typical insurance salesman look. Responsible and trustworthy.

What a dick.

I watch the man's gaze dip down to Cat's cleavage and my heart starts beating faster. She smiles, pointing and expressing everything with her hands as she recounts the story of how his son hurt himself. He reaches out and touches her bare arm and I clench my fists at my sides. It could be a reflex move, one of understanding and gratitude, but red coats my vision. Cat steps back and his hand falls off her arm back down to his side.

Good girl.

"Daddy!" I look down to find Lily staring up at me.

I bend down to her eye level and she brings her hands up, running them through my hair.

"You're a mess," she says.

I tickle her sides and she slides from side to side to get away from me. "Stop it, Daddy." She's laughing so I continue to tickle her ribcage.

"Are you making fun of me?" I stop tickling and pick her up, dangling her by her feet and swaying her from side to side.

"Watch out for the tree." She puts her arm out like I'd actually hurt her. "Daddy!" she screams then giggles.

"Watch out for Drew." I knock her lightly into a boy from her class.

He smiles and gives her a little shove of his own. *Whoa kid, this is my joke.*

"Daddy!"

I pull her up and rest her stomach on my shoulder. "Are

you going to make fun of me again?" I ask her and she giggles once more. I can never get enough of that sound. My one arm holds her secure over my shoulder as I wait for her answer.

"No!"

"Promise?"

She giggles. "Pinky promise." She holds out her pinky finger.

"That's a pretty hardcore move, Lily." I glance up to find Cat in front of us, a smile instead of a scowl on her face.

I let Lily down and she stands at my feet. "Daddy's dirty." She shakes her head then turns to me with an excited gleam in her eye. "Guess what I made?" She runs away, leaving Cat and I by ourselves.

I can't help but wonder what these other parents have been thinking for the past few weeks. I mean, while the other parents talk with the other counselors getting a run down of their child's day, Cat has been my sole go-to counselor.

"I just came from work," I remark, my hands continuing to rub down my jeans.

"I'm sure you'll feel better after you shower."

Visions of my shower jerk-off sessions to made up scenarios between Cat and me bombard my mind and I widen my stance, praying for the first time ever that my dick stays limp.

"I mean, I can't wait to take a shower after camp every day."

Now my imagination has her in the shower, water cascading over those perky tits and her round ass.

"You know, to get all the dirt off me." She's rambling and I can't bite back the smile on my lips.

"I imagine camp can get dirty," I say and her cheeks flush.

"I just mean—"

"I've never wanted to be a loofah more in my life."

Her gaze shoots to mine, that pink flush now a flaming red. She clears her throat but I don't miss the way she crosses her legs. Does she need to dull the ache? God, I hope so.

"Mr. Kent," she says back to her all-business tone.

"What happened to Marcus?"

She glances around us and then fixes her gaze back on me. "I'm your daughter's camp counselor. We can't. It's—"

"Inappropriate?"

She nods, a smile tipping up the corners of her lips.

"Yeah, I don't much care about that."

Her shoulders tense and as she looks at me, I can't decipher if it's desire or annoyance in her gaze.

"Look, I made a boat!" Lily's in front of us with a Popsicle stick boat and thrusting it into my stomach.

"Popsicle sticks?"

Cat narrows her eyes, remembering my insult the other day. However, the anger that filled them that day is no longer there, replaced with resigned amusement.

"You're a natural," I say, running my hand over the top of Lily's head.

"Just like her daddy," Cat remarks and my hand freezes on Lily's mass of blonde hair.

I stare at her but she hasn't clued into what she said yet.

"How did you know my daddy makes boats?" Lily asks.

Cat looks down at her for a split second before she gasps and covers her mouth. But it's too late.

"Um … I think you mentioned it," her eyes never meet mine as she concentrates on Lily alone.

"I never told you," Lily says, the honest girl she always is.

"Are you sure? I don't know how I would've known then." She still can't meet my gaze.

"Lily, can you go grab your lunch bag?" I ask, keeping the Popsicle stick boat in my hands.

"Okay." She skips off toward the cabin, oblivious of the tension that's now like a blanket over our little group.

She runs off, but I see her get distracted by another kid outside the cabin doors. For once I'm happy she's lollygagging. There's nowhere else I want to be right now. Well, unless having Cat underneath me is an option, or being under her works, too.

"So." My fingers run along the small pieces of wood while my eyes focus on Cat.

"Lily must've told me, or maybe you mentioned it." She's antsy and it makes me wish I had a rope and a headboard. Maybe tying her up and teasing her until she admits she remembers me would fulfill both of our needs right now.

"Cat," I say softly and lean my shoulder against a tree beside us.

A long stream of breath pours out of her mouth and she chews on the inside of her cheek for a second, her eyes squeezing shut for a moment.

I press my lips together to keep the smile from forming.

"Fine. I remember you."

A weight I hadn't known I was carrying lifts from my shoulders and I somehow feel lighter. "You do?"

"Yes," she says with annoyance and throws her hands up in the air. "And we are *not* to talk about it, okay?"

"What aren't we talking about?" I try to appear casual even though the cockiness I'm feeling that I am not forgettable to her, has me bursting at the seams.

She juts her hip out, places her hand on said hip and

stares at me deadpan. "Stop acting like that. Smugness isn't attractive on you."

Yeah, she'd love it if I backed her up into a tree right now. If all the kids weren't everywhere, I just might. I chuckle and try to stifle the amusement I feel with this situation.

"Oh, and look your friend is here just in time to make my mortification complete."

I glance behind me, finding Toby doing back flips off a bench near the play area, Dane's eyes trained on Cat.

I nod to him and he nods back. Lily runs out of the cabin with her backpack swinging on either side of her and Dane catches sight of her.

"Lily!" he screams and she looks over at him.

Toby stops trying to put himself into a wheelchair and waves at her.

"Can I go play with Toby and Uncle Dane?" Lily asks. This couldn't have gone better if I'd planned it.

"Sure." I signal to Dane that Lily's coming.

"Bye, Miss Cat." Lily waves and runs up to the top of the path.

"Since we're done pretending we don't know about each other, how about coffee?" I ask.

She shakes her head and turns toward the cabin.

I glance around and realize the only people left are the other counselors, most of whom are heading to the cabin to clean up.

I gently cup her elbow. "Wait."

She whips around and when I glimpse the shame in her eyes I fear that she's about to cry.

"I'm not her," she says.

I want to ask what she's talking about, but she seems

upset so I decide to go with something non-committal that won't push her over the edge. "Okay."

She glances behind her and signals for us to go to the side of the building. When we reach it, she tucks us behind a tree so we can't be seen.

"I'm not that girl. I've grown up."

Her meaning becomes clear. "You've *definitely* grown up." My gaze skips over her body and I realize that was a dick move. "I mean—"

"I know what you mean. I was a late bloomer, okay? But that doesn't change the fact, this" —she waves that delicate finger between us that I'd like to suck into my mouth— "can't happen."

"I suggested coffee. Figured we could catch up." I cross my arms over my chest, tucking my hands under my arms to keep from reaching out for her and pissing her off more.

"What are you going to catch up on, how my tits and pussy look now compared to when I was eighteen?"

God, her fiery temper is such a turn on. I raise my eyebrows and she bites her lip, but I know it's because she wants to smile.

"Listen, everyone does stupid shit when they're younger. If it helps, I'm just as embarrassed at how I treated you back then. I'd like to take you to coffee to apologize and start over."

This is a genuine invitation. Am I attracted to Cat? Does a bear like honey? Yes, I want to nail her every which way I can imagine and then try some shit that hasn't even been invented yet. But I need to make amends for how I treated her and I want her to be comfortable around me.

"Start over? As friends?" she asks, and the defensive stance her body is in, relaxes.

"Yeah. Let that stuff from the past just be a distant memory."

"Fine." I think I'm more surprised than she is that she agreed to this.

I pull my phone out. "What's your number?"

"You don't need my number," she says. I should've known she wouldn't give this up easily. I stare at her until she rolls her eyes, but rambles out her number. Her phone dings in her back pocket after I text her.

"That's me. So, we'll plan a time for coffee."

"Coffee." She says the word like it's a finality of sorts.

"Maybe a Danish, too."

I smile and she shakes her head, but there's a playful side to it this time.

"Coffee."

"Cat!" one of the other counselors calls out from the cabin.

"I should get going." She begins to step away.

I want to cage her in, taste those sweet lips. Have my hand venture up her shirt.

We'll get there. I'm going to make sure of it. But she needs time first.

"I'll talk to you soon," I promise.

Her cheeks flush the cutest pink color before she turns around completely and disappears around the corner of the building.

Now I just have to figure out how to get from a coffee date to my bedroom.

I stretch in bed and open my eyes for the first time since I woke up from a blissfully erotic dream where Marcus was the star. God, the things that man did to me. Does my subconscious really want him that bad? I haven't had a dream like that in like...ever.

Brushing off the last vestiges of sleep I leave the confines of my bed in search of something to eat. If I'm lucky, Ava baked last night and if it's cupcakes for breakfast, who am I to argue?

Clinking dishes tell me I'm not the only one awake in the house.

Rounding the corner past the living room, I find Charlie sitting on a breakfast stool with a spoonful of Fruit Loops about to meet her lips. She smiles with a Cheshire-like grin that says she knows something.

But instead of saying anything she places the spoon in her mouth and chomps down on the cereal.

Finding the counters bare of any sweets I frown and move to the cabinet and grab a bowl.

"So, who did you sneak out of here?" She raises her

eyebrows. Her dark hair is pulled up in a high ponytail and she has on shorts and a tank top.

"Um...no one." I pour the Fruit Loops into the bowl and she picks up her phone from the counter and acts like she's looking at the screen, but I know she's waiting to drill me with another question.

"Then you must have one awesome vibrator based on the satisfied look on your face."

I stifle my laughter and take my bowl over to the kitchen table. "More like a hefty imagination and a subconscious that wants to play it out in my dreams."

"Damn. I wish I had your imagination." She grins over her spoonful of Fruit Loops.

That's the thing about Charlie. She's kind of a cheerleader for everyone. Not the rah rah rah throw my pom-pom's in the air kind, but she doesn't seem like she'd ever wish ill will on anyone. She only ever seems genuinely pleased when someone else is happy. Being from a family in the upper echelon of San Francisco high society, I've seen my fair share of people who really don't want you to succeed or find happiness.

My face flushes and I try to bury my head into my bowl of cereal.

"So, who's the guy? An ex from back home?" Charlie rises from her breakfast stool and joins me at the table with her bowl of cereal.

I haven't had as much time to bond with Charlie since she also works some shifts at Happy Daze Tavern on top of the fact that she's a local and shoots home for family dinners occasionally. Ava has her dad here too, which leaves me with my art. Not that I'm complaining, my hotel pieces are starting to move from the sleazy rent-a-room-by-the-hour variety to the high-end resort living type.

"Not an ex." My spoon skims through the milk, stirring the small rings of colors around.

I glance up to find Charlie leaning back in her chair, her gaze on me. She's waiting for me to expand. The problem is, because Charlie is local, she'll know Marcus.

She leans forward as though we have to worry about someone overhearing us. I'm assuming Ava is still sleeping. "I know we don't know each other all that well, but just so you're aware, I'm not a gossip whore. I won't push you to talk to me, but if you want to, I'm here."

Then she stands and takes her bowl to the sink. The kitchen is silent as she grabs her purse and puts it crosswise on her body then takes her keys off the small table we have next to the backdoor to our apartment.

"Marcus Kent." I blurt out his name fast, like she's not going to hear me.

Truth is, I need to talk to someone about him and most of my other friends took the summer as a vacation before we finish the final year for our Master's.

Her Chucks skid to a stop and she slowly turns around, the smile teasing her lips looks like she's trying to bluff with a shitty poker hand.

"Well, he's definitely worthy of the orgasm you had this morning."

She sits down on the edge of the chair she just left. "He's the dad? The one with the Popsicle sticks and glitter comment?"

I nod. "Yup."

She has a knowing look on her face. "Marcus is *very* protective of Lily."

"Aren't all dads?" I ask, pushing my bowl of cereal to the side.

"Yeah, but he's different. My boss is a single dad too, but

he's more go with the flow," she talks with her hands and pauses trying to think of the word to describe him. "Let's just say he's an open book with his son. Now he's older than Lily, but when it comes to Lily's mom, everyone who's close to him is *super* tight-lipped about the situation. That's a hard line with Marcus. He never talks about it and no one ever talks to him about it."

Her eyes are filled with sympathy, as in 'don't even bother with him, you'll get nowhere'. But I love a challenge. Isn't that how I ultimately embarrassed myself in front of him at eighteen? Would I really be willing to put myself out there for him again? Especially since this time around he seems to be doing the pursuing.

"How do you know him so well?" I ask and she shakes her head, making small strands of hair fall from her ponytail holder.

"He's my boss's good friend." She's holding something back though, I see it in the way her gaze darts away from me.

"Oh, my God." My hands fly up to my mouth. "Have you been with him? Did you guys date and now I'm telling you—"

She laughs, her hand pulling mine from covering my mouth. "No. That's not it at all." She takes a deep breath and lets it puff out her cheeks when she exhales.

"Please don't tell anyone this because my boss doesn't want it to get out." She pauses again.

My mind races with a million different thoughts. Are Marcus and her boss an item? Is he gay? Is he already attached to someone?

"They're members of this thing called The Single Dads Club. But you can't say anything about it," she adds quickly.

I scrunch my nose. "What's the big deal with that?"

"A lot of people know about it, but they meet at the bar and the guys don't want that broadcast because then the single women would flock there looking for their next baby daddy."

"Whatever happened to dads using their kids to score with women? You know like they do with puppies?"

Charlie stands and opens the fridge, taking out a water. "These guys aren't those type. The kids all come first. Relationships are second and usually of the temporary variety if you get my meaning."

My heart pricks a little with her comment. So, if something happens between Marcus and I, it would be for the summer and that's all. Secret rendezvous after Lily goes to sleep is all we'd share.

"Oh, don't look so down. You might be the game changer for Marcus." She winks. "Okay, I'm off to do inventory." She walks toward the door, but it swings open before she reaches it.

In walks Ava, in her clothes from last night and nothing but her keys in her hand.

"Am I the only one that's not getting any?" Charlie says, shaking her head.

"What? I went for a walk." Ava walks to the fridge and grabs a bottle of water. "Can't a girl get a little exercise without getting the third degree?

"Does this exercise have a name?" I ask and Charlie laughs.

Ava swings around and pins me with a mock glare. "No."

"I *am* the only one not getting any exercise," Charlie laments and walks out the door, shutting it behind her.

"Wait, what is she talking about?" Ava asks.

I stand and put my bowl of cereal in the sink next to Charlie's. "Nothing." I walk up to the island counter and can tell from her just fucked hair and her inside out shirt that she wasn't out for a walk. But since I don't want her prying into the situation with Marcus, I don't bother trying to get any information from her as to where she spent the night.

"I'm going to get some coffee," I say.

"Oh, I'll join you. Just let me clean up a little."

And with that, we both do an excellent job of pretending that each of us has nothing to hide.

13

MARCUS

I'm sitting at my desk on Monday morning, after a weekend of beating off to images of Caterina in my mind.

Fucking Dane. She was right there in my hands and he had to barge in and ruin it. Not like I could've bent her over the hood of her flashy car with Lily and Ashley inside the house, but a kiss. A fucking kiss to see if she's as sweet as I think she is.

My phone rings and I glance down to it, seeing that it's Mr. Santora. Cat's dad. My stomach flips with the thought that he somehow knows about the dirty thoughts I've been having about his youngest.

I answer the shop phone, "Good morning, Bill."

"Marcus." He pauses and I swear the man could make a raging bull nervous. "I'm coming out in a few weeks with my family."

"Which boat were you looking for?"

Bill keeps three boats in our marina. He exchanges them from time to time, keeping only one down in San Francisco where he lives. I earned his trust early in our relationship after my father left me the business and he's always been a reliable client.

"Actually, I'm taking my Sweet Tahlia and my Kitty Cat both to San Francisco. My son-in-law is going to use Sweet Tahlia for the summer months. You remember him, right?"

The blond guy who never stops touching his wife. How could I forget?

"Lucas, right?" I tap my pen on the desk and lean back in my chair.

Bill Santora is either chatty or all business and if he's all business, we'd have already hung up. Today, Bill wants to talk so I sit back and try to relax since nothing seems amiss. Clearly, he has no idea about the things I want to do to his daughter.

"Yeah, he and Tahlia are expecting their second child—another grandson." His happy and proud tone ooze through the phone.

"Congratulations. Your family keeps growing."

He chuckles. "Well, at least Tahlia is having babies. My youngest, Cat—" I hear nothing else while my heart begins to race in my chest. "—she's practically being auctioned off in New York. All these galleries want her to come out there after the summer. Well, they wanted her this summer, but she said she wanted some time off before starting her career. Hey, you might run into her up there."

Yeah, we can check that box. Been there, done that and almost strapped her to my headboard.

Instead I say, "Oh really?" My voice cracks like a teenage boy.

"She's working up at that camp. I don't get why she's putting off all these gallery owners who want to sell her stuff. But Cat's always been different than her sister. Tahlia is my steadfast, reliable one and Caterina is and probably always will be, my wild child. Not in the party-all-the-time and spend all my money way, but she's always had a fiery spirit and she's never really liked the fact she comes from Santora Sausage."

Christ, this guy makes it hard not to make the obvious sausage jokes sometimes. *She comes from Santora Sausage?* The jokes practically write themselves.

"I'm sure she just wants to spread her wings, you know with her being, what now?"

"Twenty-four," he answers and a zing of excitement rushes through me.

So far past legal now.

"I'm sure she'll be heading to New York in the fall. I can't imagine that girl ever finding enough to fulfill her in a small town like Climax Cove." He chuckles. "She likes to think of herself as some regular Joe, but all you have to do is look at my credit card statements to know she likes her Starbucks and Neiman Marcus."

His confirmation of what I already know stings when it shouldn't. Why should I give two shits that she'll be gone once summer's over? It only repeats the same thinking in my head. Cat would be a summer fling that'd die with the daisies and daffodils once autumn arrives. Now, if only I wasn't the bee looking to taste her sweet nectar until there's nothing left.

"Well, Bill, I'll make sure to get the two boats ready before you arrive."

"Thank you, Marcus. I'll get you more details about when exactly we'll be arriving closer to the date, but we'll need Kitty Cat ready for the Saturday. We're spending the weekend in town and I want to take the family out for the day. We'll have lunch on the boat. I'm going to call Debbie over at Double D's after I hang up with you."

"Special occasion?" I ask, back to rolling my pen back and forth through my fingers.

"No. Just want some family time. We've all missed Caterina since she's been working at the camp."

I'd miss her too.

Fuck. Stop that.

"Well, I'll do my part to make sure it's a great day for your family." I sit up straighter.

"Why don't you join us?" he asks and I think my heart actually skips two, no three, beats.

"Well, I have my daughter and..."

"Bring her. I'd love to see that little girl. Plus, my grandson is four. I guarantee Tahlia will be happy he has someone to play with."

"It's your family time, we'd only be intruding."

Please let this go. The thought of seeing Caterina in a swimsuit again just gave me a chub. If it were him making the decision, I'd have already accepted the invitation.

"Nonsense. We'll see you then. Thanks, Marcus."

The line goes dead and I wonder where Bill Santora learned his phone etiquette.

What did I just get myself into? An entire Saturday afternoon with Cat and her family—with her Italian father and her nosy mother. The only silver lining is I that have Lily to act as a buffer. If I'm lucky she'll get seasick for the first time in her life and we'll have to cut the trip short.

THAT EVENING I walk into Happy Daze and the usual single dads are milling around the long table in the back. Summers tend to make it harder for our members to meet, what with all the kids being out of school. I approach the bar and find Charlie Shaw working.

She's Garrett's buddy's sister and though he moved away years ago, she's still always more than friendly to us.

"Hey, Charlie."

She looks up from her clipboard and sets it down. Her usual friendly smile has something more to it than normal. A tease of some kind, but I have no idea why. Maybe I'm seeing shit.

"Blue Moon?" she asks, her hand already grabbing a glass.

"Thanks." I sit down on the stool and glance up to the television.

She sets my beer down and then drops an orange on top.

"There you go. I'll add it to your tab." She turns around.

The one great thing about Charlie is she's not a chit-chat person really. She goes about her business and if there's no point to the conversation she doesn't spur one on.

"Thanks, Charlie. How is your brother?"

I'm not in the mood to join the single dads just yet.

She turns around and leans against the back of the bar. Her hair is braided to the side and she wears almost no make-up but she's got that girl next door thing down. The one a boy might just bypass for the cheerleader only to find out the right girl for him was there hiding in plain sight the whole time.

"He's in California now. Living the dream—bachelor-hood." She rolls her eyes.

I laugh. From what I know and it's really only Garrett who's told me anything about him, he's a forever bachelor. A guy who never wants to settle down and actually believes monogamy doesn't work. How different can two best friends be? Garrett enjoyed his settled down life with Sydney's mother. At least from what I can tell by the few times he's opened up about it at these meetings.

"Well, here's to your brother's simple life." I raise my beer and take a drink.

"One day I hope he'll find a girl that knocks him on his ass." She starts wiping down the bar, but her hand stops mid-stride, her gaze darting to the door.

I don't have to look back to know who's there. Everyone in town knows Charlie has a crush. A crush on the one man who'll never be available to her.

His big brooding body sits down next to me. No hello, no pat on the back in greeting.

"Hi, Garrett," Charlie says, her voice raising an octave or two from when she was talking to me.

"Hey. Usual," he says in a clipped tone.

Charlie's movements become fidgety as she opens the cooler, grabs a Miller Lite and twists the cap. "Here you go."

"Thanks." He surprises me by looking over at her.

Charlie smiles, waiting there, staring at him like he's some celebrity she's lusting after.

Garrett is the blindest man I've ever met.

"Thanks, Charlie," I say, and she comes out of her trip to Garrettville, giving her head a little shake.

"Let me know if you need anything else." Just like that she heads to the back of the bar over to the tables with the other single dads.

"What's up, man?" I ask Garrett, grabbing my Blue Moon and standing from the stool.

Lily wasn't exactly thrilled that I was leaving tonight. She's been a little clingy lately and I haven't been able to pinpoint why.

"Just Sydney. There's some dance at the camp and she

called me on the way here. She wants to go shopping with some girl she met and her mom."

"Dance sounds fun." I shrug, not seeing the problem.

"Dance equals boys. Boys equal trouble. Boys plus my daughter equals death row."

I chuckle, patting him on the shoulder.

"Hey, not all guys are bad."

He raises his dark eyebrows at me and I laugh. He's right. At thirteen, even the captain of the math team is bad. Any and all thinking goes through their dick.

"I'm sure they'll be chaperones there."

"Yeah, me." He points to himself with his thumb, standing wait for me.

We head toward the table and Dane runs through the bar doors. His white t-shirt is drenched and his shorts are hanging off his hips. What the hell?

"I'll be two minutes guys, just have to change." He holds up two fingers in the air.

"This is your club," I holler back.

He swivels around so he's walking backward to his office. "Some things are more important than a room full of dicks." He waggles those eyebrows and I wonder where he finds these women that are always up for a quickie. I mean we're in a town of less than a thousand people.

"See what I mean? Guys suck," Garrett mumbles as he passes me and says hello to the other members of the Single Dads Club.

As I take the seat next to Garrett and say hello to everyone, a blonde walks through the door and my stomach drops watching as her hips sway side to side on her way to the bar.

Charlie places a napkin down for her and the two

exchange a few words before Charlie's head dips in my direction.

Cat swivels in the bar stool, and I watch the color slowly creep up her skin until her face is dusted pink.

I tip my beer in her direction and she returns the gesture with a small wave. This might be my favorite Single Dads Club meeting yet.

W hat happens at the Single Dads Club meeting, stays at the Single Dads Club meeting. I can't tell you what we talked about, but I can tell you that as I'm half-listening to Jesse, a new member of the club, talk about some shit he's going through at home, I keep sneaking glances at Cat.

The same thought triggers come to mind each time—I shouldn't.

I shouldn't be looking.

I shouldn't be wanting.

I shouldn't be touching.

As much as I repeat it, my dick pays no attention. It wants Cat.

It wants to be looking.

It enjoys the wanting.

And it wants to be touching. Deep and hard and often.

"Why don't you go over there?" Dane knocks his elbow against my ribcage.

At some point during my diverted attention, the group

has dispersed. The meeting is over and it's time for me to leave.

"What are you talking about?" My gaze snaps back to Dane and away from Cat.

"The hot blonde at the bar with Charlie," Garrett says.

"So, you do know her name?" I say.

Garrett's face contorts into a what-the-fuck-are-you-talking-about look.

"You obviously want her, go ask her out." Dane urges. At this point he seems so desperate for me to enter the dating game that he'd throw me in front of a pack of female wolves in heat.

"She's too young." That's what I keep telling myself.

But she's not too young anymore. She's twenty-four according to her dad.

Fuck. Her dad. Reason number two and that one's legitimate.

"So, you don't mind if I hit it?" Dane asks with a grin.

My fist clenches around my bottle of water and the plastic crinkles in my hand. "No." I shrug, going for nonchalance I don't feel.

"You two act like you're fifteen years old," Garrett says, leaning back in his chair and shaking his head.

"All right. Thanks, man." Dane stands up and clamps me on the shoulder. "She's one hot piece of ass."

I try to concentrate on anything but him approaching her. I don't want to watch but more than anything I want to watch.

"Why are you letting him do this?" Garrett asks.

I start picking the label off my water bottle. Anything to stop my gaze from drifting over to Cat. "I don't know what you're talking about." I can't stop myself and my gaze slides over to them. Dane is facing me as he stands next to Cat.

I know he's baiting me. He must know how badly I want her and how pissy it's making me to watch him flirt with her.

Cat laughs at something he says and her head falls back between her shoulder blades. Her neck is exposed and I imagine my tongue sliding up that arch all the way to her earlobe.

Dane inches closer, his hand now on the back of her chair.

Charlie has no choice but to move down the bar to greet a few customers, leaving them by themselves.

Cat slides to the side to gain some personal space, but Dane bites his bottom lip and watches her lips move intently at whatever she's saying.

What is she saying?

Fuck, I don't care.

"Why are you torturing yourself?" Garrett asks.

My gaze shoots over to him. "Those that live in glass houses, man."

Again, his face contorts into a fuck you look, but he knows I'm right.

The only difference between us is that I don't think Garrett's been with anyone since Sydney's mom whereas I have my fun, but it's away from Lily. Away from anything in Climax Cove.

I sit there trying to convince myself that I don't need any relationship drama to weave into my already chaotic life. I fill my mind with the certainty that I'm doing what's right—for both myself and Lily—and then it happens.

Dane's hand reaches out and tucks a strand of her shiny, blonde hair behind her ear.

I stand up.

"About fucking time," Garrett comments.

Dane's shit-eating grin could be seen across the Pacific Ocean it's so big. He knows he made his point and he's proud of himself that he got me off my ass and trudging over to her right now.

I stop on the other side of her. She glances over and then does a double take.

Yeah, it's me Cat. Standing next to you like a damn puppy dog and wanting your attention.

"Can we talk?" I ask.

She sips her beer, which doesn't seem to fit her. I would've thought a margarita or wine but a beer girl? Not sure I saw that.

"See, I told you, it would take less than five minutes." Dane looks at his wrist as though he'd actually wear a watch. The man is a minimalist when it comes to how he dresses. Simple is always better. "I think it only took two, maybe three." He winks at her and then hops over the bar to the other side.

She places her beer on the napkin, twisting the bottle back and forth, doing anything but looking at me.

"So, can we talk?" I ask again.

I think I just felt my nuts shrivel up and die. Could I be any needier?

"This is a public bar." Her eyes meet mine and I wonder why the hell they seem so sad.

I glance at Dane behind the bar, his eyes perked up and ready to eavesdrop and there's a couple sitting a few bar stools down.

"Can we go in the back?" I ask, knowing this is a lot to ask. To seclude her.

To my surprise, she finishes her beer, places it on the bar and stands up. "You have two minutes." She walks off.

Dane raises his eyebrows with that same know-it-all smirk on his lips.

I follow and once we're in the back hallway by the bathrooms, she leans against the wall, her arms crossed in front of her.

"We can go to Dane's office. He won't mind." I motion with my hand farther down the hall.

"Yeah, no thanks. Here is," she looks around, "private enough."

"Are you interested in him?" I ask the thing that's really needling me right now.

"Who?" Her brows draw together.

"Dane," I grind out between clenched teeth.

She lets her hands drop to her sides. "You've got some nerve."

"Well, do you?"

She silently stews for a minute before she answers. "You pursue me for weeks, finally get my number, ask me for coffee, and then don't bother calling."

Relief rushes through me. She's pissed because we didn't have our coffee date? I'm just a guy and I've never really understood women all that well, but I'm pretty sure this means good things for me.

"That's why you're upset?"

She gives me a look that I can only describe as 'duh'. "Of course, that's why I'm upset. Why didn't you call?"

I shove my hands in my pockets and roll back on my heels. "I was going to. I had every intention of calling you when I asked you for coffee. Then your dad called me to tell me he's coming up this weekend and I started thinking about what he would think about his youngest daughter spending time with a man ten years her senior and I thought it was better that I leave you alone."

"You are so infuriating. I'm a grown woman, Marcus. I can make my own decisions." Her hands are clenched in fists at her sides.

It's times like this that I wish her temper didn't turn me on so much. I shift my stance to adjust the growing distraction in my pants.

"I didn't think it would be a big deal. You were the one who was insistent that we were just going out as friends." I add air quotes to the "as friends" part for emphasis.

She presses her lips together and says nothing. I can see by the way she's narrowed her eyes that she knows I have a point.

"If you just want to be friends then why are you so upset that I didn't call about coffee? Why did you act like you didn't recognize me instead of just telling me to go to hell the first time you saw me?" I ask.

A hollow laugh leaves her throat and her gaze zeros in on me, her amusement fading fast.

"I'm not that eighteen-year-old girl anymore. I'm not the girl you can crush with a few words. And I'm not the girl who will pine over you. I just didn't feel like rehashing the past. I feel like I don't even know that girl anymore. I've grown up."

"First of all, I'm well aware you've grown up, and if you'd have acted like you remembered me, I would have apologized. I was an asshole."

"Yeah, you were." She loses that defensive stance and looks down at her shoes, shuffling from foot to foot.

"You were eighteen, I was twenty-eight. I'd just found out that Lily's mom was pregnant. My life was a fucking mess. The timing was just wrong."

I remember how scared I was that despite everything going on in my life my dick still reacted to the way her perfect tits called out to be touched. How I committed the vision of her lace panties giving a glimpse of that small patch of blonde hair between her legs. She was way too young and out of my league, but I'd wanted nothing more than to have her in that moment.

"Look, it was years ago and I'm completely over it. I know we have to co-exist at camp for Lily, but this back and forth," she moves her finger between the two of us, "needs to stop."

I step forward placing one hand on the wall above her head. "Do you need me to be more direct? What do you want me to tell you? How my dick was hard for months after our little encounter every time I remembered you? That even today, you stripping down in that tiny office in the back of the restaurant is still the hottest thing that's ever happened to me? Do you want to know how I'd beat off to the memory of you topless, only to feel like a total douchebag afterward?"

She fidgets, her cheeks growing red and her gaze darts everywhere but on me.

"Should I mention how after our argument that day at camp, I beat off in my shower, imagining me stripping you down in that dingy cabin, spreading your legs wide and tasting you? How every night after months of nothing, I can't seem to get off enough and every damn time it's to you."

Her breasts rise and fall with ragged breaths at my words and although she's trying to act indifferent, I'd hazard to guess she's anything but.

I take a chance and my hand leaves my other pocket and lands on her hip. My finger grazes along the bare skin between her shirt and her shorts.

"I want you, Cat," I whisper in her ear. Her eyes close

and I inch forward, giving her no room to escape. "And I think you want me, too."

A small moan leaves her lips and though I've tried, I can't fight the inevitable in this moment. I smash my lips to hers, caging her to the wall, one hand above her head and the other digging into her hip.

She meets me with the same intensity, our tongues entwining in a newfound dance. Unable to control myself, I press harder and her hands move up to lock behind my head.

She tastes every bit as sweet as I knew she would.

I want to move her to Dane's office. I want to swipe his desk clean and fuck her long and hard so she knows she's mine and no one else's.

"I'm sorry for being an asshole. Present and past tense," I murmur against her lips and then fuck her mouth with my tongue again.

She mumbles something I swallow down and her one leg swings around behind mine, pulling me into her. I grind into her center, loving the friction on my hard cock, but knowing it's not enough. Another moan from her and a groan rumbles up my own throat.

I slide my hands down her small frame until her ass is in both my hands. I'm about to prop her up so I can carry her into Dane's office.

"Cat?"

She pulls her lips from mine and we both turn to find Victor's daughter, Ava Pearson, staring at us wide-eyed.

"I'm sorry." She takes a hesitant step forward. "I need her for a moment," she says in a small voice. She runs into the bathroom and Cat slips away from my body.

"Sorry. I should go see what's up." Cat bites the side of her lip and I want nothing more than to bite there myself.

I pull my phone from my pocket to check the time. "I gotta go get Lily anyways." I adjust myself as much as possible and I grab her hand, entwining our fingers. "I'll call you," I say and bring her knuckles to my lips.

"Okay." She nods, with no objection and I wonder if it was my lips or words that changed her mind.

Either way, I don't care. For the first time ever, I think we both want the same thing at the same time.

15

My fingers brush along my lips remembering my kiss with Marcus yesterday. He was gentle but firm. We both wanted each other and there was no hiding the fact if we'd been alone, we'd probably have ended up naked. I bite my lip and my stomach unleashes a flight of butterflies as I remember his hushed words to me in that hallway. No matter how hard I fight it, my body willingly takes what he offers.

That's the scariest part. What if all he wants is my body? I see the lingering stares at my breasts, my ass. My body does it for him and yes it gives me a thrill...but what if I fall for him?

I'm used to guys approaching me, but with my background, their confidence usually comes from their bank account.

I'm not sure where Marcus' confidence comes from. Six years ago, he had nothing. I remember my dad talking about him over our Sunday dinners—how he was working some dead-end boat mechanic job in Portland when his dad died. The house he built must have been custom and not cheap.

The small marina I remember sailing up to six years ago, now holds boat sheds and takes up the whole south side of Climax Cove's shoreline.

I'm not sure if it's his self-made success that created the confidence that rolls off his strong shoulders like honey from a jar, or just his controlling and domineering nature that seems to come naturally to him.

A vision of him tying me to his headboard flicks in my mind.

OMG. Stop it.

There's no future with Marcus. He has a daughter and clearly sees you only as a sex object. I guess the question is, can I live with that?

"Hey, Cat." Landon, a fellow counselor, sits on the picnic table with me, his group of campers now playing with mine at the park.

"Hi, Landon."

Landon Filigree, is the classic guy who's trying to boost his resume. During orientation, Victor asked us why we decided we wanted to be counselors and Landon wasn't shy in saying, "I need it to show I'm not some douche who only cares about himself." The room laughed, but he sat down and shrugged because it was the truth. He doesn't want to mold young minds or show them how much they can love the outdoors, he's here for a line on his resume. I immediately liked him for his honesty.

"Is it me, or is today just dragging?" he leans back on his hands, but his eyes stay on the kids.

"Yeah, a little." I pick at the small amount of bark in my hands that had been left at the picnic table.

"You ever go back home?" he asks.

I glance over at him. He's got the All-American guy persona down pat—short blond hair, muscles neither too big or too small, t-shirt pulling slightly across his chest, blue eyes with two prominent dimples when he smiles.

"Nah, my parents are heading here this weekend."

His eyes widen. "Seriously. To Climax Cove?" I don't know why he's acting as though that's so absurd.

"Yeah, they've been coming here for years. They store their boats up here."

"Oh, that's right. You're a rich girl." He sits up straighter and nods a few times like the two wires in his head just connected.

"Caterina Santora," I say my full name, which usually does the trick, but no recollection from Landon. "Santora Sausage."

Still no sign of the light bulb turning on. "Yeah, I'm a rich girl." I sigh. "Well, my parents are. I have maybe five hundred dollars in my account."

Not that my mom won't add more if I need it, but I'm done with my parents' charity. I need to stand on my own two feet.

He chuckles, a light and sweet laugh that brings a grin to my lips. "Well, rich girl. I'm poor boy." He holds his hand out like it's our first meeting.

I take his offering and shake his hand. "Other side of the tracks?" I joke.

He leans in close. "Does that turn you on? Want to piss daddy off?" The smile on his lips tells me he's not serious.

"Doesn't every rich girl have daddy issues?"

"Au contraire, poor girls have way more daddy issues." The gloomy look in his blue eyes says he knows this first hand.

"Well, this girl," I use my thumb to point to myself, "just wants a stress-free summer to paint and inspire kids to make more art."

He nods in understanding. "Yeah, stress-free summer sounds awesome."

The park is in the middle of where three paths converge and I spot Ava bringing her group of eight-year-olds over. It's after lunch and usually I let them expel some energy before I take them back for a game or craft.

"Would you like to go out for dinner sometime? My roommates are always on their damn Xbox and PlayStation and I wouldn't mind exploring Climax Cove a bit." I see that he's uncomfortable asking. He's shy and doesn't hold the confidence of so many who have asked before him.

The first person who comes to mind is Marcus with his perfectly mussed dark hair that only shows his natural high-lights when the sun hits the strands a certain way. His sparkling, deep dark blue eyes that have the capability to make my knees weaken when they're trained on me.

"I'd love to. As friends." Landon nods, and I don't know if he's disappointed or not but he takes my declaration in stride.

"I could use a friend," he says.

"Me too." Ava plops down on the picnic table. Correction, she lies down on top of the picnic table and buries her head in her arms.

"Tired?" I ask.

Landon looks from her to me. She picks her head up for a second and squints her eyes at me.

"Yes."

"I saw the cupcakes this morning. Yum."

This gains her interest and she picks up her head, resting it in her hands.

"Cupcakes?" Landon asks, intrigued.

"Ava is an amazing baker. She made peanut butter and chocolate last night." I rub my belly and lick my lips.

Landon holds his hands out to his side. "And here I figured you didn't do much of anything since your dad owns the camp. Figured you were a daddy's girl."

Ava scoots off the table, her legs swinging over the edge between Landon and me. "I'm nobody's girl."

Landon raises his eyebrows.

"Now, do you want to taste test?" she asks him.

"Do I look like I'm watching my figure?" He gives himself the once over and I roll my eyes.

She slaps him on the back. "Meet me at Steaming Hotties Coffee Shop tonight at eight o'clock." She changes her tone into one that implies mystery and secrets.

"Okay, although, I'm a tad scared now," he says with a chuckle.

Just then, a cry rings out and we all turn to the park.

"One of mine." I stand and jog over.

Lily.

She's bent over, holding her knee to her chest, crying.

"Lily?" I ask, bending down and placing my hand on her back.

Ben, Lily's partner in everything dangerous, comes over. "That boy over there was showing her how to do a backflip. I told her it was dangerous."

Ava and Landon both meet me at Lily's side and Ava's eyes lock onto where Ben is pointing.

"Toby?" she asks, with accusation already laced in her voice.

"Yeah," Ben says, pushing up his glasses by the middle.

"I'm going to kill him. Or his father," Ava grinds out.

I sit down on the wood chips and Lily crawls into my lap. Landon gently touches her knee, inspecting and asking her to bend and straighten it.

"Should we chop it off?" Landon asks in a mock serious voice and Lily laughs.

"Let's see what we have here. It's red and you're going to need a big Band-Aid so we should probably try that first. I don't have one here."

"I'll carry her to the first aid center," Landon offers and before I can tell him not to bother, Lily's on his back.

"Giddy up!" She uses her good leg and kicks him in the side.

"Seriously, kid?" He cocks an eyebrow at me.

I laugh and rustle my hand through his hair. "You heard your passenger, giddy up."

"I swear, this resume I'm building better open some serious doors for me after summer." He does a gallop around the park and then starts back to the cabin.

"I'll meet you there," I call after them.

He stops for a second to speak with the two other counselors for his group and then him and Lily disappear over the hill.

"What were you thinking?" Ava is yelling at Toby. "I told you to stop doing back flips and front flips and climbing every tree you come across."

I place my hand on Ava's back to calm her down because Toby looks like he's one word away from tears. She glances back and I inspect her red face. She takes a deep breath and I reassure her non-verbally it will all be okay.

Turning her attention back to Toby, she's much calmer now. "We need to talk to your dad."

"She was copying me, that's all. I told her not too. I'd never want Lily to get hurt."

I believe him, but Ava nods toward the path away from the play area. "We're calling your dad."

Toby rolls his eyes, his shoulders fall, and he mumbles something non-coherent, but he follows Ava away.

On the way to the cabin to check on Lily, I pull my phone out.

Me: *I just wanted to let you know, Lily fell at the park. She's fine, but her knee is scraped up. Don't worry, nothing we can't handle.*

By the time I reach them, Lily's knee has been cleaned and Landon is singing to her as she smiles at him like he's Justin Bieber.

By the time my truck stops, it's been ten minutes since the text came in. I didn't bother responding to Caterina. I left the staining job to Jake and sped off in my truck.

I stand outside the cabin watching Cat smile at some guy who's singing the song that Lily insists I play for her over and over again. Lily sways side-to-side while Cat places the Band-Aid on her knee.

She's fine which I had repeated to myself numerous times on the way over, but I had to see for myself. That and I had to see Caterina for myself.

Lily catches sight of me and a big smile forms on her lips immediately. "Daddy!"

The guy stops singing and Cat turns around to face me. Her eyes widen.

I walk over and sit on the back of the bench behind Lily, placing a kiss to her temple. "You okay, sweetie?"

Lily nods enthusiastically.

Cat stands. "You didn't have to come, Mr. Kent."

So, we're back to Mr. Kent again. "She's my daughter. I'll always come."

The guy who was singing looks between the two of us, with interest. "From what I know, a kid was doing backflips and Lily wanted to try one," he says.

Now I stand up. I knew this whole Ninja park shit that Dane was building was going to be trouble. I look down at Lily. "Toby?" I question and Lily looks away. "Lily?" She'll always try to protect him, which is honorable of her, but she needs to fess up.

"No," she lies. I know this because she's looking out the window and her chin is held high like 'don't question me.'

"It was." I look over to Cat and she nods.

"His camp counselor is talking to his father now," she says and her and the guy head outside.

I place my hands on Lily's shoulders and look down at her. "You okay, sweetie?"

Her indignant behavior has tampered down now and she nods. "Yep."

"Okay. You enjoy the rest of your day. I need to talk to Toby's dad."

I walk out of the cabin, Lily's hand in mine, ready to head to the office. I find Cat and the dipshit whispering about something to each other. Cat rolls her eyes and the guy has a know-it-all smirk on his lips. She continues to shake her head as if disagreeing with him.

Having elected myself as Cat's bodyguard at some point between leaving the cabin and walking down the stairs, I stomp over to them. "Excuse me, can you show me where the office is?"

She stares at me for a moment and then nods. "Landon, can you take Lily back to her group? I'll be down once I'm done with Mr. Kent." Her professional tone makes my dick twitch and if she's not careful, I'll be hiding her behind a shed.

Landon nods and a minute later, he's leaving with her on his back. She kicks him and pulls on his hair like he's her horse.

"Okay, kid, can we not pull the horsey's hair?" Landon says and Cat laughs so hard she snorts next to me.

"Do you like him?" I ask her, letting my Neanderthal brain take over before I can stop myself.

"What?" Her face is filled with indignation and I immediately feel like a dickhead.

"He's a good singer," I comment and then turn to head to the office. The office I don't need directions or an escort to.

She catches up to me and places her hand on my arm. "Is that what you think of me? That I'd kiss you one night and want to mess around with another guy the next? Nice, Marcus." She storms off, her feet heavy on the dirt path.

My head falls back and I realize I fucked up. Again.

All because this woman has me twisted up in knots and jealous over the tiniest things.

Now it's me jogging to catch up to her. We're five feet away from the office doors when Dane screeches his Mustang into the parking lot. He's got a look of annoyance on his face when he steps out of the car. He's about to be even more annoyed when my foot's up his ass.

"Your kid trying to kill mine?" I yell over to him.

He shakes his head. "Ridiculous. I told him so many times, save that shit for home. To not show off. But you know Toby. He loves to be the center of attention."

"I wonder who he gets that from?" I raise both eyebrows, earning me a middle finger from Dane before he heads to the office himself.

I shrug. It's the truth.

I turn back in Cat's direction and all that fear that Lily could have been seriously hurt dissipates. She wasn't hurt. She's perfectly fine riding on some camp counselor's back like he's her horse and she's his princess.

"What do you want from me?" Cat asks in a clipped tone.

Her question throws me off.

"I think you know what I want." I take a step forward to close the distance between us, but Toby's camp counselor chooses that moment to storm out of the office doors.

Her finger is in Dane's chest as he steps back with his hands up in the air. Toby comes out and Dane is yelling at him over the small brunette's head.

"Ava!" Cat screams and runs over there, pressing the girl's hand to her side. Cat whispers something in her ear and Ava shakes her head and says one last thing to Dane.

I'm too far away to hear, but Dane smiles. Actually, he smirks. His shit-eating grin, his signature I-find-humor-in-everything smirk that I've wanted to smack off his face more than once.

The difference between me and this Ava girl? She does it.

Toby freezes, wide-eyed. Even Cat halts all movement. Dane raises his hand to his cheek but doesn't seem surprised.

"Ava!" Victor comes out of the office doors, his authoritative voice toward his daughter causing everyone's head to swing in his direction.

She leans close to Dane and murmurs something and this time that smirk vanishes and his face pales. For the first time ever, Dane isn't finding whatever just happened humorous. Interesting.

"Let's go, Toby," he calls out, ignoring Ava, who has

already turned around and followed her father into the office.

Toby looks from me to Cat and then to his dad.

"Dane?" I call out but he holds his hand up in the air, swinging his arm around Toby.

"Later, Marcus."

And that's that. Whatever just happened between Ava and Dane, was more than a camp counselor telling the father his son was in trouble.

Cat swivels, shock stamped on every one of her features. "Well, if that's all. You can pick Lily up after camp." She walks past me and the smell of coconuts wafts behind her.

"Caterina."

She holds her hand up in the air and doesn't stop walking. "Later, Marcus," she says, sounding like an echo of Dane.

What the hell did I do?

"I want you."

Her feet stop, though she doesn't turn to face me. "You want my body?" she asks.

I step forward, looking around and spotting no one, so I reach out and run my finger down the length of the back of her arm.

"Yes."

"That's what I thought."

She steps forward, my hand falling off her arm and she walks away from me.

"Cat?"

She never answers me and I watch her until she disappears behind the building.

I guess the *honest* answer was the *wrong* answer.

I PULL in the driveway of my house and Lily runs inside as I walk toward the mailbox. The fact that Cat dodged me today when I picked up Lily has my blood boiling. If she wants me to take her serious, she needs to grow up and talk to me about whatever her issue is.

I open the mailbox and pull out the envelopes.

Damn, she looked good earlier. Her legs become more tanned every day and the tank top she had on showcased her curves.

I wasn't lying to her. I do want her. Under me, on top of me, bent over in front of me. Any and all positions would get her out of my system and give my hand much needed rest.

Flipping through the envelopes as I walk back up the driveway, I come to a stop when I see it.

If I thought my blood was boiling because of what happened with Cat, it's about to start boiling over.

The envelope I hold in my hand has the words Lancaster Maximum Prison stamped across the top. I tuck the other envelopes under my arm and rip it open then step behind my truck so I'll hear Lily before she sees me.

With the paper clenched tightly between my fingers, I start to read the letter.

MARCUS,

I KNOW it's been a long time and please hear me out before you tear this letter to pieces and go ballistic. I'm clean and sober now. Have been for a while. With my sobriety come the regrets of everything I've missed out on. I couldn't handle small town living and being a mother. I thought I wanted excitement and adventure. I regret that now.

We shouldn't have been together in the first place. Let's be truthful, you didn't love me. I didn't love you. We tried because of Lily. Maybe we were right to. I don't know.

I had no idea how to care for an infant. Half the time when she would cry at night, I faked sleeping so you'd go care for her because I never trusted myself. But that's all changed now. I know this is a lot to ask, especially since you've been so hell-bent on making me pay for my mistakes, but I want to be a part of Lily's life.

I'm asking nicely, Marcus. Bring her to me. Let me touch her blonde hair. Let me hug her and smell the strawberries from her shampoo. If I wasn't stuck in here, I'd come to Climax Cove.

Please, Marcus, bring our baby girl to me.

GRETCHEN

I CRUMBLE up the letter and stalk up the driveway, throwing it in the trashcan in the garage. I slam down the lid and take a few deep breaths. She's fucking crazy. Who does she think she is?

She left us to go party. Permanently.

The hell if I'll ever allow Lily to walk through those prison gates, past the barbed wire fence to visit a mother who cares for her about as much as a Harp Seal who leaves her young to die after twelve days. So what if I just learned that fact watching a National Geographic show with Lily the other day? The comparison holds true. The mother seal leaves her young after twelve days and they can't swim until eight weeks. I bet you'll think differently about how cute they are now, won't you?

Not everything is as it seems. Just like Gretchen's "poor me, I've changed" mantra is a load of bullshit.

Fuck her. My mind drifts back to the night it all started to go downhill—Blake's party. *What if's* surface like they do every time I think of that night. Lily was only two months old and Gretchen needed a break so I took her out hoping she'd let off some steam and be better able to deal with a newborn the next day. I've questioned that decision many times since, wondering if life placed a fork in the road and I veered the wrong way.

"Daddy?" The inside door to the house opens and my daughter's sweet voice calms me.

"Right here, baby." I take in a deep breath and will Gretchen's letter not to bother me. She's locked up and she can't get to us. At least right now she can't.

Lily's barefoot already when she tiptoes across the cement of the garage floor to me.

She's limping a little, though I'm certain her knee is okay. Whenever she's the tiniest bit hurt, she likes to make sure I'm still aware that she's been injured. That is until she starts playing and forgets about it.

"Can I watch Tangled?" she asks.

"Sure."

Lily leads the way into the house with me following close behind and when we get inside, I pick her up from behind and hoist her up. She giggles and I hug her to my body.

"I love you." I nuzzle my head into her neck, smelling the watermelon from her shampoo. Not strawberry. And I know that because I'm the one who buys her shampoo and gives her a bath every night. I'm the one who knows that though she likes to eat strawberries on occasion, watermelon is her favorite fruit. I know because I'm the one who has been here for the past five years. And I am the one who will always be here for her. I'm the one she can always rely on.

Her small arms wrap around my neck tight. "I love you, too, Daddy." She giggles again.

With her in my arms, I remind myself that there will be a time I won't be able to keep her mom away from her. A time when she'll know the whole sordid past of her young life. Will she feel abandoned? Will she hate the woman like I do? Will she forgive her? I'm the one who has a say now, but I won't forever and that scares the hell out of me.

The first face that comes to mind when I feel my grip slipping is Cat's. The question about me wanting her body. I feel her goose bumps when I touch her. The way she sucks in a breath when I'm near and her eyes look me up and down with lust. She wants my body too.

Lily wiggles out of my hold and I place her on the ground with Cat still on my mind.

What do I want from her?

Right now, after this letter, I want her hair wrapped around my fist, her ass in the air and my cock buried deep inside of her.

I pull my phone out of my pocket before I truly realize what I'm doing.

She answers.

"Ashley, Marcus Kent. I need you to babysit tonight."

C harlie's at Happy Daze Tavern working and Ava is meeting Landon at the Steaming Hotties where she's taken samples of frosting and chunks of cake to let him try. I was invited and I usually wouldn't pass up an opportunity to taste some of Ava's creations but I need some down time.

I'm sick of the highs and lows that comes with Marcus Kent. The kiss was the high and then the way he's so hot and cold toward me is the ultimate low.

I finish putting on my boy short underwear and pulling my hair into as much of a ponytail as I can get it into. The pizza has been ordered, I stopped and picked up a carton of ice cream. Let the *feel sorry for yourself* night commence.

Jogging down the stairs, phone in my hand, I put the money by the door for the pizza guy and plop down on the couch.

Just as I turn the television on, the doorbell rings. That would be about my luck for today. Then again, they remembered to deliver the pizza, so that's a good sign.

I grab the money and open the door, but it isn't the pizza guy outside my door.

"How did—?" That's the only words that come out of my mouth before he steps into my apartment and his lips crash onto mine and he kicks the door shut behind him.

Like an intruder, he takes what he wants from me, but I'm not a victim. I willingly allow him to manipulate my body until my legs are wrapped around his waist, grinding on the already hard length tucked inside his jeans. Before I can really take in what's happening, he pulls his mouth from my eager lips. His forehead rests on mine and both of our chests heave for breath. If he places me on the ground, I'm sure to crumble to the floor in a puddle of need.

"Tell me," his words are soft but demanding.

"What?" I ask in a soft voice.

He walks us over to the couch and sits down. When I try to shift off his lap, he keeps me on him.

"What do you want from me?" He takes his finger and tucks a strand of my hair behind my ear.

I look down to his hard chest and the cotton shirt stretched across his pecs. I'm unable to stop my fingers running along the length of his broad shoulders.

"I don't want to be a plaything for the summer."

There, I said it. It's out there.

A smile widens his lips, showing his perfect white teeth. His head tilts to the side and I get the feeling he's studying me. My stomach tightens in anticipation of how he's going to respond.

"Cat," my name is slow off his lips. "If I wanted a plaything I wouldn't choose my daughter's camp counselor."

The weight in my stomach lightens, but as his hand rises and he molds it against my cheek, it contracts. There's more he wants to say, so I remain silent.

"But, I can't make any promises. I don't know if this will work out between us. Lily is first for me, always."

"Of course." I shake my head. I'd never dream of coming before his daughter.

"I like *you* and as much as I love your body...I want to see where this goes, but there's no denying that I want you." His half-lidded gaze dips down to my breasts and my nipples harden.

I swallow down my insecurities and worries.

"Okay."

His thumb brushes along my cheek and I lean into the strength of his arm. "This is a first for me, Cat. I haven't dated anyone since Lily was born so I have no idea how this will go. If you'd rather wait to be physical, I understand."

I grab hold of his wrist and maneuver his hand over the top of my breast. Those amused and heartfelt eyes turn heated. His thumb rubs over my nipple and my back arches, wanting more.

"No time like the present they say."

"Thank God." His one hand slides to my back and he pushes me flush against him, his lips finding my neck immediately. His fingers skim along the collar of my tank top, slipping underneath the fabric, teasing me and making my breasts ache for his touch.

"I have a bet with myself that you taste sweet," he says as his gaze follows his fingertips along my skin.

"And what if I'm not?" I whisper.

His lust filled eyes meet mine. "Oh, you are. I know you are. The fact that I shouldn't want to taste you only makes you that much sweeter."

His finger slips into my mouth and I twirl my tongue around it. Once it's wet enough, he rubs it along my skin, making a path I hope his mouth will follow.

"What do you want, Caterina?" he says my name slow and low and the sound makes me throb between my legs.

I grind myself along his jeans and he raises his hips up off the couch, giving me the friction I need. His finger runs down the front of my shirt, over my breast, bypassing my nipple.

I groan. "I want your cock," I say.

A slow smile spreads across his lips. I'm sure he's surprised I'd use such a dirty word.

"Your want is my command." His fingers run along the hem of my tank top and then he grips the fabric and pulls it off my body.

The cool air of my apartment hits my breasts, making me feel even more exposed to him. Yes, he's seen me topless six years ago, but that still doesn't make me wonder if he likes what he sees.

When I feel him harden further underneath me, I have my answer.

"I'd like to slide my cock between these perfect tits," he says without touching them. He's just sitting there, licking his bottom lip and staring at my chest. And boy oh boy, does he make a pretty picture. In fact, there's no question in mind that Marcus likes what he sees. He looks like he'd eat me whole if he could right now.

Eventually, his hands graze up my skin, igniting a rush of goose bumps cascading across them like a wave on the shore. When his hands mold to my tits and his thumbs rub my nipples, a slow groan wrestles up my throat. He chuckles.

My hands fiddle with his belt and button of his jeans, eager to see what we're working with. He shifts his body from side to side to allow me to shed him of his pants.

Having no choice, I stand up and wiggle the jeans until they fall to his ankles.

His hands never leave my tits and I straddle him again. I can feel the heat from his stiff cock despite my pajama pants and his blue boxer briefs acting as a barrier. He grinds up into me and I wrap my hands around his neck.

"I think it's time I get a taste, don't you?" He cocks an eyebrow.

Before I can answer, I'm on my back. His lips tease my stomach and I suck in a breath, closing my eyes.

He slides my pajama pants down my legs and kneels, looking down at my center. The insecure girl inside wants to shut her legs. To hide myself from his viewing pleasure.

But his gaze could scorch every inch of skin it lands on. His want of me hasn't waned and so I spread my legs wider and slide my hand down my body until I circle my swollen clit.

His eyes combust with fire, but he doesn't move. His rigid cock strains the fabric of his boxer briefs and like he's able to reach into my mind and know what I'd like to do, he reaches down and strokes himself.

I take my finger from my self and hold it out to him. "I thought you wanted to taste how sweet I was?"

He never takes his hand off his dick as he inches closer until his hot mouth covers my finger, sucking and swirling his tongue around it in his mouth. My finger pops out of his mouth and a satisfied smile tips up the corner of his lips.

"Mmm," he moans. "That was the appetizer before my meal."

Bending down, he pushes my thighs up and out to the side. He's rough and unapologetic and God does it get me hot.

"Watch me," he orders in a demanding voice.

I try to squirm underneath his strong grip, desperate to feel his tongue on me. My heartbeat is in my throat and my breathing is labored as I watch him suck my clit into his mouth. His tongue work is complete perfection. I can't imagine anything better until it's paired with his next words.

"If you want to come, you'll watch me." His voice is threatening and a little condescending and fuck women's lib because it's a complete turn-on.

I get up on my elbows and admire the man I've thought about more times than I care to admit since our first encounter all those years ago. It's almost an out of body experience watching Marcus Kent feast between my legs.

The entire time he plays with my clit, his fingers tease my slit, never breaching the entrance. I'm desperate to have any part of him inside and eventually he gives into my unasked request as I feel his fingers plunge in. I whimper, desperate for more.

More him, more me, more anything.

He teases me with his tongue, his fingers still inside me. My eyes disobey and slowly shut closed enjoying the euphoria only he can bring me. Moments later his thumb is massaging my clit. The room is silent except for the sound of my soft moans.

"Please, Marcus." I need the relief only he can bring me.

"You want my mouth? Open your eyes," he commands and I nod, doing as he says, my entire body on fire.

He lowers his mouth and my entire being is wracked with the anticipation of feeling his warm mouth on me again.

Ding dong.

Marcus stops and looks up at me.

"Don't stop."

He smirks. "Are you expecting company?"

It takes a moment for my lust-riddled mind to recall who it could be. "Just pizza. Please, Marcus, I need to come so bad."

Without any further preamble, he curves his fingers and pushes them even deeper inside me at the same time his mouth covers my clit and sucks and circles and teases relentlessly. I grip the throw pillow, the fabric clutching in my fists as I realize that he was taking it easy on me before.

Seconds later it happens. I burst like an overinflated balloon. Stars swim in my vision as my orgasm rips through me, my moans and whimpers filling the room as I free fall back down to earth.

The doorbell rings again and Marcus' fingers and mouth leaves my body. I miss them immediately.

"Bet you're hungry now." He laughs, grabbing his jeans and pulling them on.

I sit up on the couch and quickly search for my tank top and put it back on, then toss the throw blanket hanging on the back of the couch over my lower half.

He answers my door with a shit-eating grin and no shirt so I'm fairly sure the pizza man knows why it took us so long to answer the door.

"The money is on the table," I call out.

Marcus doesn't answer and doesn't grab the money. Instead I see him dig his wallet out of his back pocket. A minute later he strolls back into the living room, pizza in hand, placing it on the table.

"I had the money ready," I say.

He smirks, walking toward the kitchen now. "Now, what kind of guy would I be if I didn't feed you after you fed me?"

I laugh, tossing the blanket aside and sliding one leg and then the other into my pajama pants.

He walks back into the room with two plates balanced on top of the pizza box and two beers.

"Yours?" he asks, holding the two beers lodged between his fingers in the air.

"They're Ava's, but I'll buy her some next time I'm at the store." I sit on the edge of the couch and open the pizza box. "You really didn't have to spring for my pizza."

"You're a Hawaiian girl?" he asks, spotting the ham and pineapple toppings. "Just so you're aware, I'm a meat lovers."

That doesn't surprise me. There's something about the men in Climax Cove. They're all so much more rugged and manly than the ones in San Francisco.

"We may have to compromise on half and half," I say with a smile, enjoying the fact that I'm seeing this new side to Marcus.

An expression of mock horror crosses his face. "Everyone knows that pineapple on even one-half of the pizza, spoils the entire thing."

I laugh. The age-old pineapple on pizza debate.

He cracks open the beers and hands me one while taking a swig of his. I watch his forearms flex with the movement and a small tinge of exhilaration hits my stomach. Those forearms just worked on getting me off five minutes ago.

"Okay, well maybe you should start eating healthier," I comment, earning me a quirked eyebrow.

He sits down and that's when I realize that everything between us all seems different. There's no uncomfortableness or awkward silence. No animosity from what happened years prior. We're like friends. Well, friends with benefits. *Amazing* benefits.

Picking up a piece of pizza, he places it on a plate and turns to me. Holding it right at my lips, he waits for me to take a bite. My mouth opens and I nibble a small piece. He doesn't move the slice of pizza.

"Eat it like I'm not here."

"But you are."

He chuckles. "Eat, Cat."

I open my mouth and take a giant bite.

"There you go." He finally removes the pizza from in front of me and takes a bite himself.

I swallow down my bite and reach for my beer. "Are you always so commanding?" I take a gulp and place it back on the table.

He shrugs. "I like control." His expression turns serious. "Not as in you-can't-do-anything-without-telling-me control. I'm not a dictator. When it comes to you, I just think I know what you want and I don't want you to be afraid to ask for it and to be yourself around me."

"Like I'd put on some act."

He finishes the piece of pizza we're obviously sharing now, but bends over and grabs another one, holding it up to my lips. "You know how it can be. You spend half the relationship with the fake version of someone until their true colors come out. People pretend to be something they think you want until they can't anymore."

I bite the pizza and lean back, watching him take his own bite.

"So, this," I point to him, still no shirt, relaxed on my couch having us literally share each piece of pizza, "is the real you?"

He shrugs again. "Other than the fact that I'm eating a pizza I don't really like, yeah. But relationships are all about compromise, right?"

We share a smile and he feeds me the pizza again.

"Is that a hint that next time you want me to eat the meat lovers?"

Again, with the damn shrug. When did this man become so indifferent? "I won't tie you up and starve you until you eat it."

The idea of Marcus tying me up sends a thrill through me. I push it aside though since we're getting to know each other better.

"Funny fact," I say. He turns in his seat, eating the rest of the slice he's so deeply offended by. "I used to be a vegetarian."

He cringes. "Oh, that might be a deal breaker." Placing the pizza down and grabbing his beer, he arranges himself in the corner of the couch, his leg casually bent and hanging off my couch.

If someone would've told me six years ago that I'd be sharing a pizza and pleasant conversation with Marcus Kent, they would have a better chance of convincing me that the Kardashian show wasn't scripted.

"Deal breaker? Really?" I chuckle.

"I love my meat. I'm from Oregon. I may not be a hunter like Garrett, but tofu and beans are about as tasty as a rice cake."

I shake my head. "You've eaten a rice cake?"

He pats his perfectly flat stomach with ripples most men spend hours at the gym to form. "Do you think I get this by eating Doritos and Oreos?"

We each laugh and I hope he isn't one of those crazy health nuts who only drinks smoothies and eats quinoa and kale.

He places his beer on the coffee table and leans forward.

"I'm done talking about our diets. How about we have

another get to know each other conversation after we expel some excess energy?"

He inches closer and the less room that separates us, the more my heart rate picks up. He's a hairbreadth away from kissing me when his phone rings in his pocket.

"Saved by the bell?" I ask, and his head falls into my lap.

"I'm sorry," he mumbles against my thighs.

He sits up straight, pulls his phone out of his pocket and his face transforms from easy going to worried and concerned.

"Ashley?" he asks.

I recall that was the babysitter's name when I stopped by the house to drop off Lily's bracelet.

"Okay. Yeah. Put her on." He holds his finger up in the air to me as though I'm going to get up and decide that now is the time to get a week's worth of laundry done. "Lily, sweetie, how are you?" He waits a second, positioning his phone in the crook of his neck and reaches for his shirt.

And...I guess the night is over.

"Does it still hurt?" His voice is nothing but concerned and caring. "Okay, sweetie, I'm coming home now. I love you."

He hangs up the phone, throws his t-shirt over his head and looks over to me. "I'm sorry."

I wave his apology off. "Is Lily okay?"

"Stomach ache. Ashley probably let her eat all her candy from the Memorial Day Parade." He stands up and tucks his phone into his pocket then holds his hand out to me.

I accept it and he pulls me up to a standing position. His hands wrap around my waist, pulling me into him. I hadn't realized how much taller he was than me, but the top of my head only comes up to right under his chin.

"Rain check?" he asks, placing a kiss on my forehead.

"Of course."

I rise to my tiptoes and he plants a kiss on my lips—nothing too deep or long, but enough to know that he wishes he could stay.

"Thanks for understanding. I'll call you."

I walk him to the door and sag against it after it's closed behind him. I can't believe what just happened. I just fooled around with Marcus Kent, the man I tried to get to take my virginity all those years ago. And the reality even better than the dream was.

18

MARCUS

The ride home from Cat's is short, but it is long enough to contemplate what just happened. The start of a relationship, or at least an attempt at one.

My only goal on the way over there was to relieve some of the sexual tension that acts like a third wheel every time we see each other. To be able to control one portion of my life. I might not be able to make Gretchen stop with her insane demands and I might not be able to stop Lily from growing up and wanting a relationship with her mom, but the one thing I could control tonight was getting Caterina Santora into bed.

That might sound like a dick move and maybe it was, but I knew she wanted me as much as I wanted her. It's there in her eyes every time I see her, even if she's spouting insults at me with her lips.

The minute out tongues touched it was game over. The more we kissed, the more I wanted. The further my hands ventured, the further I wanted them to explore. It wasn't until those blue eyes stared back to me and I saw how scared she was that I'd hurt her.

I'm not a bachelor-for-life kind of guy like Dane. I'm not the celibate type like Garrett either. I've never thought about finding a wife. I guess I figured once Lily grew up, I'd go from there. Until then, I'd enjoy the odd one-night stand and my fist and call it a day.

Lily's been my number one priority since the day she was born and that will never change no matter how much I want another woman. But Cat. There's just something about her I can't shake.

By the time I pull into my garage and turn off my truck, I convince myself that it's summer. We'll date casually for a while and see what happens. It's a good test for Lily and myself. I'm secretly hoping whatever this magic is I feel when Cat is around me fades otherwise Lily and I might find ourselves heartbroken come the end of August because Cat has hopes and dreams that don't include a man ten years her senior with a five-year-old in tow.

I walk in the door and Ashley's sitting on the breakfast stool, her phone in her hand.

"Hey, Ashley," I say, placing my keys and wallet on the counter. "How is she?"

"She's asleep now in her bed. I put a bowl next to her and made sure she was on her side." She stands and tucks her phone into her back pocket, already preparing to get out of here.

Opening my wallet, I hand over her cash and she smiles. "Thank you. Hopefully, it was just something she ate."

"Yeah, no fever, I checked her right after I called you." She walks toward the front door and I follow her, opening the door.

"Thank you again."

"You're welcome. Sorry your night got messed up."

I wave her off. "Don't be. Lily comes first, always."

She smiles and nods. "Good night, Mr. Kent."

"Night, Ashley."

She walks out to her car and I watch to make sure she backs out of the driveway before shutting the door and locking it. After setting the alarm, I walk up the stairs and into Lily's room.

Lily's blonde hair is strewn across her pillow. Her cheeks are red and her body is half lying over the covers. I admire my angelic daughter and kneel next to her bed. When I brush my hand over her forehead I notice that she feels a little clammy, but not hot, so I tuck her back in and slide the bracelet off her wrist, putting it on the nightstand.

That fucking bracelet. Maybe I should make her get rid of it like I did with her pacifiers at two, or her bottle at one. I understand the need for kids to have a comfort item, but this bracelet is becoming a problem. Her hand runs over it more and more as the days pass. I'm not convinced that it's healthy for her to be so attached to something that she feels anxious when she doesn't have it.

I shut the door just enough to leave a stream of light from the hallway peeking in on the off chance she wakes up and then head to my bedroom.

My king size bed never looked so empty.

Even though I've been the only one who's ever slept in it, tonight there's a certain blonde I wouldn't mind seeing lay naked under those sheets.

I'm not even sure if I could perform with Lily in the house. What if she had a nightmare or just woke up?

Stripping down to my boxer briefs, I brush my teeth then slide under my covers and reach for the television remote. But it's my phone that's calling my name.

The conversation inside my head goes something like this...

Horny Me: For Christ's sake don't be a pussy just call her.

Practical Me: I literally just left there.

Horny Me: Phone sex could get rid of this hard-on.

Practical Me: You haven't even had real sex with her. Why would she have phone sex with you?

Horny Me: She could relieve all that pressure that's been building since you first saw her in that parking lot at camp.

Next thing I know, my thumb is hovering over the green call button.

Horny Me: Press it.

Practical Me: You're going to scare her off.

Horny Me: You saw how much she wanted it and you only have the summer anyways.

My thumb presses on the screen. Horny me wins. My heartbeat slams in my ears as the phone rings.

"Hi," she answers and her sweet voice puts my indecision about calling to rest. "How is she?"

My heart shouldn't warm because the fact she asks me about Lily first, but it does anyway.

"She's sleeping."

"Oh good." I hear rumpling behind her.

"Your roommates back yet?" I ask.

"No. Charlie works late at Happy Daze and Ava's out with a friend. She's pretty into this baking thing."

"What are you doing?" I prop up a pillow behind me and lean back against my headboard.

I haven't talked to a woman on the phone just because in at least five years.

"I just got into bed."

"What are you wearing?" The question escapes through my mouth without funneling through my brain first.

"Why, Mr. Kent, how very kinky of you. I like it." Her voice drops into a seductive tone that practically pumps my dick up into full salute. "I'm wearing a pair of boxers and a tank top."

"Where did your pajama pants go?" I ask because that's how I had been visualizing her.

"I get hot at night."

"So does—" I stop myself before telling her that so does Lily. I'm sure there's no better mood killer than bringing up my five-year-old daughter. I'm a jackass.

"Who?" she asks.

"Never mind. How tight is the tank top?" I ask, switching gears.

She giggles. "Remember that lesson about SnapChat?"

I roll my eyes, thinking back to that bride and groom shit Polly played. "Yeah."

"I'll send you a picture, but only SnapChat."

"Why?" There's nothing I want less than a SnapChat lesson, but if it means I'll get some racy pics of Caterina? I'm down.

"Because it's only good for ten seconds. That way you won't be able to share it."

"Nor will I be able to beat off to it." I can't help the disappointment in my voice.

"It's SnapChat or nothing," she teases in a sing-song voice. I can tell that she already knows she's got me.

"All right, walk me through this thing."

"Okay, we're going to have to use a landline. Do you have one at your place?" she asks.

"I do." I give her the number and a minute later she calls me from the landline in her apartment.

"Put me on speaker," she says.

We go through the whole setup process and then her

picture comes up as my friend. Immediately, ten other people ask me to be their friend.

"How do these people know me?" I ask, seeing Dane's name pop up as the only one I recognize.

"You must have chosen to have it inform your contacts that you're now on SnapChat. Sometimes random people will friend you."

I accept the friend requests since it doesn't matter one way or the other. After tonight I'm not going to be doing jack shit on here.

"All right, I'm all set up. Now where's my reward?" I ask.

She giggles again. That one that makes my entire body feel warm and at ease.

My phone dings and I see a message from her. I click on it and the picture is of her shoulder with the tank top strap pushed over as though she's about to strip it off. I'm able to see the crest of her tit and her hard nipple poking through the thin fabric.

"I think I like this SnapChat thing." As I stare at the picture I move my hand down under the waistband of my boxer briefs and stroke my dick a few times.

"The courteous thing is to send one back." There's humor in her voice and for some reason, it only makes me harder.

"All right." I sit up straighter, holding my phone as far away from me as I possibly can while trying to keep my thumb on the button.

"Anytime now." She laughs and I imagine her hair falling forward in her face like I've seen it do so many times.

"Beginner's curve, okay?"

Snap.

I send off the picture of my rippled stomach. The one women admire when I take Lily to the beach. The same set of abs that made Cat moan when her fingertips brushed down them.

"Sent," I say, proud of myself. Maybe you can teach this old dog new tricks after all.

"Um." She chuckles.

My phone dings with a notification.

"You already sent me another picture?" I ask. I'm eager to see what she's got for me.

"No. I didn't." She's full on laughing now and sounds like she's having a hard time catching her breath.

"Who did then?"

"Um, Marcus." She's laughing again.

I glance down at my phone and Dane's face comes into view, but it looks like he's sent me a video. I press the button and the video starts. "What are you going to send me next? A dick pic? What the fuck man?" The video dies with him shaking his head.

A sinking feeling weighs heavy in my stomach. "What happened? I don't understand."

"You sent it to all your contacts, not just me." I can tell that Cat is trying to keep it together now.

Relief washes over me like a wave. "Okay, that's not that bad. The only person I'm friends with that I really know is Dane. Maybe technology isn't my thing." God, those words leaving my mouth make me feel ancient compared to Caterina.

"It's a learning curve. Let's try again and this time I'll walk you through it," Cat offers.

"I'm still wondering why you haven't sent me another picture," I say with mock disappointment.

My phone dings and when I check it waiting for me is a picture of her chest without her tank top on. Her tits are displayed in full glory and I squeeze the tip of my engorged cock for a small piece of relief.

"Now, how about that dick pic?" She's challenging me and damn if I don't want to live up to the challenge.

"I'm not sure I want Dane to get that picture," I joke.

"He won't. Stay on this exchange and it's just me and you."

There's something about when 'me and you' leave her lips. I like her referring to us as a unit. Unbidden, I envision her in my bed after a day at the park or out on the water in the boat. Her putting lotion on as she makes her way to bed. The blonde strands sticking out of her small ponytail as she folds the comforter open to slide into bed next to me. Her hands raking my stomach as she snuggles into my side.

Whoa, whoa, whoa. I just went from we'll see what happens to side-by-side burial plots in ten seconds flat. This girl has dreams. Dreams that need to be fulfilled before she'd ever consider playing house with you and Lily. Even with all the red flags flapping in my mind, the invitation leaves my lips.

"Would you like to come over for dinner next Friday?" I ask her.

"I'd love to." She accepts without hesitating.

All those red flags just faded to white. I give up. I'm done trying to resist the hold this woman has on me.

After trying on ten outfits, pairing them with shoes and accessories, I decided on a yellow sundress and flats. Leaving my hair down, I throw some waves in it, but I still feel unsure about it. I chopped my hair off right before summer started. Long hair was nice to pull away from my face, especially when the humidity makes it a frizzy mess.

As soon as I leave the confines of my bedroom, the heavenly scent of Ava's baking hits me. Come fall, I'm going to miss having the place I'm living smell like a bakery. Of course, I'll probably end up ten pounds lighter for it.

A whistle echoes through the room before I clear the bottom step of the stairs. Charlie's sprawled out on the couch watching a marathon of Younger. It's her first Friday night off in two months and she plans on doing "fuck all." Her words, not mine.

"I'd totally bang you, Cat." She winks and pops a handful of popcorn into her mouth.

"Thanks." I blush because I shaved every hair off my body with the hope that's exactly what will happen. I'm trying not to get my hopes up. I have to remember that he has a daughter at home and there's a chance the new vibrator my sister's best friend sent me to test out will be the lucky bastard this evening. Caveat: she runs a sex toy company, so it's not as weird as it sounds.

I pass through the archway into the kitchen and there's Ava with purple glitter in her dark hair and on her cheeks.

"Smells amazing as usual," I say, moving to the table by the back door where we keep our purses and keys.

"You smell absolutely edible." A knowing smile crosses her lips.

"Not as edible as that cupcake." I eye her tray of pink and purple cupcakes and lick my lips.

"Maybe if you frost yourself, your night will be magical." She winks and pumps the frosting on her second set of cupcakes. "They're unicorn cupcakes." She pinches some glitter from a bowl and sprinkles it across the tray of frosted cupcakes.

"You really need to sell these." I grab my keys and my purse. "What did Landon say the other night?"

She releases a long breath. "He said he wouldn't pay four dollars for a cupcake." She rolls her eyes. "But he also added that he's a cheap ass. After that, I went and drowned my sorrows at Happy Daze."

I giggle. From the short conversation I had with Landon, it was clear he doesn't come from money and spending four dollars for a cupcake isn't on his list of necessities, but there are plenty of people that would.

"In San Francisco, these cupcakes would probably go for five dollars each." I hold one up, the colorful frosting and glitter making me so close to taking a bite.

Charlie walks in and sits down at the breakfast bar in front of the cupcakes. "Okay, I'm on a break between season two and three. What do you have for me?" Ava grabs a plate of five different cupcakes from behind her and places them in front of Charlie. "Are these the ones you brought into Happy Daze last weekend?" Charlie asks.

"Sort-of. I tweaked the recipe after all the feedback."

Charlie looks over to me and I check the microwave clock to see that I still have some time. The last thing I want is to get there early and seem like an eager beaver. Since I hardly ever get to spend time with both my roommates at once, I take a seat on the stool next to Charlie.

"Did this little sugar dealer tell you that she passed around cupcakes the other night? The customers were going crazy," Charlie says around a bite of cupcake.

Ava cringes, continuing to frost and sprinkle. "I hope you didn't get in trouble?"

Charlie rolls her eyes. "Hell no. Dane wants you to be a weekly thing. He said he almost came in his pants with the caramel cocoa one." She shoots Ava a smile that says 'you're in there like swimwear.'

Ava blushes. "Oh good. Which night do you think is better, Sunday or Monday?"

Charlie laughs. "Let me talk to Dane." She chomps down on the vanilla cupcake with pink frosting.

"Isn't Dane, Toby's father?" I ask, swiping the frosting from the bowl and sucking my finger.

Charlie nods, her mouth full and Ava sighs. "Unfortunately, yes."

"The one you told off the other day?" I ask, surprised.

"Wait!" Ava freezes and narrows her eyes at Charlie. "Does he know it was me with the cupcakes?"

"First of all," Charlie mumbles and then swallows. "You told Dane off? Second of all, no, I just told him it was one of my friends."

Ava's shoulders lose all the tension. "Toby caused Lily to get hurt and I might have overreacted. Do me a favor, Charlie and don't tell Dane the cupcakes are coming from me?"

Charlie's perfectly arched eyebrows furrow as does mine. "Why?"

The buzzer on the oven goes off and Ava quickly turns around. "I like unbiased opinions and so many people know my dad. They'll just say they're good even if they suck."

Charlie holds the cupcake up in the air. "These things do not suck." Charlie chomps down again.

"Who cares if he knows?" I add in but Ava remains quiet.

"That goes for you, too, Cat. I know Dane and Marcus are friends." She starts positioning the cupcakes on a plate and wraps some foil over it. "Here." She thrusts them at me. "Get Lily's opinion and don't tell Marcus where they came from." Her warning voice is kinda scary.

I nod. "Okay, but I don't see the big deal."

"Me either. What the hell Ava? You're acting like you're going to cut our fingers off if we snitch." Charlie places the cupcake down.

"I don't mean to be demanding, it's just...trust me. It's better if Dane Murray doesn't know I'm responsible for the cupcakes." She focuses on the plate as she transfers the cupcakes from the hot pan.

"Well, I'm sure Lily is going to love this. What kid doesn't love unicorns?" I change the subject because Ava's reasons aren't my business and I don't want to push.

She looks up and smiles but it doesn't reach her eyes.

"Everyone loves unicorns." Charlie grabs one of the unicorn cupcakes now. "I might as well go shop for bigger sized shorts. Seriously, Ava, the freshman fifteen I gained in college and finally lost will be nothing compared to this summer." She dips her finger into the glitter and frosting on top of the cupcake. "Here's a tip. An early Christmas present for me would be a muumuu."

I chuckle remembering my sister and her friends. The Unicorn Cock vibrator Tahlia's friend Lennon invented a few years ago comes to mind...the swirling colors and the small glitter beads that twirl around. By the time I'm back to the present, both Charlie and Ava are staring at me.

"Sorry, we're talking about unicorns and it got me thinking about how my sister and her friends had this whole thing about finding your unicorn cock." I wave off my statement and stand to get going.

"Unicorn cock?" Charlie asks, her gaze moving between Ava and me. She pats the seat I just got up from. "Do tell."

My gaze veers to the glowing numbers on the microwave and Ava follows my vision. "You have five minutes."

Reluctantly, I sit down. "They have this theory that there's a perfect cock out there for everyone. One that'll give you orgasms you never dreamed were possible. They all refer to their husbands as their unicorn cocks. One of my sister's best friends invents sex toys and she created a Unicorn Cock vibrator a few years back. That's what I was thinking about." My cheeks heat because it sounds ridiculous when I say it out loud.

Charlie laughs, almost falling off the stool and pounds her hand on the counter. Ava shakes her head and continues to frost the cupcakes in front of her.

"That's the best thing ever! I need to find my unicorn cock fast because I've had a bunch of dull screwdrivers lately." Charlie pulls her phone from her back pocket and thrusts it at me. "Pull up the vibrator on here and I'll buy it right now."

I do just that, finding Lennon's site and even putting it in the cart for Charlie.

"Perfect. In one week I won't need to find my perfect man because I'll have my very own Unicorn Cock," she pauses and looks at me with a stern glare. "She didn't use her husband as like a model or anything like that, right?"

I chuckle and shake my head. "No way. Lennon would never share Jasper's cock with anyone."

Charlie lets out a relieved breath.

"Okay, now I really do have to go." I stand, grabbing the plate of cupcakes.

"Maybe Marcus Kent is your unicorn cock," Charlie says.

"Come on. I don't believe in that crap." But I cross my fingers as I say it just in case. A girl can never be too careful.

The meat is on the grill, the vegetables are on the stove and the bread is in the oven. Lily's running around the backyard as I check on the meat. Caterina should be here any minute.

"Miss Cat isn't here yet." She runs back into the house to wait by the window again I assume. She might be even more excited than me.

Of course, her excitement isn't like mine—I feel like I'm battling the nerves of a pitcher in a no-hitter game.

What I feel when I'm in the presence of Cat could go down in a ball of flames tonight.

I move the meat onto a plate, turn off the grill and then head inside to cover dinner until she arrives. I come through the doorway and my fingers loosen, the plate almost slipping out of my grip.

She's here. And she's breathtaking.

"Lily let me in," she says, standing in the kitchen of my house.

Her hair is out of its usual ponytail, falling to her shoulders with a slight wave. The natural make-up she wears only accentuates her already delicate features. A yellow sundress makes her sun-kissed skin look even more delicious and smooth. You'd think we're about have dinner beachside in Hawaii rather than on my deck.

A grin I can't contain lifts the corners of my lips. "Great. Dinner is about ready." I head to the kitchen, with the meat, trying to convince my own meat to settle down.

Jesus, she's hot in pajamas, she's hot in a swimsuit, she's hot in a pair of shorts, but in a dress? I might as well call her dad and confess all the dirty things I want to do to his daughter right this very minute.

I glance at the kitchen table, finding a foil covered paper plate.

"I told you not to bring anything," I say, slicing the meat.

"They aren't for you, they're for Lily."

"Me?" Lily screeches, plopping down in the chair, stripping the foil off the plate. "Wow!"

Her amazement makes me turn and look. Cat joins Lily at the table.

"Cupcakes, Daddy!"

"I see." Cat's eyes catch mine and we share a smile at Lily's shocked excitement.

"They're unicorn cupcakes."

I abandon the slicing in favor of watching the two of them interact with each other. Lily's propped up on her knees, her face an inch away from the plate of cupcakes. Cat taps Lily's nose and Lily smiles. My heart warms and I quickly turn around to concentrate on anything other than how nice it is to see Lily interact this way with a woman.

I serve the meat, grab the salad out of the fridge, and put the vegetables in a bowl. The two of them giggle and I don't say anything when I see Cat allow Lily a taste of the frosting off one of the cupcakes.

"Ready for dinner?" I ask, holding the three dishes like I'm a waiter.

Maybe my years of being a server at Denny's in high school came in handy for something.

Cat looks up and stands before heading for the patio door. She slides it open and I pause before stepping through to my deck.

"Thank you." Our eyes lock and maybe I should've had her over without Lily being home. But they already know each other and Lily is a part of my life. The biggest part of and most important part of my life and I'm serious about not using Cat as a nightly booty call. Who the hell knows what will happen at the end of the summer? I'm just going to take it one day at a time right now.

"Hey Lil, grab the salad dressing," I call out to her. I hear her bare feet scamper across the tile in the kitchen.

I set the plates down on my large outdoor table under the pergola on my deck.

"What can I do to help?" Cat asks, and the wind blows her hair across her face.

She grabs a hold of it and I'm wondering if I made the wrong choice by eating outside.

I step forward, unsticking the hairs that have shellacked themselves to her lip glossed lips. Lips that are begging for my attention.

"Would you rather eat inside?" I ask.

The scent of her flowery perfume is like an aphrodisiac. My cock is painfully aware of her proximity and it's not going to be happy to continue this evening without any attention. I look over her shoulder, seeing Lily placing every salad dressing we have on the counter.

"No. This is beautiful." Cat's looking at me, not at the glimpse of the Pacific Ocean behind us.

I lean in and kiss her cheek. Her skin is just as soft as I remember.

"You're beautiful. Thank you for coming."

I walk into my house and leave her and her red cheeks outside to admire the view.

"Lil, we only need the one I made earlier. The cucumber ranch one."

She slams the fridge, ignoring me completely. Picking up the jar of salad dressing I prepared earlier today, she runs outside, not willing to miss a minute with Cat.

The two sit on the loveseat outside, though Lily's excited voice is the only one I hear through the open patio door.

With a bottle of red wine and a juice box, I head out to join my ladies for the evening, but my feet stop right outside the door. Lily is on Cat's lap as they look out over the trees to the clear view of Climax Cove. Lily's pointing out everything below as though Cat doesn't know what's down there. Each time, Cat makes sure to sound surprised as though she didn't pass each and every restaurant and shop on her way to our house.

I clear my throat and Cat turns, while Lily continues talking about Toby and Dane.

"Is red okay?" I ask, holding up the bottle.

She nods. "Let's go eat," Cat says to Lily.

She jumps off Cat's lap, skipping to the table. Lily's happier than I've seen her in a while. She jumps up into her seat, pushing her straw into the juice box and like always, squeezing too hard to make it happen so that some of the juice overflows onto the table.

I open the wine bottle and pour two glasses then hold out Cat's chair for her to sit. She accepts, tucking her dress underneath her with the grace of a socialite who's done it a thousand times before.

"Daddy." Lily climbs out of her chair. "Do me?"

Cat and I laugh at Lily's demand, but I do hold the chair out for her and tuck it back into the table. She hops up on her knees, her face crumpling up in disgust as she looks at the food.

"Oh, I'll be right back." I run into the house and grab Lily's chicken nuggets from the toaster oven.

By the time I come back, Cat is cutting up a piece of the carrot for Lily.

"Carrots make you so smart. I try to eat them every day," Cat tells her.

Lily's fork is piercing a slice of carrot, inching it toward her mouth. I wait, knowing that if I interrupt and agree with Cat, Lily will not get near that carrot.

Lily places it in her mouth and exaggerates her chewing to the point that I want to tell her to close her mouth, but I stop myself.

"It's good, right?" Cat places a piece of carrot in her mouth. "Your daddy makes good carrots."

Lily's head bobs back and forth not quite agreeing with Cat's assessment.

Cat laughs and then catches me watching. She straightens her back and places her hands in her lap. "Sorry, we started a little early," she says.

"No, please." I place Lily's chicken nuggets in front of her.

"Yay! Chicken nuggets," she screams, and I shake my head while folding myself into my patio chair.

"The meal looks delicious," Cat says.

I pick up the plate of flank steak and hand it over to her. As we pass the dishes back and forth, Lily continues to chomp down on her nuggets, her eyes flickering between the two of us.

"Daddy's a good cook, right?" Lily asks Cat.

"Shh," I say to Lily. "Don't put her on the spot."

Cat wipes her mouth with the napkin and places it in her lap. "He is."

Lily smiles a proud grin that gives me a warm feeling in my chest because it's her my-daddy-is-the-best grin.

"Wanna watch *Tangled*?" Lily asks Cat.

"Sure." Cat answers.

I wish I had her alone.

"Flynn is so funny," Lily carries on, talking about the movie.

She's just about done eating and I know she'll be bored soon.

"Do you cook every night?" Cat asks me and then takes a bite of her steak.

My knife and fork pause. "Usually. It's healthier for Lily." I glance down to her frozen chicken nuggets. "But some nights I'd rather have a nice dinner than an argument." I wink at her.

Cat laughs. "My nephew is the same. Tahlia always says that mealtime is the most stressful time of day in her house. I swear she chases him around the room with food on a fork."

I nod, chuckling because I've done my share of that in the past.

"Speaking of family, I talked to your dad earlier this week." I wipe my mouth with the napkin and place it in my lap before grabbing my wine glass.

"Oh, you did?" She sounds surprised and a little wary. She probably feels the same way I do about her dad knowing about us.

"He's coming in next week to pick up the two boats."

She nods. "My mom called me a few days ago. I hear Lucas is going to take one back?"

"Yeah."

"Daddy, can I go in and get my iPad?" Lily interrupts.

Seeing her plate is now clear and not wanting to bother lecturing her about interrupting right now, I simply respond, "Sure."

She stands up and jumps off the chair onto the deck.

"Lily!" I begin to scold her for almost hurting herself when I remember we aren't alone. The last thing I want is Cat to think I'm some quick-tempered father.

"Sorry," Lily says, running into the house.

"She's so great," Cat says and leans closer. "Don't tell anyone, but she's my favorite."

My lips spread open. "I'm glad she doesn't cause you too much trouble."

"I didn't say she wasn't trouble. The girl talks non-stop, she's always running around and jumping, but she's such a sweet and loving little girl."

"She's nothing like me."

Cat studies me for a few seconds and then concentrates back on her meal. "Why do you say that? You're fun and you're obviously sweet."

I place my fork and knife down, again, reaching for my wine glass. "I'm pretty sure fun and sweet have never been used to describe me before." I chuckle.

"You have responsibilities, so it's not like being fun can be bungee jumping or skydiving. You can't go out every night and get smashed and wake up with a hangover, but I bet you have pillow fights and go to parks. You and Lily probably make day trips to explore different places."

I nod in agreement though I'm surprised that a woman Cat's age would describe all that as fun.

"And as for sweet, well, Mr. Kent, you invited me here. You made me dinner and set a table outside on your deck to watch the sun set." She glances to the door and leans closer. "I think we both know you didn't have to wine and dine me like this, and the fact that you did it anyway makes you sweet."

She has a point. Dane takes his dates to Breakers, a fish restaurant that hands out plastic bibs. And that's only if he wants to invest in her. Otherwise, it's a stroll on the marina and maybe a drink at Happy Daze. And Garrett. That guy hasn't been with anyone in years.

"I'll be honest. You're the first woman I've done anything like this for. I guess I only do this for the ones, or one as it were, that I want to."

She smiles, pushing her plate away from her. "Thank you. I'm glad I'm wanted."

"You're definitely wanted."

Our eyes lock and I cup her cheek, pulling her lips to mine. I taste the wine on her tongue, but as always when you live with a five-year-old, interruptions happen. I hear her little footsteps running our way and so I pull back.

"Look at Flynn!" Lily thrusts her iPad into Cat's lap.

"Lily." My voice has that note of warning and Lily picks up the iPad from Cat, but Cat stops her.

"It's okay." She looks up at me. "It's okay."

While she's watching the video my phone rings in my pocket. I pull it out and glance to see that it's Ashley.

"Hi, Ashley," I answer and Cat turns her head my way.

"Can I talk to her?" Lily asks, running over to my side, jumping up and down.

I hold my finger up in the air and she jumps side to side like she has to go to the bathroom.

"Hi, Mr. Kent, I'm sorry, but I won't be able to babysit tomorrow. I think I'm coming down with something."

My head falls back and I suck in a slow breath as disappointment sets in. I was supposed to go rock climbing with Dane and Garrett tomorrow.

"Okay, I understand, Ashley. I hope you feel better."

"Thank you and I'm sorry." We hang up and I tuck my phone into my pocket. I'll have to message the guys later.

"Sorry."

"I wanted to talk," Lily whines.

I pat her head. "Sorry, Ashley doesn't feel well so she can't watch you tomorrow."

"Can I go with you now?" Her eyes light up.

"No, but now you get me all day." My fingers tickle her and she cries out in laughter.

"Yay," she squirms and I pull her onto my lap.

Rock climbing would have been nice, but spending time with Lily isn't something I'd ever complain about.

"I can do it," Cat offers and both Lily and I stop and look over to her for a second.

"Can she? Can she?" Lily turns to face me, waiting for an answer.

"I can't ask you to do that on your day off."

She waves me off, holding her arms out to Lily, who happily shifts over to her lap.

"I'd love to."

Lily wraps her arms around her neck and gives her a tight hug.

"Thank you," I say, a little in awe that she'd even offer.

Cat looks at me over Lily's shoulder. "You're welcome."

"Let's play Monopoly!" Lily screams, hops off Cat's lap and runs into the house.

"I thought we were watching *Tangled*?" Cat calls out after her.

"Welcome to the wonderful world of Lily," I say and chuckle. "I really appreciate you watching her. I'm going rock climbing with Dane and Garrett. Shouldn't be gone too long. Maybe I can make you dinner again?"

She stands up, stacking the dishes on top of one another. "Maybe *we'll* make you dinner."

I reach out without thinking twice. Before I contemplate if Lily is going to run back out here. My hand cups her cheek and her breath hitches in her throat.

"That sounds amazing," I say.

My lips are millimeters away from hers when I hear the playroom door slam shut which means Lily is going to be out here any second.

"To be continued." I let her go.

Lily comes outside and we both pretend we were clearing the table instead of about to make out like a couple of teenagers.

21

This might be the first date I've spent playing the Frozen version of Junior Monopoly, and making my own sundae. Most of my dates in the past wined and dined me courtesy of their trust fund or daddy's credit card. A lot of those ended with him expecting too much in return and curse words thrown my way as he walked down the hallway of my condo building after I shut him down.

I watched my sister get screwed over by a rich boy who thought the rules didn't apply to him. Not that I typecast all the guys who attended my private school, but I witnessed enough shit the guys in my inner circle did to know that's not what I want for my future.

Tonight, I wait in a pink and purple room with butter-flies hanging from the ceiling for a little girl to brush her teeth so I can tuck her in at her insistence. I've gone from frat parties to play dates.

"She really likes you," Marcus says. He seems nervous as we stand alone in Lily's room to say goodnight.

I'm not even sure she understands I'm here for a date

with Marcus. She's talked my ear off the entire night and made sure my attention was focused solely on her. Which isn't horrible, I meant what I said to Marcus. I like Lily. A lot. And she is one of my favorite campers, but interacting with kids when their parents aren't around is much easier. I keep worrying that I'm doing something wrong or he's judging me on how good of a mom I'd be if we got serious. There's a whole other level of things to stress about that isn't usually there when I date someone.

"Thanks," I say, my gaze continuing to skirt around Lily's room.

For a guy, Marcus has done a surprisingly good job of decorating Lily's room. Besides the butterflies, there's a mural of a tree with dark pink birds and owls on the branches. Fairies are painted on the four walls. Right above her nightstand, words are written in script. I step closer to read them and my heart fills with warmth for Marcus.

From the moment they placed you in my arms, you snuggled right into my heart.

Swallowing past the lump currently lodged in my throat I look over my shoulder to find Marcus leaning on the wall, his intense gaze on me.

"Wow," I say, tears pricking my eyes. He loves her so deeply and I'm not sure I realized until this moment, what a big step this must have been for him. That he hasn't gone into the decision of bringing me here lightly.

Lily runs into the room and jumps onto her bed, shuffling under the covers. She grabs a book off her nightstand, holding it out to me. "Will you read me my goodnight story?"

I look over to Marcus who's still leaning against the wall. I've never met a man whose thoughts were so hard to read.

"Sure," I say, hoping that's okay. I take a seat beside Lily in bed and stretch my legs out in front of me.

"Come, Daddy." Lily pats the mattress on the other side of her.

My breath lodges in my throat when the bed dips and the scent of Marcus's crisp cologne reaches me. In the moment, it feels suffocating in the small space Lily has placed us in.

Together, from an outsider's view, we're a family, but in reality, they're the family and I'm the outsider. I can only hope that my presence doesn't threaten their happy bubble.

By the time I finish reading and close the book, Lily's eyes are droopy. I press my finger to her nose and I'm rewarded with a soft giggle. "Night, Lily," I say and stand up to leave the room.

"Night, Miss Cat." She yawns.

I circle around to face her, stepping backward out the door. "I promise to bring some fun things for us to do tomorrow."

"Yay," she says, her eyes shifting to her dad's with a look that says, tomorrow's going to be amazing.

I wait in the hallway outside her room for Marcus to finish saying goodnight.

"Let's just take it off for the night," I hear Marcus say.

I'm positive they must be talking about the bracelet.

"No, Daddy."

"Okay, okay. Night, Lily Lu, see you in the morning," Marcus says and the nickname Lily Lu surprises me. Marcus doesn't seem like the type to nickname someone, but then again, he doesn't seem like someone that would paint the quote about his daughter snuggling into his heart.

It's almost as if he holds his emotions captive inside of him.

"Daddy?" Lily asks.

"Yeah?" Marcus' voice is closer now.

"Can Miss Cat be my mommy?"

All my muscles tense and my breath catches in my throat. I'm certain my heart sputtered over a beat or two.

"Miss Cat is here as our friend, sweetie. But we'll talk about that when we have more time. Love you, Lily Lu,"

"Love you, Daddy."

He steps out of her room, his hand on the doorknob, freezing on the spot when he sees me.

"You heard?" he whispers, letting go of the doorknob and walking toward me.

"Yeah," I whisper.

If Lily is anything like my nephew, Alexander, she's not asleep yet. Hell, she might surprise us in a second by cracking open that door.

Marcus continues walking, his hand grabbing hold of mine and leading me down the stairs. "Let's go have another glass of wine."

Following him down the staircase, I admire the way his lean, muscled body moves. His movements are controlled and suave, as usual.

My skin tingles in anticipation of his touch. My nipples have been able to cut glass almost all night and my panties are soaked. I want Marcus so fucking bad that I'm half tempted to make the first move. I don't think he'd complain, but he shut me down all those years ago and that's not a feeling I can easily forget.

He guides us to the kitchen, pulling another bottle of wine out of his wine fridge, his hand never letting mine go. He navigates us around the kitchen until he detours to the family room, grabbing a blanket off the couch, finishing up by walking back onto his deck.

It's a spectacular view, although right now it's in darkness except for the lighthouse and a few restaurant and bars still open in the downtown part of Climax Cove.

Marcus lets go of my hand and I saunter over to the edge of his deck. It's so high up on stilts that it might make some people nervous, but all I can think about is what a great spot it would be to paint. I hear the cork pop out of the wine bottle, but my gaze refuses to divert from the view in front of me as I wish I had my paints and canvas.

"I don't suppose you'd mind if I locked myself up here for a few hours to paint this view one night?" I look over my shoulder and Marcus is closing the distance between us, the blanket in his hands.

He wraps it around my shoulders and cages me in against the railing between his two arms. "You're welcome anytime."

I lean back into him, his strong chest taking the weight of my body with ease. "What made you build up here?"

He brushes my hair off my shoulder. "I wanted to be the king of Climax Cove." Before I can ask if he's serious, he laughs into the crook of my neck. "My dad owned the land, it made sense."

His lips touch my temple and my eyes drift closed as I relish in his touch.

"It must be nice to be so remote." Although, I'm not sure how much more remote you can get than Climax Cove.

"It's nice not to hear the fisherman in the morning. We used to live downtown right off Main. Close to your apartment."

I tilt my head and he gets the hint, his lips traveling along my skin, his hands still on either side of me gripping the iron balcony.

"Yeah, they can be loud in the morning, but I love

painting them when they come in for the day."

He tenses behind me. "Do I need to be worried that you like fisherman?" The tone in his voice is light, but there's still a slight edge to it. I hope he's catching on that I only do have eyes for him.

I circle around, allowing his lips to fall from my skin. "I like men who build boats more."

He steps forward, so we're chest to chest.

"I'm trying really hard right now to tell myself that this balcony was built properly and that I won't plummet to my death." I laugh, but he only moves further forward, making me bend over the edge.

"Trust me, Cat, nothing bad will happen to you if I'm near." His eyes hold the conviction of his words and without the thought of repercussions or rejections, my hands grab a hold of his cheeks and I plant my lips to his.

His urgency meets my own, swiping his tongue along the seam of my lips and I open to him. The taste of red wine comes off his tongue and I dive deeper, needing to feel how much I unglue him. As if he can hear my thoughts, his hands wrap around my waist and he lifts me up, carrying me over to the loveseat.

My arms slide around his neck, my fingers fisting in the strands of his hair on the back of his head. Breaking the kiss, he sits down on the loveseat, taking my hand and guiding me down so I straddle him. His gaze fixates on my movements and when I sink down on top of him he growls, his hands landing on my ass and pressing me into him.

The hard erection hidden under his khakis isn't a surprise, but I never thought I'd crave it this much. I want to unbuckle his pants, freeing the beast that teases me. See what it can really do and how it will leave me panting for breath by the end of the night.

Not missing a beat, Marcus's hand slides up my back, finding the zipper of my dress and dragging it down. The cool night breeze hits my overheated skin and I shiver, arching my back.

"If you want me to suck on your tits, just tell me." A smirk teases his lips and he pulls down the sleeves of my dress, leaving me in only my bra from the waist up.

I wore a demi cup bra so my nipples are about a millimeter away from the edge of the fabric. Marcus wastes no time in pulling the cups down and his mouth closes over one nipple, devouring it while his thumb and forefinger pinch my other one.

"What about Lily?" I ask, my eyes closing and my arms wrapped around his head as my body rocks back and forth, grinding into his lap.

My nipple pops out of his mouth and he looks up at me, his hair a tousled mess.

"Please don't mention my daughter's name right now."

He smiles then buries his head back between my breasts. My skin has never burned the way it does now. The small amount of stubble on his face tickles as it rubs along my skin.

"What if she wakes up?" I whisper.

He pulls away from me and this time he leans back on the love seat. "She's a deep sleeper."

His eyes say 'trust me on this, I'm her dad,' but I can't help the fear that I'm going to look through that glass door and find her face pressed to the glass. We'd ruin her for life and only years of therapy would fix her.

He blows out a breath. "You aren't going to relax, are you?" he asks.

I bite my lip and shake my head. "I'm sorry. I just don't want her to see us."

He inches forward and I pick up the sleeves of my dress, my hand reaching to my back.

"Don't zip up." His callused hand covers mine. "This isn't exactly what I wanted for our first time, but I need you relaxed when I fuck you."

He entwines our fingers, grabbing the wine and the blanket, walking us through the patio door. He shuts and locks it then pulls me through the house to another door— one with a deadbolt lock on it. The door opens and reveals an office.

"We could play therapist and patient," I say, letting go of his hand and falling onto the brown leather couch along the window.

He laughs, placing the wine bottle on his desk.

"I'll be whoever you want me to be." His determined footsteps come straight for me and he has that cool and debonair look to him again that makes my insides tingle and zing and sizzle. You'd think I was some kid with the most wanted toy just out of reach.

"Well, doctor," I shimmy my arms from the sleeves of my dress again, my tits out to play since I never tucked them back into my dress. "I have an unhealthy obsession." I drop my voice to a seductive tone and lick my lips.

"Not all obsessions are bad, Caterina." He sits next to me, his arm hanging on the back of the sofa, his cologne filling the space between us.

"He's," I lean forward, "older," I whisper.

His finger grazes along my bare shoulders and shivers run up the back of my neck.

"With age comes experience." I watch his gaze dip to my breasts and the pulsing between my legs vibrates through my entire body.

"So, it's okay to want an older man?" I bite back my smile

because in all honesty, I don't see Marcus as an older man. I get that he's ten years older, but he's still hot as hell.

His head falls forward, his lips capturing my earlobe and my back arches. I lean into his mouth, goose bumps overtaking every inch of my skin.

"I think I'd heavily endorse your obsession."

"Figures. All men are alike." I fall out of the patient role, needing him to touch me and calm the overzealous arousal burning inside of me.

"We are a hungry breed." He nibbles on my earlobe and then bites down until I almost scream. His mouth stays next to my ear, his hand sliding to my back to undo my bra and then along my ribcage. His large palm covers my tit and he squeezes. "Now Cat, let me show you the perks of an older man."

He places his weight on me until I'm against the back of the couch.

"Well then, Mr. Kent, do show me what I've been missing out on."

My eyes drift closed as his hands venture along my ribcage and my legs part, making room for him to ease between my thighs.

He says nothing else although I know the dirty words will start pouring out of his mouth soon. His mouth covers mine and his elbows rest on either side of my head while his lips press to mine in an unexpected gentle and loving manner.

Just when I think Marcus went sentimental on me, his hands slide down to my hips. His warm, wet lips leave my mouth and he flips me on my stomach.

"Ass in the air," he demands.

I swear I drip down my thigh.

I should go slow. I should treat her like a princess and circle my hips at a leisurely pace, but with every moan from her parted lips, my urgency increases. Taking her gently right now isn't going to happen.

When I slip my finger between her slit and feel how drenched her pussy is, it's clear that she likes me dominating and commanding in the bedroom. Which is a good thing since that's the only way I know how to be. Don't get me wrong, after I smack her ass I'll soothe it with a rub.

My fingers grip the sides of her panties and I pull them down her legs, allowing her to help me by lifting one leg at a time. I bring the lacy fabric up to my nose and inhale. God, she smells fucking sweet. I toss them behind me readier than ever to be inside Caterina.

"Is there nothing about you that isn't perfect?" I take her ass in my hands, molding and squeezing every inch of smooth skin. My dick is painfully hard as the urge to slip into her wetness and let her know who owns her ratchets up a level.

"Marcus," she whines.

I chuckle. "Something wrong, sweetheart?"

I stand and with shaking fingers, I unbutton and unzip my pants until they fall to my ankles. I step out of them, stripping my shirt off at the same time so I'm left only in my black boxer briefs.

"I need you inside me," she says, her head tucked between her elbows on the arm of the coach.

I'll never be able to use this office again without remembering this moment and picturing her splayed and ready for me.

"In time, in time." I trail my fingers along the globes of her ass again, wanting her anticipation to build up to a fevered pitch and then I smack my hand down.

She yelps, her head swinging up, her back sinking and her chest rising like a cat.

I lean forward, casting small kisses to her now sweat pebbled skin. Her dress is still wrapped around her waist and at this point, it's in the way. Grabbing the yellow fabric, I pull it down past her hips and her legs.

She sighs when it joins my clothes on the floor.

"I need to see all of you," I whisper in her ear.

She flips around and I wait to see her on her back, sprawled out, but instead, she sits up on the arm of the couch. Her legs are pressed together and her tits sit on her chest like two perfect raindrops. She's so fucking gorgeous and hot as sin I'm not sure how much longer my dick can play this game of delayed gratification.

She crooks her finger to me and I'm like a dog with a bone, sliding across the leather. My hand eases between her legs and I nudge them open, crawling up to kiss her.

"We can play games later, Mr. Kent, I need you inside of me." Her voice is tender and sweet which I love. I prefer to be the one in charge, the demanding lover. I'm not into being tied up and hit with shit. My assumption is that's Dane.

Taking her head in my hands, I pull her face to mine and that dance we're starting to perfect intensifies as our tongues meet. I hoist her up by her hips and she lands on my lap. I don't know if I'll be able to be slow, but either way, I need to see and feel all of her while we fuck.

She holds my body tight to hers and I use a free hand to pull my boxers down, realizing I need a fucking condom.

Ripping my lips away from hers, I pick her up in my arms, gliding along the floor until I can step out of the boxers wrapped around my ankles. "Sorry, need a condom."

I prop her on my desk and she keeps her legs tight around my torso as I dig through the drawers searching for one measly condom. It's been awhile but surely, I have one.

"Marcus," she says.

"Yeah?" I answer, my hands scrambling through pens, staples, papers and rubber band balls.

"Marcus," she says my name again, this time in a sing-song voice.

I glance up at her as my hands continue blindly searching for a damn foil packet. She shakes her head and places her hand on my forearm to stop my efforts. She's crazy because I am not leaving this office until I know what it feels like to be inside her. We both need relief from the tension that's been building for weeks.

"I'll run to the store if I have to."

She laughs, her head tilting to the side and her hair falls over her face in the most carefree, flirty way.

I need her now.

"Are you clean?" she asks.

I briefly wonder if this is what happens now-a-days because most dipshits would lie.

"I've only had sex with a condom since Lily. Promise, but—"

She shakes her head again. "I'm on the pill and I'm clean, too. Just pull out."

She's so matter of fact and comfortable with this conversation that a self-conscious part of me from the past, time warps into the present. I'm a long way out of college and my curiosity as to how many and what caliber of partners Cat has had during her exploratory phase makes me consider for the first time tonight that I might not compare.

Who am I kidding? I've got ten years on those little shits she's probably used to dating. Back when I was twenty-four, I was only concerned about my own pleasure, almost never the girl I was with. Guys that age are greedy and I'm sure that hasn't changed.

"So, can we go without?" She uses her heels to push me closer to her and the slick heat of her core presses against my engorged cock.

I'm seconds away from lining up my engorged tip with her entrance when I hesitate.

The phone call from Gretchen six years ago telling me about her unexpected pregnancy playing in my head. I do not need another baby mama in my life. When I have another child, I want it to be in a committed relationship with the woman I plan on spending the rest of my days with.

Talk about a mood killer.

"If you're not comfortable, we don't have to." A small smile forms on her lips, but I can see a little of her confidence draining away at my hesitation.

I can do this.

"You're sure?" I clarify one more time.

I don't believe Cat is the kind of girl to try to get pregnant on purpose. What would be the point? Her family has more money than God and the only thing I can offer her is myself and Lily.

"Marcus." Her hands warm my cheeks as she waits for me to focus on her. "I promise you, I have never not used a condom. I was tested right before I came here during my annual exam."

Does she really know me well enough to know that a part of me is freaking out, while the other part is raising my foam number one finger in the air in celebration?

"Okay." I smile at her and she returns it with a full wattage smile of her own.

I grab her legs and pull her forward on my desk so her ass is right at the edge. The tip of my dick lands right where I want it to, teasing her clit. She falls back, her palms pressed to the hard wood on top of my desk.

Her skin is glistening from the heat we've caused in the small room and I imagine what her tits will look like when I spray my cum all over them when I finish.

I arrange my tip at her opening and slide in, inch by glorious inch, until she takes all of me. She's tight as a fucking fist and my eyes nearly roll back in my head.

"Marcus," my name falls from her lips like a plea and a prayer all in one.

Once I'm fully seated inside her, I circle my hips so she can get used to my size. Damn, I forgot what it feels like without a condom. So hot and silky and wet. Not to mention a hundred times better than with that thin sheet of plastic covering my dick, and about a thousand times better than my fist.

My hands grip her small hips, my fingernails pressing into her flesh. Her eyes zero in on our point of connection and we both watch as I withdraw slowly and then slam back into her. We both moan out our pleasure as I do it again.

She drops so she's propped up on her elbows and I swing one of her legs over my shoulder and thrust into her. She cries out.

"You like it like that?" I practically growl.

She nods her head frantically up and down as I continue to pound into her.

Fuck. She's warm and wet and slick and if I don't concentrate on something else, I'm sure to blow my load in two point two seconds.

She brings her elbows out from under her so that she's lying on the desk now. One hand snakes down her body and she starts massaging her clit. Since my gaze won't veer away, I concentrate on her movements, committing them to memory so next time I do it just how she likes.

Her teeth bite down on her lip and although I wish could scream from the rooftops, we both know we don't have that pleasure tonight. We'll have to save that for a hotel room at some point.

Needing to free her bottom lip and wanting to swallow down her cries, I lean forward and capture her mouth with mine.

Our tongues collide and our mouths mesh as though we've gone hundreds of years without human contact. I never stop pumping and her body never stops arching as items fall from my desk, landing on the floor.

One hand reaches behind her and she grabs the edge of the desk to use as an anchor to push back against me, only gaining me deeper inside of her.

"Oh, shit. That's it," she says, her eyes drifting closed and her back arching off the desk.

I take my hand and plant it on her stomach to keep her down so that she has no choice but to take every inch of me in her slick pussy.

The intensity switches gear the closer we are to coming and somewhere, in the midst of searching hands and exploring mouths, our kisses become gentler. Her leg falls off my shoulder to wrap around my waist and I'm leaning forward, swallowing down her sweet moans. Cat's arms are wrapped around my neck, fiddling with the hair on the back of my head.

"I'm going to come," she announces in a breathless voice as I'm licking my way up her neck to her earlobe.

"Come all over me," I whisper.

And she does. Her body convulsing around me as she cries out before she eventually slows and her body lies limp beneath me. Satisfaction fills my chest as I gaze down at her knowing her orgasm was a result of my efforts.

Her eyes drift open and a lazy, Cheshire-grin slides across her mouth. "Keep going. Don't stop until I'm sweet *and* sticky."

She's got to be fucking kidding me. Those dirty words mixed with her innocent appearance would drive any man to the limit.

Not needing any further encouragement, I slam in and out of her at a ferocious pace. She clings to me tighter and when my lower back starts to tingle and my balls clench, I drag myself out of her and use my fist to finish the job. I decorate her tits with my cum while she looks on, sucking her lower lip into her mouth as if she enjoys seeing it as much as I do.

Once I've milked myself dry, I step back and grab a tissue from the holder on the other side of the desk. I take a second to admire my handy work before I start wiping down Cat's tits and stomach.

My dick is still hard and I'm almost positive I could have her all night and not be sated.

She sits up and I remain between her legs, cupping her face in my hands and bringing her lips to mine. We share a sweet kiss that doesn't speak to the raw sex we just had, but I'm not sure I've ever shared anything like that with a woman.

The emotions between us were hot and fast and then slow and sweet. Hell, if there was a synonym for the phrase 'perfect woman,' it'd be Caterina Santora. She works my dick like fucking magic and makes my heart swell at the same time.

"You don't think Lily heard us, do you?" She covers her mouth now, looking a little shy, as though the moaning from moments before wouldn't have already stirred my five-year-old.

"And there goes my hard-on." It shrinks down to a half chub with the one word Cat can't seem to stop using when we're undressed.

She giggles and scoots off my desk. Never will I be able to work in this room without reliving this night. I step back to give her space and we both venture back to the couch where our clothes are. I wish I could stay naked with her for the rest of the night and get a few more positions under our belt. I want to find the hidden spots that drive her crazy and help her discover new areas she doesn't even know about. But that's not happening with Lily here.

I throw on my pants and shirt as Cat zips up her dress, but I catch her bra in my hand as she's swinging it up from the floor.

"Stay a little longer?" I ask, placing a quick kiss on her lips.

She nods with a smile. A smile that makes me regret every frown I ever put on her beautiful face.

"I'm going to run up and check on Lily. Why don't I meet you out on the deck?"

"I'll grab the wine."

I give her another chaste kiss and somehow resist the urge my body has to take it further. I open my office door and head up to Lily's room. I can hear Cat moving around downstairs and I stop outside Lily's room realizing how weird that is—having someone besides Lily and I in the house at night.

Peeking in, I see Lily is on top of her comforter, her arms tucked under her pillow. Her face is a little flushed so I turn on her ceiling fan and shut the door quietly. I run down the stairs like some teenage boy who's afraid his date might leave.

When I step out to my deck, Cat doesn't turn, instead she continues to face forward looking up at the moon lighting the sky. I slide in next to her, placing my arm over her shoulders.

"She's asleep," I tell her and a look of relief crosses her face. She really thought I'd take the chance of Lily finding us. Never if I can help it. She's a sound sleeper, but Cat's idea to be somewhere with a locked door was a better idea than me screwing her on the deck with only a screen door between us and my five-year-old.

The scent of Cat's shampoo lingers around me when she places her head on my shoulder and snuggles into me. I forgot what it was like to have a woman around. The softness of her curves, the scent of her hair and how it tickles your nose when they snuggle close. The warmth of her hand on your waist. I forgot all the good that comes with having a woman you care about being a part of your life and I'm not sure I want to go back to the other way.

"Daddy!" Lily screams in my ear.

Somehow, I manage to pry one eye open and glance at the clock. "Eight o'clock." Well, it's better than six o'clock I guess. Regardless, I'm still going to be dragging ass like I drank a bottle of tequila last night. No way will I be able to hang from a rock, and poor Cat has to watch Lily. She didn't leave until three this morning.

"I made breakfast," Lily says, with a proud smile on her face.

"You did?" I try to sound as excited as she is.

Please tell me she didn't touch the stove or oven.

"Cheerios and milk and banana." Her wide smile stretches across her face.

I sit up, keeping the blanket over my boxers. Lily and her questions these days. I'm thinking we need some new boundaries about privacy and shutting doors.

"Great, I'll be right down," I say, but she jumps on my bed, grabbing the remote off the nightstand.

This has always been our routine. I went into the bathroom, got ready while she watched cartoons in my bed, but now I need to figure out how to get from bed to bathroom without Lily seeing my morning wood.

"When is Miss Cat coming?" she asks while she flips through the channels.

"Lily, do me a favor and go downstairs to see if we have enough ice cream for tonight, okay?"

Now, I have no idea about ice cream or if we'll even eat it tonight, but I do know that one of the only things that might get her out of here is ice cream.

"We have lots. Remember we had sundaes last night?" She gives me her 'silly daddy' expression and I smile back.

"Just check so I can stop on my way home from rock climbing to grab some more if we're running low."

She settles on the channel she wants and leans back on my pillows with her ankle resting on her knee, apparently not feeling the role of Daddy's helper this morning.

"Lily?" I question again, my tone on the exasperated side.

"I don't wanna go downstairs by myself." She shoots me her sulking eyes and sticks out her bottom lip.

This is proving to be much more difficult than I first expected.

"You were just down there when you made breakfast," I counter and she presses the button on the remote changing the station to yet another damn cartoon.

"I'm scared," she says in a small voice.

I rack my brain for another tactic.

"Miss Cat is so pretty," she says.

Fucking A, can we cool it with the Cat talk?

"Sweetie, I really nee—"

"Can she be my mom?"

My head is pounding, my stomach is churning and my

dick is growing harder the more she says Cat's name. Today is not the day for the mother talk.

"No, I need to get ready. Lily, we've talked about privacy and Daddy needs privacy right now, sweetie." I try the gentle approach.

She drops the remote and looks at me with narrowed eyes. "You look sick," she continues to stare at me and not moving a muscle to leave the room. "Are you sick?"

I can only imagine what my face must look like. "No, I'm not sick. I was just up late."

"With Miss Cat? She's nice."

Again, with the Miss Cat talk.

"That's why I pick her for my mommy. That's how you get one, right? You pick them?"

I take a deeper breath and expel all my anxiety out in that one. "No, that's not how you get a mommy. Miss Cat can't be your mom unless we ask and she agrees and that's not happening anytime soon."

She stares blankly at me without any idea of what I'm talking about. Of course, she doesn't and that's exactly why she'll have no fucking clue what I'm talking about if I tell her real mother is in prison.

"I have to get ready, we can talk about this later, okay?"

She scowls and scrambles off my bed and starts walking out of the room.

"Lily?"

She turns around by the door. "I want a mommy, not just a daddy." Her voice so indignant I'm surprised she didn't slam her foot down when she said it.

"I'm sorry, sweetie, I am, but you have me. You'll always have me. Some kids don't have dads. Imagine not having me in your life."

She says nothing and I wait for a smile or a sweet word

from her, but she turns around and slams the door behind her.

Great start to a Saturday morning.

———

I'M DRESSED in my shorts and t-shirt, grabbing my climbing gear out of the garage when Cat's car pulls into the driveway. I zip up my bag and erase the distance between the two of us.

"How is it you look even more beautiful after last night and I look like death?" I take her in my arms and give her a quick kiss.

"I'd say it's probably the ten-year age difference." She stretches, her shirt rising and giving me a view of her bare stomach—her stomach that had my cum all over it last night. My dick twitches with the memory.

"Now I don't feel so bad leaving you with a five-year-old for the day."

She rewards my comment with a small laugh. "So, I should've told you my head is hurting and I want nothing more than to have stayed in bed?"

I wrap my arms around her waist. "Is that true?"

She laughs, her smile widening. "No."

"Good. It just means that when we go out, Lily will be your responsibility the next day. So the old man can sleep it off."

I walk her backward until her back hits my truck. "Has last night been replaying in your mind all morning?" I'm putting myself out on the broken branch, praying to God last night was as amazing for her as it was for me.

"Let's just say, my vibrator got quite the workout this morning." She winks.

Unable to stop myself, I slam my lips to hers, my tongue plunging in immediately. She raises on her tiptoes, her hands landing on both of mine attached to the side of her head. Our tongues duel for control and she lets out a moan I can feel in my balls.

Then a fucking horn honks. Blares actually, and I don't need to remove my lips from hers to know who it is.

Cat slides out of my hold, pulling away from the kiss and looks over at the driveway.

Garrett's pickup truck sits there with Dane inside leaning across Garrett, his hand pressed to the horn while Garrett attempts to push him away. He finally relents on the horn and hangs out the window of Garrett's truck, pounding on the roof.

"Fuck man, stop banging up my truck!" Garrett screams. A rare occurrence.

"Oh please, your truck's been used and put away wet for years."

Cat snickers behind me.

"Let's go lover boy. I'm not scaling in mid-day heat," Garrett snaps.

"Why is pretty boy worried his hands aren't as strong as he thinks?" I call out.

Dane exaggerates pounding on the hood again in fake laughter, spurring Garrett to storm out of his truck.

"Get the fuck in the truck," Garrett's tone is his usual when he's unamused by Dane's antics.

"Daddy's mad, I better stop," Dane says in a high voice and pretends to cower and slinks back into the truck.

I see him attempting to calm Garrett down, but the amount of head shaking from Garrett says his attempt has failed.

I chuckle.

"You should go," Cat says and I grab her hand and lead her into the house.

"Let me say goodbye to Lily. She's playing Barbies." I stop right before I open the door.

Her pink plush lips calling to me one more time before I have to put on my daddy role and ignore my libido.

"Keep doing that and you're never going to leave," she says, smiling up at me.

"If I had my choice, those dipshits would be babysitting Lily and I'd be taking *you* somewhere secluded."

"Secluded? As in a place people take other people to murder them?"

I scrunch my eyebrows at her. "You're insane, you know that? Secluded, as in a place you can scream my name in pleasure until your vocal cords give out."

"Hmm." She rises to her tiptoes and plants a kiss on my lips. "I do like the sound of that."

"Seriously, stop the smoochy-smoochy and get your ass in the truck!" Dane yells and I open the door, dragging her in behind me.

"Lily, look who's here," I call out.

She barrels down the hall with a pair of scissors and a Barbie. "Um, Lily, did we buy a Sinead O'Connor Barbie?"

From the look on her face I know she doesn't understand what I'm saying. Hell, Cat is probably wondering who Sinead O'Connor is at this point. I'm only aging myself.

"You aren't allowed to use scissors." I try my best to not imagine her falling with them in her hand and stabbing herself in the heart.

If you're not a parent that'll sound crazy, but trust me. Kids make crazy things run through your mind and it's usually you imagining the worst situations happening to your child.

"They're kid scissors." She holds them up and I notice the dull top.

"Why did you cut your Barbie's hair?" I ask, bending down to inspect exactly what she's done.

"I want Barbie to look like Miss Cat." Lily glances over my shoulder, holding the Barbie doll up. "See?"

I look behind me and see Cat trying her best not to laugh or smile.

"Well, you don't need to cut your Barbie's hair when the real Cat is right here for you." I stand, holding my hand out as though Cat is on display.

Lily walks up to Cat and holds the Barbie doll up in the hair like a proud parent. "You like it?"

Cat bends down and takes the Barbie from Lily's hand. "I'm very flattered."

"What's flattered?" Lily asks with a crinkled nose.

Cat looks from me and then back down to Lily. "I'm glad that you like me so much that you wanted your Barbie to look like me, but Barbie's hair isn't going to grow back."

"It isn't?" Lily's entire face droops. I know tears are on the horizon.

Garrett's horn honks again.

"Go, I've got this," Cat urges and I teeter between the door and Lily.

"So, she's never going to have long hair. My hair grew. When I was a baby, I had a mullet, right Daddy?" she asks.

I laugh. "Yeah, but Barbie's not real, right sweetie?"

"Yes, she is. She's right here." Lily's foot stomps on the hardwood floor.

"Don't, Lily," I warn, my voice growing sterner.

She crosses her arms and runs out of the room.

"You," Cat stands up, turns me to the door and lightly pushes. "Can go."

"But—" I start to turn and she flips me back around.

"I've got this. You go have fun with your boys."

"You don't understand. She can be temperamental."

"Just like her father," she says in a wry tone. "I've got it handled." She opens the garage door, fists my t-shirt and pulls me to her. She kisses me hard but short and then nudges me out the door.

"Be safe, bye, bye." The door slams and I hear the flick of the lock.

"Did she really just lock me out of my own house?"

"Yes, I did. Now go," she says through the door.

Reluctantly, I grab my bag and head to Garrett's truck.

"Mary Poppins got the kid?" Dane asks when I open the back door and climb into the quad cab truck.

"Fuck off," is my response.

He looks around the cab like he's surrounded by a bunch of zombies. "Why is everyone in such a pissy mood today?"

Garrett looks at me through the rearview mirror and rolls his eyes and then backs out of my driveway.

"So, have we nailed the nanny yet?" Dane asks.

Sometimes parenting Dane feels harder than parenting my own child.

I'm halfway up Pilot Rock when Dane starts flapping his mouth again. I managed to dodge all his questions on the ride up here. Finally, I got him channeled into coming up with new names for the bar, but now as I'm literally hanging by my fingertips and he's holding the rope below, he's started up again.

"I'm just curious, what made you take the plunge? It was me, right? Hitting on her at the bar?" he asks.

"No," I scream below me and try to get my foot placement just right so that I can get a little higher.

"What's the plan now? I mean once you screw the nanny?" Dane's mouth is like a tsunami—unstoppable.

"She's not the fucking nanny." I don't know why I even bother responding to his banter, it only encourages him.

"Garrett? Did we not leave that pretty little thing at his house to watch his daughter?"

I glance down and see Garrett raise both his hands up in front of him. "I'm not getting involved. I do think you need to worry about Lily growing attached to her though."

These two are regular Dear Abby's today. The local paper should give them their own advice column.

"She's literally watching your kid, so, she's the nanny," Dane calls out.

I turn to look over my shoulder, losing my grip for a second before I grasp another spot.

"Will you please just focus?"

"I think a summer fling will be great for you. Enjoy her while she's here. That's what I'd do." He shrugs and I return my attention back to the giant wall of rock in front of me.

"That's because your only interest is what your dick wants. And he doesn't tend to get stuck on one thing for too long," Garrett says. "There is Lily to consider."

Lily, Lily, Lily. These two should know that she's always the first thing on my mind.

"What are you thinking will happen between you two? You see marriage in your future?" Garrett asks and I'm wondering when he found his voice box. Especially, when I'm half asleep, climbing a rock and my life rests—literally—in Dane's hands.

"Lily always comes first, but there's something between Cat and me. Something I've never felt before, but I can't put my finger on it. Lily knows Cat and she's comfortable with her. I guess I acted without thinking it through entirely, but don't I deserve that once in my life? It wouldn't matter who I was dating, there'd be no guarantees."

The more I think about that, the more I decide to hang on to that theory. I stayed. I fucking stayed and worked day and night to support Lily and give her the kind of life I want for her. Changing diapers and waking up for three a.m. feedings and then heading to the shop wasn't easy. And I did it on my own. I'm not asking for a medal, but I think if I decide to test the waters with the first woman who's sparked my interest, I should be able to, without having to have every scenario figured out like I usually do.

"That's not the way fatherhood works. As soon as you stuck your dick in Gretchen without a condom, you chose to put your needs after your daughter's." Garrett and his words of wisdom again.

"I don't believe that. I mean, sometimes the heat of the moment makes you temporarily insane," Dane argues.

"You seriously need help. Listen, Marcus, do what you want, but I'm telling you, if this doesn't end in church bells, you'll have one upset little girl."

I climb up another shelf of the rock, contemplating what he's saying. I'm not sure I agree with him. Lily will face heartbreak and I do wish I could save her from that experience, but my life can't stay on hold until she's eighteen. Especially when she's made it abundantly clear lately that she wants a mother. I'm not saying Cat is that person, but if I never try with someone, I'll never know.

Then again, Lily's tears are my kryptonite.

The cord slacks and I glance below to see four girls sauntering by. Each one in yoga pants and a sport bra. Dane's eyes are focused on them, and even Garrett is taking the time to appreciate the view.

"Tighter, Dane!" I yell, but get nothing from him.

My fingertips are inches away from the ledge of the rock when my body slips and falls a foot. Quickly, the rope is tightened.

"DANE!" I yell, pissed.

"Sorry," he mumbles but when I look down again, he's now stopped the girls to chat.

I start my climb in the same spot for the second time and I'm almost to where I was when the cord loosens again, except this time my entire body flies out from the rock.

"Dane!" I scream, but by the time he tightens the rope, my body slams into the face of the rock wall. "Fuck!"

"Sorry, man." His voice does sound concerned but damn it to hell.

My hand reaches to my forehead and when I pull it back to take a look, sure enough, it's covered in blood.

"Bring me down. I'm fucking bleeding," I grind out between clenched teeth.

He lowers me and I kick off the rock as best I can to speed up the process. By the time my feet are back on solid ground, my legs give out. Garrett props me up and walks me over to a boulder to sit on.

I ease myself onto the rock and the girls 'oh and ah' as they peer down at me. I must be as banged up as I feel.

"Dane, what the fuck?" My anger isn't missed and the girls all say their goodbyes and head down the trail.

"Sorry. I got distracted," he says, another lame excuse like he always has.

"You're about as responsible as an infant." I stand, but my leg is shooting with pain and Garrett hurries to hold my weight up. "Take me fucking home."

"HE'S OKAY, HE'S OKAY," Dane says as Cat's wide eyes watch them help me into the house.

"Daddy!" Lily rushes over, but Cat gently takes her hand, keeping her back.

"Let them get Daddy to the couch," she says in a soothing voice.

"I'm fine, sweetheart," I tell her.

"What happened?" Cat asks.

As we're making our way over to the couch, I spot the

kitchen. It's a disaster with flour everywhere and baking dishes out. Cat and Lily are both wearing as much flour as the counter.

"I could ask you the same." I chuckle.

She pats down her hair and apron that says, 'Hot Daddy'. I'm still not sure what my mom was thinking when she helped Lily pick that out for one of my Father's Day gifts last year.

"I hope you don't mind." Her hands move behind her neck to pull the string loose.

"Not at all. Leave it."

Her hands drop to her sides. Dane and Garrett take a seat on the couch and Lily sits on the ottoman right in front of me, staring at all the cuts and bruises on my body.

"What happened?" Cat asks again on her way into the kitchen.

She pulls a few beers out of the fridge and brings them over to the table. Twisting the cap off each one, she hands one to Dane and Garrett before giving me the last one.

I'm happy to take a beer over a kiss right now. She looks adorable playing Suzie Homemaker.

"What happened is Dane can't hold a rope." I glare over at him and he rolls his eyes.

"Marcus can't climb." He swallows down a hefty gulp of his beer. "May I just say, you're a very hospitable nanny." Dane tips his beer in her direction.

"Nanny?" she questions, joining Lily on the ottoman.

"Are you okay, Daddy?" Lily's voice cracks and a frown mars her pretty face.

I pat my lap for her to come over. She crawls up and I wince from the pain.

"Lily, maybe you should..." I hold my hand up to Garrett.

If being on my lap helps her not to be scared that I look like I lost a fight with a scrappy raccoon then so be it.

"See, I'm okay. I just slammed into a rock because Uncle Dane got distracted."

She eyes Dane and he holds his hands up in the air in defense. "Hey, now, it was an accident." He covers his head with his hands. "Please don't hurt me, Lily."

His defensive act makes Lily laugh and soon so is everyone else.

"Lily, why don't you get the cookies?" Cat suggests. "Maybe they'll make your dad feel better."

Lily jumps off my lap and runs into the kitchen. A second later, she's placing a plate of chocolate chip cookies on the ottoman. Dane grabs one immediately.

"Hey, how about the patient first?" I shake my head.

He chomps down on one, with no regard to what I just said. "If you're the patient, then Cat's the nurse. What do you think, Cat? Can you kiss all his boo boo's and make them better?"

Lucky for him, Lily's attention has turned to the television, but if it wouldn't take so much effort, I'd hit him over the head.

Cat picks up a cookie and hands it to me.

"Maybe a sponge bath would be good." Cat looks at me and I can't tell if she's playing Dane's game or if she's serious. I hope to hell she's serious. I might be a little battered, but I'm not down for the count just yet.

"There you go." He pats her on the back, standing up with his now empty beer bottle. "Here you go, big guy." He throws a cookie Garrett's way and he catches it. "They aren't as good as these cupcakes that Charlie's been bringing in lately, but you're pretty decent in the kitchen." He looks over to me. "I'd give her a seven."

"Excuse me?" Cat asks, standing up and following him into the kitchen.

"That's a compliment. It means you can prepare food and it's edible."

"I'd be careful, there's knives in there," Garrett calls after them and I laugh, sharing a smile with him.

"Uncle Garrett, where's Sydney?" Lily distracts him as I watch what's transpiring in the kitchen.

"And I'll rate you about a two for boyfriend material," Cat hammers back, starting to clean up the counter.

"Try a one, baby, I don't commit, which is rule number one for a boyfriend. I am, however, number one in the bedroom." He tips his new beer to her and a look of disgust crosses her face.

"You're maddening and disgusting."

I glance over to Lily, happy to find she's talked Garrett into doing a puzzle on the floor.

Dane leans against the counter. "For your information, I drive them back to their cars the next morning *and* I offer my shirt, you know, after I've ripped theirs off them."

Cat freezes and stares blankly at him. I'm not sure if she's about to slap him or knee him in the nuts.

"I'm not having this conversation anymore. My time is much too precious." She turns around and throws out the flour she scooped into her hand.

"I know you might not like to hear it, Cat, but I make no promises. The women I date know the score before they agree. It's not a surprise." He downs another swig of his beer.

"Maybe you two should just agree to disagree at this point," I holler out and Cat looks over at me.

"One day, the clouds will clear and you'll realize what you're missing."

"When I'm buried six feet under." Dane smiles and it's apparent he's enjoying the banter, but Cat is not amused.

She walks back into the family room and leans down to talk into my ear. "I'm going to make dinner."

I shake my head. "We can order something."

"No, no, I'll make dinner for you and Lily and then I'll get her to bed before I leave." She smiles and her hand lands on my arm in the most natural way. My gaze shoots to Lily, but she's busy with Garrett.

"Thank you."

"That's a nine for wifely duties," Dane leans in and says as he passes us, obviously eavesdropping on the conversation.

"I can still kick your ass. I'm not hurt that badly," I threaten and he laughs, throwing himself down on the couch.

"Daddy, that's a dollar," Lily says but doesn't get up to collect.

"That's right Lil, hit him in the pocketbook." He chomps down on another cookie, as crumbs fall from his mouth onto his shirt. "Yeah, these aren't nearly as good as those cupcakes I had. Seriously, they dissolve in your mouth and the frosting, oh, the stuff I could do with that frosting."

A smile crosses Cat's lips as she listens to him speak. "Who makes them?" she asks and as I study her features, I get an inkling that she already knows who it is.

"Charlie's friend. I think whoever it is should buy The Bread Box Bakery. You heard that Georgie's moving to Arizona and closing the shop, right?"

"She is? Lily loves her zebra cookies," I say.

Even Garrett turns around. When a company closes in Climax Cove it's a big deal and Georgie's is a staple for the tourists who come here each year.

"I took Toby there for her jimmy cakes the other day and she said she can't do it anymore and she has no help."

"Her son? What was his name? Chris?" Garrett asks.

"Moved to San Francisco."

"So, she's putting the shop up for sale?" Cat walks back in from the kitchen, intrigued by the conversation.

"Yeah. At season's end," Dane says.

"Does she have any prospects?" Cat asks.

Dane looks over. "Not that I know of. Why? You interested?"

"No, but I might know someone who is." She leans back on the couch and stretches her legs out so her bare feet are close to mine on the ottoman. Her feet are so tiny and feminine compared to mine. Her pink toe polish stands out on her tanned feet and compared to my battered-up feet we look like a before and after example. The image of our feet close together warms my heart somehow and I wonder what it would be like to come home to her every night.

"Well, then get snappy. Climax Cove needs another bakery by next tourist season," Dane adds before grabbing yet another cookie.

Makes you wonder how many he'd eat if they were a ten.

25

"Sit down," Cat demands, pointing to the chair with the plate of food in front of it.

Lily scurries up and climbs into her seat and looks down at her plate.

Lasagne and garlic bread.

Her eyes widen in surprise. I'm sure to her Cat walks on water, so she shouldn't be too surprised that she can put a mouth watering dish on the table.

"This looks delicious, Cat," I say, sliding out of my chair to grab a bottle of wine to enjoy with dinner.

"Stay," Cat points to the chair. "What do you need?" she asks.

I laugh and Lily joins me in.

"She can get bossy," I say in a teasing way toward Lily.

Cat's stance widens and she places her hands on those narrow hips. My apron is long gone now, leaving her in yoga pants and a t-shirt. Both articles of clothing are clinging to her curves.

I hold my hands up in the air. "I was going to get us a bottle of wine."

"I've got it." She scrambles to my wine fridge and pulls out another bottle of red. I sit at the table as instructed and watch her move around my kitchen. "Lily, tell your daddy what we did today."

Lily's eyes light up. "First we played Barbies and Cat did all their hair different and we got them dressed up for a big party."

"That sounds fun," I say.

"Then we went for a walk on the trail." It's apparent that Lily enjoyed having Cat to herself with the way her eyes are beaming.

I glance from my daughter over to Cat. "I should've told you, we've seen a few black bears over the years. I usually take protection with me."

Protection would mean a gun and I don't tell Lily I have it on me when we go.

Cat looks back at me as she stands on her tiptoes to grab two wine glasses from the cupboard. Her calves are flexed and the arches of her feet are straight up in the air, causing her t-shirt to raise enough for me to catch the glimpse of her stomach.

"We were fine," she says.

"Next time you go with me."

"We saw a frog and then Miss Cat scooped it up into her coffee mug and we put it in the stream."

I chuckle. Lily seems very proud of their accomplishment.

"Nice," I say.

Cat comes back over and places the two glasses, wine bottle and the opener on the table. I pull the bottle and opener over to me, fully capable of opening the bottle of wine for us. She smiles at me, letting me know that she'll let me have that one and disappears again over to the fridge. A minute later, a juice box is placed in front of Lily. Man, she's sure made herself comfortable today. Surprisingly, I find I kind of like that.

"Oh, and Daddy! We made our own playdoh." Lily hops down from her chair and runs over to the counter where the mail sits. "Look, Miss Cat made the flower and I made a butterfly."

I look them over, and realize that Miss Cat can do more than just paint, she can sculpt too.

"Then we made the chocolate chip cookies." Lily smiles. "Miss Cat even let me try some of the dough."

"Lily." Cat's eyes widen and Lily's hand flies up to cover her mouth. Cat looks over to me. "That was our secret. I know what they say about raw cookie dough but it was just a small piece." She even holds up her fingers to show me the exact amount.

"It's fine. I'm glad you guys had such a great day today. I'm upset I missed it."

Lily shares a look with Cat and they both smile. "We missed you, too, Daddy," Lily says.

"Now both of you eat," Cat says, pointing to our plates.

Lily and I pick up our forks and start eating the lasagne. Then I realize, I need to cut Lily's up but when I place my fork back down and bend to reach for her plate, I see her scooping a piece into her mouth. Cat already cut it up before she brought it to her.

Huh, I glance to Cat's lips that turn up as she chews.

I take a sip of my wine, admiring the table and the people seated at it.

I'm one lucky man.

LATER THAT NIGHT, I'm flipping through the mail from earlier in the week while Cat gives Lily a bath and tucks her into bed. My hands freeze when I see an envelope with the return address of the prison in the upper left corner.

Another fucking letter from Gretchen.

Not bothering to open it, I shove it in the middle of the stack and place it on the table. I know what she wants and she can chill the fuck out and wait for a response. The problem is, did Cat see the letter sitting there?

Cat tiptoes into the living room a moment later. "Okay, I think she's down," she says, falling back onto the couch. "Bath done, story down, goodnight hug, check." She does an imaginary checkmark with her index finger.

She's been a trooper staying the entire night to help me out as much as possible.

"What are you watching?" she asks, glancing at the television.

"Some cooking show." I hold my hand out. "Come join me."

She sits up, crossing her legs under her and shakes her head at me. "I don't want to hurt you."

I reach for her. "You're not going to hurt me. Come on."

She crawls over to my oversized chair and gingerly sits down on me, swinging her legs over my lap.

"You look exhausted," I say as she lays her head on my shoulder.

"I'm tired but good. This is nice." Her arms wrap around my neck and she kisses my cheek. "Do you need anything?"

I've got everything I need right here.

"No, I'm good."

She wiggles her feet in front of us and gets comfy on my lap. A small spot of flour is still on the side of her head and I swipe it off with my finger.

"I'm a disaster." She chuckles and buries her head into my neck.

"You're beautiful." I lean in and kiss her temple.

I refrain from telling her what I'm really thinking. I stop myself before I ruin our moment, but I can't deny it...motherhood looks good on Caterina Santora.

"Stay the night?" I ask instead.

"Are you sure? What about Lily?"

I place a chaste kiss on her lips. "I'll handle it. We can say you slept in the guestroom because you weren't feeling well. I want you here in the morning with us."

"Okay." She nods.

I know I'm crossing a line here that I can't hop back over, but I've never been more excited not to have it all figured out in my life.

26

Lucky for us, Ashley's sickness was a twenty-four hour bug, because the following Thursday evening, Marcus invites me out to a picnic dinner. We leave right after camp, drop Lily off at home and then he drives us out of town to where we're going to hike through the bush to a waterfall.

I've seen many things in my life—been privy to trips to Europe, Africa, and China. But nothing could have prepared me for the view when we pushed through the thick trees.

Water overflows onto rocks below and then flows into a pool of water as green as an emerald.

"How do you know about this place?" I ask in awe, my feet still not moving from their spot on the edge of the water.

"I found it on a hike and brought Lily last year."

He places the picnic basket down on one of the larger rocks and sits down. I join him and he hands me a bottle of water. The hike I complained about was well worth this view. I swear it beats the sunset in Africa over the plains and the giraffes off in a distance.

"Thank you," I say to him and he smiles, pulling out a Tupperware container full of strawberries.

He holds it out to me and I take one. "You're welcome. I knew you'd enjoy it."

"There's no one around?" I ask, glancing at the forest surrounding us.

He shakes his head. "That's why I wanted to come during the week. It can get crowded on the weekend. Let's eat and we can swim for a while before it gets dark. Then we need to get out of here."

I lean forward over the picnic basket, his lips too tempting not to kiss. "Before a bear eats us?" I shake my whole body in fake terror.

"You laugh, but it's a real threat." His face is stone cold.

"Do you have a gun with you?"

I hadn't even thought about it until now.

"Yes." He's confident and cocky and for some reason, it turns me on that he knows how to use a gun. Or maybe it's the protective side of him that I'm liking. Either way, I enjoy the feeling that he'll look out for me should some-thing go wrong. The guys from the city would probably just pull out their nail files to try to defend us against any wildlife.

"So, what do we have in here?" I ask as I rummage through the picnic basket.

"We've got antipasto salad skewers, those strawberries and if you're really good I made my own chocolate chip cookies." He winks and my stomach does what I've come to think of as the 'Marcus flip' over the past few weeks.

"Are you trying to compete with me?" I ask, narrowing my eyes in a playful manner.

He chuckles and shakes his head. "No way. Yours are better."

We sit on the rock while he feeds me the antipasto skewers.

"Can I ask you a question?" There's something I've wanted to know and now seems as good a time as any to ask since we're alone.

"Sure." He chews and swallows, shifting the picnic basket to the side and sliding over so we're right next to one another.

"Have you had a lot of women since Lily?" I study my water bottle, my finger picking at the label.

"No. If you haven't been able to tell, I'm very protective of her."

Interesting. "Has she asked about me? Why I'm around a lot more?"

Marcus swings his arm around my shoulders. "No, I don't think she really understands, but surprisingly hasn't really said anything since the first time you came over. I think it's because she likes it though."

"Do you have plans on telling her about us?" I bite my lower lip. This is unchartered territory for me. I'm not even sure *what* to tell Lily.

"Yes," he says simply and leans in to kiss my temple.

I swallow hard and ask the question I've really wanted an answer to, even more to how many people he's slept with since his daughter was born. "When did her mom leave?"

His body tenses and his lips don't leave my temple right away. "Three months after she was born."

My stomach suddenly feels like there's lead in when I picture Lily as an infant without a mother's love.

"And she never sees her?"

He takes his fingertip and pushes up my chin to the side so I'm looking directly at him. "I don't want to ruin today by talking about Lily's mom."

He's opened up more than he has in the past about it. Baby steps I guess. Still, the fact that he won't discuss Lily's mom with me still cuts like a jagged knife to the heart.

I'm falling for Marcus more each day I share with him. And Lily, she's already weaseled her way into my heart whether her dad and I break up today or years down the line. But if Marcus can't be honest with me about his past, I'm not sure we have a future.

Trying to move things back into safer territory, I ask what I think is a mundane question and will garner a mundane answer. "So then tell me, what do you love so much about Climax Cove?"

He blows out a long stream of air. "I hated it when I first came here, but it's grown on me. Maybe because every sidewalk, every building, and every season or holiday reminds me of Lily." He looks off into the distance for a second before continuing. "Take for instance during the summer festival...I was sitting at a table with Lily, bouncing her on my knee to the beat of the music. We were having a great time and then she threw up the first funnel cake she ever had all over my legs and feet." He laughs and I love the twinkle in his blue eyes when he talks about his daughter. "As frustrated as I was, I always remember that time with a smile. Don't get me wrong, people are up in your business all the time here, and you can never just run an errand without it taking an hour. Which I think I've grown to tolerate more than enjoy." He leans in close. "But don't tell Betty, the town librarian that, she's usually the one stopping me."

A tear pricks the corner of my eye. I'm envious that Marcus has found where he belongs. I think I'm still finding my way. It's not San Francisco, whether it be my high school or Berkley friends, I always felt restless. It's just never felt like it was where I belonged—like it was home. Home is a place where you're accepted for exactly who you are. So, for me, home is the studio, when I'm producing my art. My parents are great and they've grown used to my art, but I'm not sure they would feel the same if I was a starving artist selling my stuff at flea markets around the country.

"Hey." He inches forward, his hand caressing my cheek. "Did I say something?" For a man who runs hot and cold, he's very attentive and warm right now.

I shake my head. "No, I just..." I shrug. "It must be nice to know you're exactly where you want to be."

He gives me a small smile that has a sad note to it and he shrugs. If I'd recorded what he confessed a minute ago, he wouldn't be acting like Climax Cove might or might not be that place for him. It wasn't only his words, but the sentimental tone of his voice while he spoke them.

"And where is that for you, Caterina Santora? Where do you want to be in the art world?"

Isn't that the question of the year?

"New York, I suppose." My voice holds none of the confidence his did when he spoke about Climax Cove.

"I guess that's the place for an artist to be, right?" He picks up his plastic wine glass and looks off to the right.

"Yeah." I pick at the loose gravel on top of the boulder. "I've had a few galleries interested in doing a showcase, but they're more about testing the waters. I don't see my stuff going for a very high price. New York just sounds like San Francisco. A lot of people, a lot of concrete and a lot of germs." God, I sound like Ava.

He chuckles, stabbing a piece of strawberry with his fork and holding it up to my lips. I accept it and chew. "They'll be lucky to have you." He winks.

I've tried to keep the worry of what happens to us at the end of August at bay. There's the long-distance option, which is maybe successful in what, one in a million cases? Or the 'hey, it's been real, see you next summer' option. But Lily always comes to mind. What will she think when I sail off to New York come fall?

Feeling the weight of all the inevitable decisions we'll have to make bearing down on us I decide to lighten the mood. I glance from the inviting, emerald water and back to Marcus. "How do you feel about skinny-dipping?"

Marcus' eyes widen and he shakes his head. "I'd prefer not to get arrested today."

When I begin to strip off my t-shirt, dropping it on the rock beside me, his eyes widen even further. Not in surprise this time, but in lust.

"Oh, come on. There's no one around. You said so yourself, 'it's dead out here through the week.'" I stand and begin to unbutton my shorts and his eyes track my movements. "Mr. Kent," I lower my voice a few octaves, shimmying the shorts down my legs.

He bites his lip, his eyes smoldering as he takes in my bra and panty clad body. Reaching around, I unhook my bra and it falls to the rocks, joining my shirt and shorts.

"Cat," he says my name with a warning. I love the way his normally controlled façade is slipping away.

I shake my head, my fingers dipping into either side of my panties and sliding them down my legs. Leaving them on my toes, I fling them and they drop in his lap.

"Come and get me, Mr. Kent." I step to the edge of the rock. I shouldn't dive because I have no idea how deep it is here. Honestly, I should slowly wade into the water until I'm sure, but I look over my shoulder, finding Marcus still sitting, an amused grin on his face. He knows all the questions filling my head right now. Damn him.

I let one foot dangle into the water and retract it right away.

What is this glacier water?

"Cold?" he asks.

I turn back around. "No."

Do this. Come on. You can be sexy, Cat.

With my back turned, my eyelashes fluttering and my teeth chattering, I step into the water, every inch forcing my toes to curl a little more. And not the kind of toe curling I enjoy.

By the time I'm fully submerged, goose bumps cover me from my head to my toes, trying to warm the body I'm punishing.

"Come join me?" I say, trying not to let my teeth chatter.

"Need someone to warm you up?" he asks, an I-told-you-so smirk on his lips.

"No. I just thought maybe we could do some stuff to scare away the fish."

"There's no fish in there." He raises his eyebrows.

Smartass.

"Fine, I'll just enjoy the water myself."

Truth is the longer I'm in, the warmer the water becomes. Or maybe it's just that my skin is frozen and I can't feel it anymore.

"You sure you aren't cold?" he yells out to me, but I swim to the other side of the water, and prop up my elbows up on a rock ledge so my chest is completely exposed.

"Do I look cold?" I say, thankful the sun has decided to shine down through the trees.

"Either that or you're remembering the way you rode me

last night." He stands and toes off his shoes, then removes his socks.

"Changed your mind about joining me?"

He shrugs. "Maybe I'll just put my feet in."

Pulling something out from behind his back, he drops it in the picnic basket.

"Only your feet?" I question, sinking lower into the water.

He looks at me long and hard, and the goose bumps return, but this time it isn't the temperature of the water.

"Do you want me to join you?" His hands are resting on the button of his pants.

"Nope. You know exactly what I want and if you don't want it, then that's your loss." I circle around, back floating and acting like I don't really care if he joins me or not.

I'm back to the other side, wondering how long he'll let this go on when I hear a splash seconds before waves rock me back and forth. A small smile crosses my lips and then two hands grab my hips and a big, hard body pulls me flush against it.

"Fuck. It's freezing!" he yells, shaking his head from side to side. "You definitely need a big strong man to warm you up." He pulls me even closer, so there's not even a millimeter between us.

"Were you really not going to join me?" I hate the small-ness of my voice, but in my mind, I've twisted this game back to six years ago when he refused me.

He chuckles a deep throat laugh. "Oh, Cat, sometimes the guy has to play a little hard to get, too."

"I think six years is long enough," I deadpan.

"Hey, no one ever said big strong men were smart."

With that comment, his mouth descends on mine and I hang on to the rock ledge for dear life because I could easily forget that we're in the water—the outside world just falls away when we're together.

After a minute, he pulls away. "Come over here." He leads us farther down the rock ledge and I realize it's getting deeper. By the time he stops me I'm not able to touch the bottom, but he is.

Without warning, he grips my waist in his hands and props me up on the edge. I let out a yelp of surprise that quickly fades when I see the way he's looking at me—like he's a starving man and I'm the buffet.

"Spread your legs and scoot all the way up to the edge," he orders and I do as he says.

Because why the hell wouldn't I? This can only mean good things for me.

He wastes no time, licking his lips he glances up at my face and watches my reaction as his mouth descends on my clit.

"Oh fuck." I buck up into his mouth, unable to stop myself.

"Not yet, but soon." He winks and continues to rain pleasure down on me. Alternating between sucking and flicking until I don't think I can take much more.

His blue eyes watch me intently the entire time, missing nothing. When he can tell I enjoy something he gives me more of it. I'm a panting, writhing mess within minutes and all I want is for this man to fuck me into oblivion.

When he pulls hard on my clit I fall apart, moaning and arching up off the hard rock as I ride out my climax. I come on his face and he moans, taking his time licking up every last drop of my pleasure.

"Back in the water. Now."

His command makes my pussy clench and I quickly hop back down into the water, unfazed this time by its temperature. I can't reach the bottom so I grip the side and tread water.

"Turn around and face the wall. Hold on to the side."

Marcus lines himself up behind me and I let out an eager moan the moment I feel his hard cock press against my ass.

"I'm not going to be gentle. Make sure you tell me if I'm hurting you."

I nod so that he knows I've heard him and seconds later feel the mushroom tip of him push into me. He continues until he's fully seated and pressed up against my back and I let my head drop back onto his chest.

The feeling of him filling me up isn't something I can describe, it's just...pure bliss. He begins thrusting in and out of me, dragging his hard cock from me and hitting every nerve ending in the process. Water splashes around us and the sound of our grunting and panting and moaning fills the air around us.

He hammers into me and I manage to put enough resistance into my arms that I'm not crashing up against the rock ledge I'm white knuckling. His feet are planted wide and I let my legs drift back and around his waist. There's something to be said for weightless fucking in the water.

Marcus angles his body in a different way and I cry out each time he thrusts because he's hitting a spot that steals all control from my body.

"Come on, baby. I want us to come together."

A few more thrusts and Marcus gets his wish as I moan and he growls, holding himself against me while he empties his cock inside of me. My pussy milks his cock as I finish and a minute later we're both left shaking and panting from the strength of our orgasms.

He leans over my shoulder and kisses my temple. "Told you that you needed a big strong man to keep you warm."

I let my head fall back behind him. "Remind me never to doubt you again."

We both laugh and afterward we continue our swim, happy to enjoy whatever this is that's developing between us.

27

MARCUS

"You are thirty-four fucking years old. You have a daughter and a successful business. You don't need his approval, nor does it matter if he likes the idea that you're dating his daughter." I repeat the same lines that I've been telling myself the last few days into the mirror.

"We're going on a yacht?" Lily runs into the bathroom in her t-shirt and shorts. I've done her hair in braids and gave her a bath this morning. She looks like the perfect little girl.

"We are."

I pick her up and plop her on the bathroom counter. She grabs my cologne and knowing the drill, spritzes one squirt onto my neck.

"Thanks," I say.

"Daddy?" she says my name with that tone where I know a bomb is about to drop in my lap.

"Yes, Lily..."

"You said later, and it's later."

I wrinkle my forehead. "I'm sorry, what?"

"About Cat being my mom. Can she be my mom? Mallory's mom cooks and bakes and plays games and she used to sleep in bed with her daddy just like Cat does."

I blow out a stream of air. "Oh, Lily Lu." My shoulders droop and I swear I can feel the weight of the entire solar system on them. I knew this moment would eventually come at some point in Lily's childhood. "Cat did those things because she's a good friend of ours."

"So, good friends sleep in your bed?"

"No." It's amazing how fast an image of your college-aged daughter letting some weasel sleep in her bed because of some dipshit thing you told her when she was five, can flash through your mind.

"Cat slept in your bed the other night."

My jaw drops to the floor. "No, she didn't," I argue and for the first time, I outright lie to my daughter.

"Mmm-hmm," she nods her head. "I saw her."

I look up at the ceiling. I can play this a few ways—claim she must've been sleep walking, or that it was a dream, anything but admit that Cat was in my bed.

"When do you think you saw this?"

Though I know when.

"The night she watched me, and Uncle Dane and Uncle Garrett brought you home. I woke up in the middle of the night and I was gonna crawl in with you."

Damn it all to hell. I remember thinking I should lock the door, but the last time Lily got up to sleep with me was six months before when she was so congested the humidifier didn't work and she couldn't sleep. Other than that, my little girl is on a routine schedule and never wakes up in the middle of the night.

"Well, she had a tummy ache." The minute I hear the sentence out loud, I could face palm myself. That's the best I can come up with? I'm screwed when she asks me about sex.

Lily's nose scrunches and I wait for her to call me on my bullshit. I'm not bragging, but she's a helluva lot smarter than to think an adult with a tummy ache needs to sleep with someone.

Instead of saying 'Daddy, that's crazy', she hops off the counter without saying anything else.

My heart stops thundering in my ears and I'm thankful I dodged a bullet on that one. But that doesn't stop me from coming to the haunting realization that I'm going to have to come clean with Lily sooner than later. As soon as I figure out what the hell Cat and I are doing, I'll be sure to do that.

A HALF HOUR LATER, Lily and I are at the marina in town. We're waiting on a bench watching a couple of my employees put the finishing touches on Bill's boats while the Santora's finish up breakfast at Double D's. Bill and his wife Bree came in last night with their other daughter and son-in-law.

Cat and I already decided that maybe this isn't the time to talk about us with her father, so although it's completely chicken shit of me, I agreed we'd hold off.

I sip my coffee from Steaming Hotties and Lily sits on the bench, swinging her legs back and forth downing her frozen hot chocolate. Sometimes when it's an already stressful day, you gotta pick your battles. Fighting with Lily in the middle of the coffee shop on why she can't have a frozen hot chocolate at ten o'clock in the morning wasn't one of them.

"Jack," I call out as he walks out of the boathouse. He's got the rags and spray ready to do one last swipe of every surface before the Santora's climb aboard. We put one of the boats in the water last night and while we're out for the day, Jack and the guys will go ahead and get Sweet Tahlia out of the shed and into the water to sail out tomorrow.

He turns in my direction and makes his way over to us so I stand.

"Hey, Lily!" He raises his greasy hand to high five and Lily doesn't miss a beat, slapping his palm. "You're going to have a blast today."

Jack is like a kid himself. He's the youngest of three and if it wasn't for having to look after his ailing mother after his two older brothers left town, I wonder if he would've stuck around here.

"I'm going to make a new friend," she says with a smile from ear to ear.

He winks. "Man, scratch a blast, and make that a super duper stupendous day."

Lily giggles. "You're silly, Jack."

He nods and taps her on the head. "I know." Then he turns to me and Lily throws her now empty frozen hot chocolate in the trashcan. That was a record finishing time. "What's up, boss?"

"Can you make sure there are two bottles of champagne chilled in the fridge? I have it on good authority that Bill likes his toasts."

Jack nods with a smirk across his lips. "You sure you aren't thinking of popping the question?"

I laugh. Well, I laugh and choke at the same time. "Don't know what you're talking about."

He looks at me long and hard. Now, Jack is about my height but probably has an extra twenty pounds of muscle on him. "You do remember that the Climax Cove gossip chain is still in full-force, right? That you can't go parking your truck outside a certain someone's apartment on the regular without someone else noticing." He raises his eyebrows up.

"She's my daughter's camp counselor."

"And she makes house calls?" He walks away backward, knowing this is a useless conversation. I'll dodge his comments as much as I can.

I glance from Lily and back to Jack. "Let's just keep it on the down low for right now."

"Sorry, boss, gossip is at a full five-alarm forest fire level. You're the talk of the town and so is that blonde coming up behind you." He nods his head and I turn to find Caterina walking up with a small boy at her side.

She smiles and I smile, then she diverts her footsteps to Lily.

"You stress me out. We'll be leaving in fifteen," I say.

Jack salutes me with two fingers, which he knows I fucking hate and then he walks down the pier to the yacht.

I didn't think it would be a secret, but I did think I'd been more discreet. It's not like my truck sat outside her apartment every night and when she comes up to my house, there's no one that comes up that high on the hill unless they're there to see me.

"Hey." Cat's sweet voice says from beside me and that warmth that hits every drop of my blood in my veins, warms my entire body.

I glance to my side. "Hey. How was breakfast?" Looking further off, I spot Lily and Cat's nephew sitting on the park bench, not really talking.

"It was good. They're paying now. Tahl had to go to the bathroom for the fifth time since we sat down." She pauses for a second before continuing. "So, we'll still keep us quiet?" she asks.

"Yeah, it's for the best, right?"

She nods a few times, and even though she was the one who brought it up to me last night, if I had to guess right now, she's upset we're not coming out as a couple. "For sure." She smiles and her sad frown disappears.

"So, you do remember each other." Bill's voice disrupts us before we have a chance to talk anymore. He wraps his arm around Cat's shoulder, pulling her into his side. "You guys met years ago when you had just taken over the shop," he says to me, as though I don't remember.

I nod, eyeing Lily. "Yes, we did." I smile and glance over at Cat. She has a horrible game face. If her family really knows her they'll know something is going on with us.

"You've met these two as well, but just in case, this is Lucas and Tahlia." He lets Cat go and she fists her fingers together.

He points to a guy an inch taller than me and looks like bicep curls are his usual daily gym routine including weekends and holidays. He looks like the classic all-American guy and he smiles and holds out his hand.

"Marcus, right? Nice to see you again." We shake and he doesn't do the whole alpha handshake some guys do. Next, he places his hand on the back of another blonde's back. "My wife, Tahlia." I'm not sure I've met a man before where I could see how enamored he is with his wife within the first few minutes of knowing him.

She takes my hand and leaves her other one on her protruding and very pregnant belly.

"Nice to see you."

After we all say our hellos we're all standing around making small talk and I try not to look at Cat, but it's like trying not to look at a car accident.

"Where's the Mrs.?" I ask, rolling back on my heels, stuffing my hands in my pockets.

"She got distracted by some shop. You know how women are," Bill says.

Truth is the female species I know best these days are the five-year-old versions.

"So, that's your daughter?" Tahlia asks, observing the two kids talking on the bench.

"Lily, yes. How old is your son?" I ask.

"Caleb is four," Cat answers the question and Tahlia looks quizzingly at her sister.

"Yeah," she says slowly. "He's four."

Caleb and Lily look like they belong on some high-end kid's clothing magazine with their matching blonde hair and light eyes. Lily's blue to Caleb's green, just like his father's.

"And one on the way?" I ask.

Tahlia places her hands on her stomach, staring over at Lucas.

"Yeah, I'm about two months away from having control of my body again. And this one," she points to Lucas with her thumb, "wants to spend it on a boat this summer."

"I'm a firm believer that spending time on a boat when you're little makes you less prone to seasickness," Lucas says.

Tahlia rolls her eyes at him. "You're just lucky I don't get nausea. Remember Lennon? She had a rough go."

"I'm pretty sure people still remember her bitching about how uncomfortable she was. Didn't stop her or Jasper for getting it on though. Jasper's one helluva a guy, I tell ya." Lucas chuckles.

She slaps his shoulder. "Stop it, she's my friend."

"Hey, she's my friend too, baby, but she's the devil when she's pregnant."

Tahlia laughs. "Well, I think we can be thankful that the

experience inspired her to launch a line of toys especially for pregnant women." Tahlia smiles at her husband and his lips curl into a knowing smirk.

Gross.

"Ew," Cat whines and points between them. "Keep your bedroom shit to yourself."

"Language, Caterina," Bill snaps, but seems lost in the conversation other than his daughter just outed his other daughter's sex life.

"We're married, Cat," Tahlia says. "I think Dad knows we have sex."

"Tahl," Lucas warns.

Tahlia points to her stomach. "Hello." Her head falls to the side in a give me a break look. "Did Caleb just sprout to life in my stomach?" She concentrates on her dad. "You do know that Lucas and I sleep in the same bed, right?" she jokes.

"I understand how babies are made yes, Tahlia, but I don't need the details of your sex life." Bill glares at Lucas before turning and walking down the pier toward Kitty Cat.

Lucas throws his hands up in the air. "There goes that six years of progress with your dad." He stalks off, following Bill down to the yacht.

A second later, they're talking about the boats.

"I don't even know why he cares. Like Dad doesn't think of Lucas as his own son," Cat says.

Tahlia's hands land on her stomach once more. "I know, right? I think he might actually pick him over us."

Cat laughs with her sister and I realize that their relationship is much different than it was years ago. The first time I met them I didn't get the impression that they were close at all.

"That's the truth," Cat says.

Jack walks off the boat, signaling to Bill and Lucas that they can board.

"I guess we're ready," I say, stepping back and holding out my hand for them to go first.

Tahlia glances toward Main Street. "Finally, here comes Mom."

Bree walks down the sidewalk with five bags hanging off her arms. She pats Caleb and Lily on the head and continues until she reaches us.

"You do know we're docking back here this afternoon?" Tahlia says.

"It was a sale and ever since your dad opened his big mouth about Climax Cove, so many people come up here. Especially on a Saturday afternoon and I'm not about to miss out."

Cat glances into the bag. "What was so direly needed?" She pulls out some utensil. "This cuts up herbs." Her eyes shine like she found a pirate's treasure in the depths of the ocean.

Tahlia and Cat share a look of what the fuck happened to Mom.

"You don't cook," Tahlia says.

But Bree isn't listening. She pulls out an apron and hot pads. "I got these for Lucas." She holds up bear claw hot pads. "And you." She tosses an apron at Tahlia and she holds it up. It has a sexy woman in lingerie painted on it.

Tahlia's gaze flies to Caleb and then she folds it up. "Mom, a little inappropriate."

Bree laughs. "I thought Lucas would enjoy it until you got your figure back." Then she takes both items from Tahlia's hands, shoves them in the bag and walks over to the boat.

"For your information, Mom, Lucas loves my stomach," Tahlia calls out while Cat and I try to not laugh.

"I'm sure he does, sweetie, but food for thought."

"Has she seriously lost her mind?" Tahlia looks at Cat.

Cat shakes her head and stares at her sister.

"I should double check the boat." I wave my hand in the air. "Lily, let's go."

Cat and Tahlia continue to talk about their parents and I dodge the conversation by walking away.

"This is my friend Caleb, Daddy," Lily introduces me to the boy who's the exact replica of his dad.

"Hi, Caleb. Are you ready for a day at sea?"

"Can you drive the boat?" he asks, the two of them walking alongside me.

"Yes, I can."

"Because you have a penis?" Caleb asks.

I spit out some of my coffee and Lily's head swings to Caleb so fast I worry it will continue to spin around.

"Why would you ask that?" I use my hand to wipe up the coffee dribbling down my chin and try to remain calm since we're approaching where Lucas, Bill and Bree are all standing around looking at the boat.

"My daddy, my Uncle Jasper and my grandpa all can. They all have penises. Because boys have penises. Girls don't."

"I can see why you'd think that, but no, that's not why. It's because I learned."

"Yeah," Lily says, her hands on her hips and her face in his. "I have a bagina and my daddy lets me steer sometimes."

Caleb shrugs, obviously over the conversation, not understanding why Lily is upset.

I tap her head and her arms fall to her sides. "Let's get on the boat."

I lift Caleb first and Lucas grabs him and we do the same with Lily.

"Beautiful day," Lucas comments.

I take in the blue sky with only a few wisps of clouds and nod. "It is. We should have great weather."

We each help Tahlia by each holding a hand out for her and she gets on the boat, but when it comes to Cat, it's just me left to help her.

My hand grips a little firmer, and I don't pull away right away. We exchange a smile and I look her up and down, loving her short shorts and tank top.

"Now, now, Mr. Kent, let's keep my panties dry," she whispers in my ear.

I should be concerned that my dick twitched so hard in my pants, I'm about to give us away, but my dick went into hiding when I notice Tahlia's spying eyes flare in our direction.

28

CATERINA

The day *is* beautiful. The sky is clear. What could possibly go wrong?

The fact that my sister witnessed a moment between Marcus and me two seconds into this trip is what.

How she figured it out so fast, I'll never know. She must be taking lessons from her BFF Whitney, the investigative reporter back in San Fran.

So, I've done what any good sister would do—I've dodged her. She's tried to corner me several times to drill me with her list of questions. A list she probably handwrote so she wouldn't forget. Let me tell you, my sister is anal with a capital A.

I slide by her after I throw away my plate, her big belly in the way of the garbage can. If she thinks she can corner me with her unborn earthling, she's got another thing coming.

"Cat! Cat!" Lily rushes in, saving the day. "Come outside." She grabs my hand, pulling me from the galley.

"Boy, she seems very fond of you," Tahlia murmurs under her breath as she follows behind us, but I ignore her, following Lily to the back of the boat where we just had lunch.

My dad is standing there with a champagne glass in his hand, my mom, Lucas and Marcus following suit. "To Cat."

Lucas hands me a glass and then a flute with what I suspect is apple juice to Tahlia.

"What?" What reason could they possibly have to toast me?

"You've made me so proud. I never thought you could make a living off an art degree. I thought your dream of painting was some hippie-dippie dream you'd grow out of. I'd hoped you'd come join me and maybe I'd have *one* daughter who wanted to stay in the sausage business."

"Technically, Tahl never left the sausage industry." Lucas grabs Tahlia's hand and eases her onto his lap.

"Enough about your sex life," I say, rolling my eyes, although I wouldn't mind this conversation veering away from me.

Like always, Dad just carries on, ignoring Tahl and my banter. "The fact your artwork will be in New York City this fall and you'll be making a living from something you love shows how hard you work." He raises his glass and everyone does the same, including Marcus.

"Congratulations, Kitty Cat, you're about to get everything you've dreamed of." My dad smiles and tilts his glass back for a sip.

I down my champagne while staring at Marcus. Something is up. His entire energy seems a little melancholy now.

"Congratulations, Cat," Lily says, and drops her empty cup of apple juice on the table next to Caleb's and the two run off.

"Whoa, you two." My mom stands to chase after them,

pausing briefly to kiss my cheek. "I'm so proud of you, sweetie."

I walk over to the table and my dad's phone rings. Holding it in his hands he leans in to kiss my cheek and then holds up his phone. "See, you don't have to worry about these emergency calls when you decided on art for your future."

I take the comment on the chin and sit down at the table.

"Congratulations, Caterina," Marcus' deep voice pulls me from my surprise that my family is actually proud of me.

Tahlia gets off Lucas' lap much to his dismay and sits in the free chair. "So, Marcus, where's Lily's mom?" she asks.

"Tahl?" My jaw practically hits the table.

"Oh, I'm sorry, I guess that's a personal question." My sister feigns embarrassment, but I know her better than that. She's working an angle here.

Marcus clears his throat and sits up straighter. "No, no."

My ears perk up like I'm a dog that just heard the word 'walk.' Marcus has been quiet on anything to do with Lily's mom.

"She's not in the picture. Decided a child wasn't really for her." His eyes scan the area behind us, looking for signs of Lily I assume.

"So, you've raised her by yourself her entire life?" Tahlia continues to pry.

"Tahlia," Lucas chimes in, placing his hand on her arm.

"Yes." Marcus' back is as straight as a rod iron, his eyes steady on Tahlia.

"That's admirable." Tahlia leans back. "Takes a pretty great guy to do that."

I'm sorry, exactly how crazy do your hormones make you when you're pregnant?

"Thank you." Marcus is gracious and polite, but I know him well enough to know that he doesn't need anyone else's acceptance of what he does. He knows he's a great father.

"You're welcome. I'm not sure Lucas could do it." She looks over to her husband.

Lucas and his face scrunches before he rolls his eyes and tips back his beer. "You know your sister, aka superwoman." He smiles. "As soon as her hormones get back in check, I'll fight back for myself." He winks at Tahlia.

"Oh, sweetie, stop the sweet talk," Tahlia coos, sarcasm dripping from her tone.

Marcus glances over to me and raises his eyebrows, probably thinking my sister and her husband are a psych case.

The four of us sit and talk about kids for a bit. Marcus having much more in common with Tahlia and Lucas than I do. They complain about bedtime routines, how a red sock instead of a blue sock can cause a total meltdown in a toddler and the nighttime stories they read. A small amount of jealousy rests in my heart. Though they're spouting out complaints, it's clear that none of them would change it for the world.

My gaze finds Lily dancing along the deck of the boat. Her braids with a slight curl at the ends blowing in the wind as she pretends she's a ballerina shifting her weight from one foot to the other to the rhythm of the music playing through the speakers. She's beautiful and I wonder what my life would be like if Marcus and I worked out.

I scratch the thought of a future as soon as it floats to the surface, there's no way this could work long term. Sure, we're having fun, more in the bedroom than out, and even with our interesting conversations and cozy nights in front of the television, he's never said anything about a future with me.

"What are you day dreaming about?" Tahlia looks over to me and then follows my gaze to Lily.

"Nothing."

I overhear Marcus and Lucas talking about baseball and the Giants.

"She's a very pretty girl," Tahlia remarks, while I'm still staring at a carefree Lily.

"She is."

I'm startled when I look up and find Tahlia's blue eyes on me—assessing and appraising and letting me know the gig is up.

I nod to her unspoken question and the corner of her lips dip. She glances at Marcus and then at Lily and finally back to me. Her chest rises and falls with a deep breath, but she says nothing.

If there's one thing I know, it's that my sister doesn't stay quiet for long. If we could just get off this boat before she speaks her mind, I swear I'd clean-up the glitter at camp for the rest of the summer.

Once we dock, Cat takes Lily to Swirly's Ice Cream Shoppe with Caleb and her family as I double check that Sweet Tahlia is on the water and ready to go for the next morning.

I'm not in my shop more than five minutes before a blonde strolls in. And not the one I'd like to be checking up on me, but the one currently in hormonal imbalance. I glance over, knowing this conversation could be coming, but hoping I was mistaken on seeing Cat and Tahlia share a look across the table.

"What exactly are your intentions with my sister?" She pulls out my office chair and plops herself down.

I look up from the messages scribbled down next to the phone in Jack's chicken scratch. "Excuse me?"

Gretchen was bat shit crazy when she was pregnant so I proceed with caution.

"Don't act dumb, Marcus. I know there's something going on and I'm here to tell you that it needs to stop."

"Excuse me?" This time I'm wondering why she thinks she can come into my shop and dictate my life decisions.

"Listen, you seem like a good guy, but you're what thirty-five?"

"Thirty-four." I try not to show my irritation that she thought I was a year older than I am.

She rolls her eyes and gives me a same-difference look.

"My sister is twenty-four and it took a long time for her to get her head on straight."

Looks like we're going to do this.

"Maybe it's always been on straight. Maybe it just wasn't pointed where you thought it should be." I cross my arms over my chest.

"That's not it."

"How do you know? You two are obviously very different." I remain my usual calm self even though I want to say 'you're a planner down to the tiniest detail and Cat is a follow a wisp on the breeze kind of girl.' But this is Cat's sister and regardless of my feelings, I need to show her the respect she deserves.

"We *are* different, but that's good because then I can keep guys like you from trying to trap her into playing house up here in the middle of nowhere. She has dreams to fulfill. Goals to obtain."

I hold my hands up in the air. "You think I'm looking for a mommy for my daughter?"

She huffs, standing to her feet now. It takes her a minute to get there. I would've offered to help her myself, but I get the feeling it wouldn't have been welcomed.

"I know how hard it is to raise a kid and I'm sure it's exhausting to do it on your own."

A dry laugh rumbles out of my throat. "Listen Tahlia, my daughter has a mom. Not a very good one. She got the raw end of that deal which sucks, but that doesn't mean I'm going to trap some girl into sticking around. I get that Cat has aspirations that will take her far away from Climax Cove. I promise you, I'm not going to persuade her to stay here past summer."

"So, she's a summer fling?" She juts out her hip and then holds her stomach. Obviously, her sass has had to take a downturn with the baby thing.

"No." I run my hand through my hair. "Isn't it supposed to be your dad who nails me to a cross?"

Tahlia laughs for the first time. "My dad is blind, especially when it comes to Cat. Listen to me," she steps forward. "All I ask is that you think about what you want from this thing with Cat. I'm sure you don't want Lily hurt in this either, but if the two of you walk around like you're oblivious that there's an end to your time together when decisions will have to be made, that's exactly what will happen. Except it won't just be Lily and Cat hurt." She points her finger at me, jabbing it in my chest. "Oh, and if you hurt her, I will sic every boxer I know on you. Do you understand me?"

I chuckle at her attempt to strong-arm me. "Understood."

She narrows her eyes and stares at me until the door opens. We both turn to see Lucas coming through to join us.

"Sorry, Marcus, she escaped." He swings his arm around his wife's shoulders and turns her to leave.

"Oh, quit treating me like a head case." Tahlia tries to push him off her but he's not having it and instead entwines his hand with hers. "See Marcus? Are you sure this is what you want? The Santora women go crazy when they're pregnant."

Lucas looks over his shoulder, nodding enthusiastically. "Think twice," he jokes and Tahlia smacks him in the stomach.

"Come on, baby, I'll get you a cinnamon roll when we get back to the city in the morning."

"You always think food solves everything."

"So, you don't want one?" he asks, raising his eyebrows as he holds the door open for her.

"I didn't say that." Her voice is anything but nice.

A minute later, they're gone and I'm alone to process what Tahlia just said. Guess it's about time I act like an adult and realize that there are ramifications to my involvement with Cat.

LATER THAT NIGHT, Lily is fast asleep and a naked Cat is lying on top of me. My fingertip brushing along the length of her arm.

"Hey," I say, now that we've both come out of our orgasm fog.

She peeks up, placing her chin on my chest.

"Yeah?"

My hand moves to her hair, smoothing down the just fucked strands in different directions.

"Tell me about your art."

A smile graces her lips and a pinch in my heart forms from the fact I've never asked her before and what a dick move that was.

"What do you mean?" she asks.

I stare down at her. She's beautiful and my gut twists knowing that the end of our time together is drawing near.

"Your art. Your future. You're heading to New York in the fall?"

Her smile falls and her gaze dips down to focus on my

chest. Her fingers outline the planes of my muscles for a bit before she answers.

"That was the plan, yes."

"Was?"

The tiny glimmer of hope beginning to sparkle inside of me should not be there. I don't want this girl to give up her life's ambition to live in a small town like Climax Cove. If Gretchen taught me anything, it was that you can't force someone to want to be here.

"Lately, I've been thinking a lot about it. I've been wondering if New York is the best place for me." Her unsure eyes reach mine and I can't help but swallow down the feeling that she's leading to a question.

"Why?" I ask in a quiet voice.

Her shoulder lifts. "I'm not sure that's where I belong."

I sit up straight, my back against the headboard, needing space. Cat sits up, placing the sheet in front of her to cover her breasts. Probably from the cold rush I just brought in this room with my change of attitude.

"Cat." My hand lands on her cheek. "You can't stay in Climax Cove for Lily and me."

As much as I want to beg and plead with her to stay, to tell her I can make her happy, I'm reminded that she's not mine. She never has been and the last thing I want to do is trap a girl again because this time it won't just be my heart that's devastated by the loss, it will be Lily's too.

Her gaze dips down and a jagged fracture rips up my chest because I've obviously hurt her.

"Who said I would stay here for you? I never said I was going to stay in Climax Cove, I just said I didn't think New York was the place for me." Her tone is curt and if I didn't already believe I've hurt her, I'm positive I did now.

"Hey," I say in a soothing voice.

She looks at me, tears pooling in the corner of her eyes.

"I can't have you settle by staying here. Lily will always come first in my life. I know that might make me sound like an asshole, but she comes first. Her life is here in Climax Cove and I'm not going to disrupt that. Don't get me wrong, I love what's going on here, and I don't want it to end, but I know come September, you have choices to make. I need you to make those decisions for yourself, not for me or Lily."

She nods, letting the sheet drop and exposing herself to me. Her hand holds my hand to her cheek and her eyes fall closed. No words come out of her mouth. No empty promises of what will happen. Of what she'll choose.

When the shimmering blue hues I love to look into are visible again, the vulnerability I saw minutes ago is gone.

"Thank you," she says softly.

"For what?"

"For your honesty. I know it's probably hard for you to tell me, but I appreciate knowing where I stand." There's no hint of anger in her voice. "For the record, I would never expect to come before Lily. Ever. And if this became more than fun, it would be the same for me. Her needs would come before you."

Jesus, what single dad wouldn't want to hear that the woman you're falling for loves your child enough to put her first?

"Maybe we're getting ahead of ourselves. Just promise me as you're contemplating your decisions, you'll do what's best for you."

She nods. "I promise."

"Now, how about round two." I glance back to make sure my door is still locked. "If you leave me in the fall, I need to have lots of material for the spank bank."

She squeals as I pin her to the bed and my lips descend to her neck.

"Wait," she cries out. "Let me up."

I do, concerned that I might have hurt her, but she pushes me onto my back with a wide grin on her face. I watch as she straddles my legs and brings her mouth down onto my cock.

"Fuck, Cat. Your mouth is exquisite."

She runs her tongue along my crown and I clamp one hand in her hair, gripping it tightly. When she sucks her cheeks in and pushes all the way down until I can feel the back of her throat I can't help myself. I start controlling her movements with my fist in her hair dragging her up and down my cock.

I don't worry about what's going to happen at the end of summer. I don't worry that she may very well break my heart, or me hers. I can only concentrate on the pleasure she's gifting me in this moment.

All the concerns Tahlia threw our way have been sealed by placing a Band-Aid on top. And somehow, I know that Band-Aid is going to hurt like hell when she rips it off.

30

CATERINA

"Show me the chair that the throwing up incident happened," I tell Marcus as we walk with each of our hands clasped to Lily's around the Climax Cove summer festival.

"Right there." Marcus points to a table filled with people that rests just under the street light. "That's where she threw up all over me."

Lily laughs. "Daddy, you always tell that story."

I look over at him. We share a smile and then face forward again.

After our conversation last week, there's an underlying fissure in our relationship. Almost like he's waiting for me to blurt out a decision and I've wondered more than a few times whether he really wants me here or not.

I wanted to scream at him that of course Lily comes first. I would never assume she didn't. But I've learned over my time with Marcus, he has a fear of being hurt, left behind, but what really keeps him one arm's length away from people is the fear of Lily being hurt.

"Mallory!" Lily screams, and let's go of our hands, running toward a red-haired girl about her age.

"That's her friend," Marcus whispers in my ear.

"I've seen her at camp. So, her mom is single?"

A smirk forms on his lips and he nods. "She is."

"And she's hit on you?" The ugly green monster rears her head as I notice the woman's eyes focus on our joined hands as she approaches.

"Never."

He winks, and I roll my eyes. The Bachelor of Climax Cove, Marcus Kent, ladies and gentlemen.

"Hi, Viv," Marcus holds his hand out to the mom.

I realize when I get a better look at her that Mallory is the exact replica of her.

"Hi, Marcus." The girls talk non-stop next to us about the cotton candy and rides. "Don't you work at the camp?" she asks me in a sugary-sweet voice that suggests she's purposely pointing out the age difference.

"I do. Caterina." I hold my hand out and she takes it, shaking it lightly.

"Nice to meet you." I'm no body language expert, but even I can tell that the smile on her face does not suggest that she's happy I'm here.

"You too."

Each of our hands drop and Marcus quickly grabs hold of my free hand. Again, Viv's eyes zero in on our connection.

"Why don't I take the girls for a bit?" she offers.

Marcus and I look to one another and he's quick to nod. "That'd be great."

"Okay, Mallory's been bothering me to ride the rides, but my ass can barely fit in those rides, so let's meet back here in about an hour or so?"

Is there some magic bug that bites you, morphing your

personality to the opposite end of the spectrum? Why is she being so nice?

"Perfect, Viv, thank you."

"No problem." Her eyes linger up and down my body once more. "You two go enjoy yourselves."

Marcus bends down to talk to Lily, instructing her to pay attention to Mallory's mom. She nods, not hearing a word he says because she just wants to go.

Lily hugs him and tells him she loves him. And just as we're about to part, she rushes over to me and wraps her arms around my stomach, tight. "Be right back," she says. I don't get an I love you, or much else, but her actions. Her actions speak so much more than words.

Viv watches the scene and I should remind her there are flies around so she might want to shut her mouth. Her reaction doesn't throw me, but Marcus's eyes move from Lily to me and it's in this moment I know that if I leave for New York, I'm going to crush two people that I've grown to love having in my life.

"Let's go." Marcus drags me away, but he can't hide the reaction he had from me.

"Viv sure didn't hide the fact that she's put off that I'm in the picture," I say as we make our way through the crowd. "How long has she carried a torch for you?" I try to keep the jealousy from my voice, but it's useless.

Marcus covers his mouth with his free hand and starts laughing.

"What's so funny?" I ask, a little perturbed that he finds it so funny. He keeps laughing and eventually I give him a playful smack on the arm. "Seriously, what's so funny?"

"I think Viv's probably more annoyed that I'm holding *your* hand." He wipes at the tears under his eyes from laughing so hard.

I stop walking and pull him back to me so we're facing each other. "I don't get it."

"Cat, she's a lesbian." He chuckles again. "You have nothing to worry about. But based on the way she was checking you out, I might." He grins at me and I return the gesture.

"Oh, I didn't know," I say and laugh.

He leans in and gives me a chaste kiss. "It wouldn't matter anyway. Come on, we have a date with a Ferris wheel."

A few minutes later, we're on the Ferris wheel that overlooks the small downtown area and ocean.

"It really is a beautiful city," I say.

"Town. I'd say Climax Cove is a town. A small town at that," he says.

I elbow him in the ribs.

"Hey now, you break a rib and you'll be the one punished when I can't give you those earth-shattering orgasms anymore." He chuckles, wrapping his arm around my shoulders.

"I would miss those." We sit quietly for a moment taking in the view as we move slowly around the circle. "You're always so quick to pick on this town. I thought you loved it?" I turn to face him, but he transfers his attention back out to the view in front of us.

"I do love this town, but that doesn't mean it's for everyone."

"If I didn't know better, I'd assume you wanted me to pick New York," I say.

He takes my face in his hands and stares into my eyes. "Believe me Cat, I want you here with us, but that doesn't change the fact that I can't promise you anything. You need to be where you have a real shot at the future you want."

His lips tip down at the corner and there's defeat in his eyes. Normally I wouldn't pick on someone when they're down but I'd love to cock back my fist and slam it into his face. Strike that, I'd like to go all MMA on his ass.

He can't promise me anything? I may be ten years younger but even I know there's no such thing as a future that's promised to us.

His lips press to mine and if only I could deny the magic that swirls between us when we touch, I would speak my mind. But what there is to say until I make my choice, I don't know.

For now, I choose to enjoy the present and pretend the future will never arrive.

31

I t's midweek and I'm at the shop, finishing up a boat for a client I have coming in this weekend. My plan was to take Cat and Lily out on my own boat for the day on Saturday, but business comes first. This is a whale of a guy from Portland that I need to cater to if I want him to refer me out to all his rich friends.

"Marcus," Carl, the mailman, peeks inside the door.

"What's up, man? Come on in." I wave him in, dropping the stain and brush on the side table and wipe my hands on my pants.

"I have a certified letter for you. I knew you weren't home, so I was over at Double D's for lunch and thought I'd try you here." He holds out a piece of green cardboard paper. "I need your signature."

Using his pen, I sign and we exchange the green cardboard for the envelope. There's an attorney's return address on it. What the hell could this be about?

"Well, nothing good usually comes from those. It's not like they send you a letter telling you, you won the lottery," Carl says, backing up toward the door.

"That's the truth. Thank you, Carl." I wave and he leaves quickly, leaving me alone with what feels like a grenade with the pin pulled in my hands.

I rip open the envelope and pull out the single sheet of paper. I start to scan the words and instantly my heart rate kicks up and my breathing becomes labored. I see nothing but red. Red volcanic lava is probably squirting from my ears.

"Fuck her," I mumble, reading the letter from some lawyer, Mr. Bushwell, stating that Gretchen wants to enact her parental rights and have visitation with Lily.

What kind of loon did she hire? Hello, she's in prison. I didn't know they had a park for the convicts to play with their children.

"Jack!" I scream.

He casually walks through the archway from the second building wiping his hands on a rag. "What's up?"

"I'll be back, I need someone to finish staining." I point to where I abandoned my project.

"Sure thing."

I grab my cell phone, and right before I'm out the door, I go back to my desk and pull my checkbook out of the desk drawer. I don't care how much this fucking costs me, Gretchen will *never* see Lily if I have anything to say about it.

"You okay, boss?" Jack calls out behind me as stomp toward the door again.

I don't bother responding.

Two minutes and three people later, I'm in Mike Polar's office, my lawyer. I open his door, slam the piece of paper on his desk and then start to pace.

"Why, hello, Marcus, how are you this afternoon? Me? Well, I had a nice BLT for lunch and business is going well.

Thank you for asking." His sarcastic tone doesn't lighten the mood.

"She wants fucking visitation." My fists ball at my sides.

Mike picks up the letter, reading it and sighs and groans over what he's seeing.

A lot of people in town know what happened with Gretchen. Well, they don't know that I'm partially responsible for the fact that she got to where she ended up, but they know how she left me, never to be seen again. And they know she's currently in maximum-security prison. It's one of those things that everyone knows, but out of respect for Lily, no one ever discusses.

"Sit down, Marcus," Mike instructs, but I shake my head, my mind in a frenzy of fury.

"Here." I pull out my checkbook from my back pocket and toss it on the desk. "I don't care how much it is, I'll fight until I'm broke."

He slides the checkbook to the edge of his desk and leans back in his chair, steepling his hands in front of him.

"Marcus, you're going to have to face this head on. Money is not going to solve the issue." He presses his lips together and shakes his head. "I doubt a judge would be okay with a kid being dragged into prison to see a mom she doesn't know, but who's to say? If she can show she's turned herself around, she could have a case. And then once a month you'll be driving your five-year-old upstate to visit her mom."

"This is fucking insane!" I yell. "How is there even a remote possibility that Gretchen has a leg to stand on?"

"Look, she's Lily's biological mother and she never signed her parental rights away." He sighs again. "My suggestion is that you handle this yourself. Go up there and talk with Gretchen."

That's not what I wanted to hear.

"I've raised Lily. I'm the one who cuddles with her when she's sick or makes sure she has clothes, food and a damn roof over her head. No judge would allow her to get visitation." I continue pacing, hoping I wear out a line in his office from his lack of help.

"You don't know that. Why take the chance? I'm sure the two of you can come to some resolution that won't be court ordered. Maybe letters should be exchanged first. Does Lily even know about Gretchen?"

I walk up to his desk, the edge of the top gripped in my palms as I lean toward him. "Why does everyone give a shit about what Lily knows? I'm her dad, I'm all she has. I'm all that matters to her." I grab the piece of paper. "If you're not going to help me, someone else will." Taking the letter and my checkbook, I stomp off.

"You need to be reasonable," he calls out after me.

I flip him my middle finger and slam the door behind me.

32

CATERINA

"Why do people eat with these?" Lily asks, trying her hardest to use chopsticks.

"It's part of their culture," I say, positioning them in her hands the correct way for the tenth time.

"What's culture?" she asks and a noodle slips from the sticks.

"Why don't you use your fork?" I chuckle and slide it closer to her but she shakes her head.

"Nope. You use them, I want to, too." She continues to struggle with the chopsticks and I glance over to Marcus, who is staring into his General Tso's chicken, his own chopsticks just moving the pieces around.

"You okay?" I ask, placing my hand on his forearm.

He retracts his arm and hides it under the table. "I'm fine. Bad day."

"Okay," I say softly.

Lily and I discuss our day at camp and how Ben is goofy with his songs and all the dances he's always doing. She asks me about San Francisco and if I like living there. My entire dinner conversation is with a five-year-old whose only concern is picking up a piece of meat with two sticks. Marcus sits there, eating nothing, saying nothing, but hey, he's on his third beer. Stellar night.

"Can we watch a movie?" Lily asks while I'm putting the Chinese food in the fridge and placing the silverware in the dishwasher.

I toss Marcus' two empty beer bottles in the recycling and cork the bottle of wine for another time.

"Actually, you've been up a long time. How about a bath and a story and bed?"

Lily's face droops. "That sucks."

I bite my lip trying not smile. Zombie Marcus finally becomes alert.

"What did you say, Lily?" His tone is not one I've heard him use with her before. It's borderline close to anger.

"What?" she asks.

"Don't play me, you know what you said."

Lily slides away from him, her face falling. "Sucks," she says so softly a mouse would have a hard time hearing her.

"Where did you learn that word? At camp?" He pins me with an accusatory stare.

I hold my hands up in the air.

"No one," she says and then runs away and up the stairs.

"Lily!" he screams, but her footsteps on the stairs only speed up.

"Marcus, are you sure you're okay?" I ask.

Both his hands entwine on the back of his neck and he pulls hard. "I'm fucking fine."

"Look who's using the bad language now."

My words were meant to be a joke, but when he stares

up at me, it's clear he didn't take it the way I thought he would.

"What is your problem?" He moves past me and right to the fridge.

"I'm sure another beer will solve your issues," I sneer and he looks at me, shakes his head and continues to twist the bottle open.

"You have no idea," he mumbles.

"And why is that? Because you won't tell me." I cross my arms over my chest.

"It's not your concern. You wouldn't understand anyway. I wouldn't have at twenty-four." He chugs back some of his beer.

"Jeez, Marcus, you weren't complaining about how young I was when you were fucking me over the back of your living room couch the other night." Heat seeps into my cheeks as my anger gets the best of me.

If looks could kill, I might have just been stabbed to death with the death rays shooting from Marcus' eyes.

"What if Lily heard what you just said?" he says and I know I should have kept my mouth shut. Lily doesn't need to overhear that, but her door slammed as soon as she went upstairs.

"Is this about Lily's mom?"

The beer bottle cap flings across the room, landing on the kitchen counter.

"No."

"Marcus." I approach him like a Lion trainer afraid to become the prey. "I saw the letter. Lily's mom...is she in prison?"

He lifts the beer bottle to his lips, his eyes focused on me the entire time as he drains the bottle.

"Did you snoop through my stuff?" He slams the beer bottle down on the counter.

"No, it was when I was babysitting. It was on the counter in plain sight. I'm sorry, I've tried to wait, but something is clearly bothering you."

"Wait for what?" His feet start moving, back and forth between the stove and the table.

"For you to tell me what happened and stop with all the secrets surrounding her disappearance." I take a seat at the breakfast bar, hoping we can resolve whatever the issue is together. "I'm here for you."

He stops, his hands wrapping around the edge of the counter. "You're here until September."

"Give me a break, Marcus. You don't even respect me enough to tell me the truth." I'm trying to be gentle but I feel that this is going to get out of hand quickly if he doesn't relax.

"Why? What do you understand about *real* life? You live off your daddy's money, you drive a car *he* bought you. I have *real* problems. A mortgage, a business, and a daughter to raise. You think you know how I should raise my daughter? Why? What gives you the right to tell me what Lily can handle? Your art degree?" The distaste in his tone when he says the word 'art' reminds me of the first time I told my dad I wanted to be an artist—like it's unproductive and brings nothing to the world.

"If you think for one second that you're helping her by letting her think she doesn't have a mother, you're clueless. One day she's going to hate you for lying to her. As far as how I choose to live my life, it's none of your business."

I push back the stool and stand. "But isn't that the problem, Marcus? I'll always be little Caterina Santora in your eyes. You'll never look at me as an equal. You'll always see me as some young dumb girl who you have to lead through life." I round the counter, completely sick of his face at this moment. "I thought we'd put the six years behind us. I actually believed you thought I'd grown up, but I see now you just liked the way my tits and ass filled out. Or maybe it's the curve of my hips so you can grip on and drill deeper inside of me. Is that it?"

He shakes his head and points over at me. "Just don't tell me how to raise my fucking daughter!" he yells.

I back step out of the room, grabbing my purse from the back of the breakfast stool.

"I can't do this. I can't be with a man who can't be honest with me because he's not honest with himself. You're stuck, Marcus, and until you can unstick yourself, there's no room for a third person in this mix. Be careful though, at some point, Lily will realize what you've kept from her and then there might only be one."

His eyes grow hotter and he clenches his fists.

"Stop!" Lily runs down the stairs, tears streaming down her face.

The color drains from Marcus' face and he races over to her, scoops her up in his arms, and tries to soothe her to calm down.

"Stop yelling," she murmurs and his blue eyes meet mine.

Tears prick the corners of my eyes at seeing the cost of our anger on Lily. "Bye," I wave my hand in the air. "I'll see you at camp tomorrow, Lily."

She squirms out of Marcus' hold and he eventually lets her go. Her small arms wrap around my waist. "Bye, Miss Cat."

I can still hear her sniffles, and I hate that we've upset

her, but when she leaves me to go back to her dad, I know this is the best for everyone involved.

The door shuts behind me, and instead of the door to the past, it feels more like the door to my future slamming shut in my face.

33

MARCUS

I t's been three days. Seventy-five hours since I saw Cat last. I even dodged taking Lily to camp today and asked Dane because I'm a pussy and a wimp.

I was an asshole and a jerk and whatever other name you can think of.

Now, as I knock on her apartment door, my stomach churns, sweat is beading on my forehead and anyone looking at me might think I have the stomach flu from how pale I am. I'm about to ask Cat for a second chance. Strike that a third if I count six years ago.

God, I am such a dumbass.

Knock, knock.

She peeks out the side window and then the door slowly opens.

"Hey," I say, by way of a lame ass greeting.

"Hey." She doesn't open the door with an invitation to come in, so I bite the bullet.

"Can I come in?"

She steps out of the way as her answer, but the knob is

firmly in her grip, as though telling me she holds the power here. Which she does.

"Are your roommates home?" I ask.

"No. Charlie's at Happy Daze and Ava is wherever Ava goes. Do you want something to drink?"

"A fifth of whiskey would be great," I joke, but other than a small upturn to the corner of her lips, she says nothing.

"Sit down." She does so herself, taking a seat in the far corner of the sofa.

I sit on her couch, leaving an empty cushion between us. Oddly familiar to the first time I barged in here. In many ways, I wish we could be back there.

"Listen." My fingers knot together as I rest my forearms on my legs. "Lily's mom, Gretchen, is in a maximum-security prison for armed robbery."

She doesn't gasp or even react at all, so I continue. "Gretchen and I were never meant to stay together. I found out she was pregnant with Lily the same night you came on to me six years ago. After not having any real relationship with my father my entire life, I wanted to make it work. Make a family work. Gretchen moved down to Climax Cove and I thought we were doing okay. I mean, I wasn't head over heels about her and we fought a lot, but I figured it was the stress of having a baby. When Lily showed up it got worse. Gretchen was so withdrawn. Motherhood was stressful on her. She couldn't handle it."

I glance over to make sure she's still with me. Her legs are crossed and her hands are also fisted together as she listens.

"Anyway, when Lily was two months old, I got a babysitter and we went back up to Portland to a buddy's party. Gretchen needed a break and I thought it would help her relax, realize there's still lots of fun to be had even if you're a mother. I figured it might help the two of us to reconnect since that's where we'd met originally. My buddy gave Gretchen what I thought was a joint but it was laced with cocaine."

"And she got hooked," she finishes for me.

I nod. "She started making more trips up to Portland and eventually I clued in, but by the time I admitted it to myself, heroin was her drug of choice. Lily was three months old when I gave Gretchen the free pass she wanted —to abandon us in Climax Cove and get on with her party girl lifestyle. But Cat," I turn my head to lock gazes with her, "I've always blamed myself for the fact that Lily doesn't have her mother in her life. Because of that one joint, her entire life spiraled out of control. Three years ago, she was desperate for her next score and she held up a liquor store with a loaded gun."

There, it's out. I squeeze my eyes shut again and when I open them to my surprise she meets my eyes. "It was never about not letting you in, Cat, it was about me being ashamed. I never wanted you to look at me like a failure or like I let Lily down."

She slides closer and places her hand on mine. "I would never think that. You might have taken her to the party, but you didn't make her smoke the joint. If she knew she was developing a problem she could have reached out for help." She squeezes my hand and her easy acceptance of the situation makes me wonder why I didn't do this to begin with. I should've trusted in what we had.

"The night we fought…" Her gaze leaves mine for a second and she looks away. "What had you so worked up?"

I let out a long sigh. "Gretchen wants Lily to visit her at the prison. She's involved a lawyer and I'd gotten the letter that day. I'm sorry for everything I said. I couldn't stop thinking about how it would affect Lily if I had to drag her up to the prison every month to visit a woman she doesn't even know." I remove my hands from under hers and stare into her eyes so she knows how truthful I'm being. "I don't see you as a young girl, Cat. I see you as a woman. And I don't think your art is silly, I think it's amazing. You're one of the lucky few who is able to follow their passion and make a living from it."

She nods as a slow tear trickles down her cheek. I use my thumb to brush the tear away as my stomach clenches over the fact that I'm the cause of it.

"I want us to try again," I say and hold my breath waiting for her to say something.

She's quiet for a moment and my anxiety grows until it's a hard rock in my throat that I can't swallow past. "I appreciate you saying that and I accept your apology. But Marcus, I don't think you're ready to allow someone in yet. You're so scared of someone hurting you and Lily. I get it, I do. Lily's heart matters most."

Panic seizes me. "I'm not afraid anymore, Cat. These last few days have been agonizing and all I've wanted to do is hold you."

She nods a smile gracing those lips I love so much.

"I have to thank you," she says.

I crease my forehead in confusion.

"These past weeks have helped me realize that what I want is to settle down and have a family. I don't want to live in a city where no one knows who I am. I want to give myself to someone and share a future with them, but it's not just us here, Marcus. It's Lily. Unless you can stand here and look me in the eyes and admit that you trust me one hundred percent with Lily's heart, there's no point in continuing our relationship."

My gaze skirts down. She's asking for the one thing I'm not sure I could ever give anyone again. Gretchen had that trust and look what happened. I'm reminded every time Lily asks about her mom or stares avidly at another daughter and mother interact that my mistakes have consequences— for my daughter.

"You're looking for certainty," I say.

"I'm searching for faith. I need all of you, Marcus, not just half of you. I get that Lily comes first, but I refuse to be a cast-off. Either you step in the circle with me or not." Another tear slips down her face because we both know, what she's asking me to do is damn near impossible for me.

"I do trust you. I can do this," I fight, although it comes out weak and with less conviction than I would've liked.

She shifts her body away from my side. My gut twists and my head screams to tell her how I feel. That I'm going to lose the best thing I ever had, but my heart cinches desperately grasping onto the past, unable to open to the depths Cat wants it to.

"Until you can look me in the eye and I see no doubt, there is no us, Marcus." She stands and walks silently to the door.

I meet her there a moment later. "You're looking for me to march in on a white horse."

She huffs and smiles. "Yes, I am."

"It's fairy tale, fiction, not real." I shake my head. "Princes and princesses don't have bills and differing career goals. Love can't conquer all in the real world, Cat."

She shrugs. "It doesn't change what I want."

"The prince confessing his love."

"No," she shakes her head. "I want a man who has two feet in my circle. One who can't breathe without me. One who trusts me not to hurt him."

I shake my head, disagreeing with her on the realities of life. I step out her door and turn to see her standing with the knob in her palm once more.

"I'm not sure I'm him."

"Then I wait for him."

The door shuts and all my hopes for what might happen here tonight come crashing down.

SULKING after my conversation with Cat, I end up at Happy Daze with a Blue Moon in my hand courtesy of Charlie, who's being a little snippy to me. She made me pay instead of putting it on my tab and then proceeded to shove my tip back at me, saying she didn't want my money.

Solidarity sister.

"You're making a mistake," Garrett chimes in across from me, his eyes focused on the Giants game.

"You're the one who told me to think about Lily. Make sure she doesn't get hurt."

"See, you took this too far." Dane shakes his head like I'm an idiot. "The sleepovers were too much. You gotta nail her and then get the hell outta Dodge. Otherwise they get feelings and they want more." He's rolling his eyes, his head bouncing from side to side.

"You do love her, right?" Garrett again, asking the deep questions. When the hell did he become the Dr. Phil of the group?

"I'm not sure I've ever been in love," I confess. I thought maybe I might be with Gretchen once upon a time, but if I truly loved her I wouldn't have set her free, I would have fought for her.

"Bullshit." Garrett takes his eyes off the television.

"You guys are getting way too sentimental here." Dane stands and goes to the bar to talk with Charlie who's trying to not stare at Garrett. He snaps his fingers in front of her dazed gaze focused in Garrett's direction and she blinks and shakes her head, re-joining us on planet Earth.

"You loved Sydney's mom, right? How did you know?" I ask.

He shrugs. "You just know. You're in denial." He tips his beer in my direction. "You gotta get the Gretchen thing under control, first. You've got too many balls in the air. Control one."

Dane sits back down, handing Garrett a beer. "Courtesy of Charlie." Dane nods in her direction. Garrett follows his line of vision then turns back.

Dane looks at me and rolls his eyes. "He'll never see it." I shrug, not in the mood to bust each other's balls like usual.

Garrett's attention is back on the Giants game now.

"I know I don't want this to end with Cat. I like her, I do."

"You need to admit that like is love, Marcus." Garrett swivels in his seat. "You let her spend the night after your second date. You had sex in your house with Lily home. You've made her dinner. You've taken her to your favorite hiking trail. These are all things you've never done with anyone else." His gruff tone is pleading with me to see the light. "You love the girl, you're just scared that she'll wake up one day and wonder why the hell she's in this small town. She's not Gretchen, man."

"Did you know that Cat placed some of her paintings in the summer art festival?" Dane asks and I shake my head. I've never even seen a piece of art she's done. "How about that she's doing an art lesson one Thursday a month down at the craft store?"

I shrug. And then wonder how Dane knows all this shit and I don't.

"That she worked with Betty to get a few more art books into the library for people who want to learn to paint and draw," Garrett chimes in.

"She likes this town and I think you're so worried she feels trapped you haven't seen how much she's embraced all the reasons you love living here," Dane says.

I shake my shoulders. "Jesus, when did you guys become so talky-feely?"

They both stare dead at me. "Deal with your shit, Marcus. Fix the Gretchen crap, and then go win over your girl." Dane is giving me the same gears now. "I'll find you a white pickup truck somewhere to drive off into happily ever after land."

As I contemplate their words of advice, much of it ringing true, I know they're right about the one thing. Gretchen needs to be dealt with.

Dane is nice enough to take Lily to camp again so I can be standing where I am—outside the prison gates.

The guards let me in and once I'm through all the standard practices of going in to visit an inmate, I sit at a table waiting for Gretchen. My leg taps on the floor while my fingers tap on the table. I'm not sure I'll even recognize her. It's been years since I've seen her.

A guard opens a door and five women file out, four of them with smiles. Apprehension radiates off the fifth woman as she walks across the room.

Gretchen looks the same, only years older. Her once glowing skin is now pale with a greyish hue. Her round face now seems sunken. Her shiny long blonde hair is now dull and cut to her chin. Even with her difference in appearance, I still can pinpoint every feature Lily shares with her mother.

I stand when she nears.

"Hi," I say.

"Marcus." My name almost comes off her tongue curtly,

and I'm two seconds away from turning around and forget-
ting this entire thing.

We both sit down and my leg bounces uncontrollably.

"Still have that nervous twitch?" she asks, with a small,
teasing smile on her face.

I stop my leg from moving and decide to get right to it.
"Why do you think Lily should come here?" I look around at
the guards posted at every entrance. Her in her orange
jumpsuit. The hard-plastic chairs. The dreary gray concrete
covering every surface. "What kind of mother-daughter
bonding do you expect to happen? Mommy and daughter
cavity searches? Bonding over metal detectors? Do you want
her to ask the guard why her mommy can't leave with us?"

I'll admit, my tone is mean and spiteful, revealing just
how much the anger still burns like a hot coal inside of me.

"I want to know my daughter and most of all I want her
to know me." Her voice is low and meek and has lost all the
toughness from her original greeting.

"This is hardly the environment." I motion to the space
around us.

Her gaze focuses down on the table.

"How are things in here?" I'm not sure why I care or why
I'm asking, but I'm curious.

"I've grown used to it," she shrugs. "I'm clean," she adds
hastily.

"I've seen shows where things get snuck in."

She rolls her eyes. "I'm clean, Marcus. I get why you'd
question it, but I've worked hard and I have it together."

"What happens when you get outside that barbed wire
fence?"

Sure, it's not hard to stay clean when a shot of heroin
isn't on every street corner you pass. None of your dealers or
friends tempting you to take one last hit. I'll just get Lily

attached to her and then she'll get out and I'll be explaining how an overdose works.

"I guess we'll see in thirteen years."

Sometimes I forget she carries such a heavy sentence, but that's what happens when the person you rob a store with fires the weapon. Gretchen had a gun too, probably with no expectation to use it, although she was so addicted back then I don't really know.

"Maybe you'll get parole."

She shrugs and brushes the idea off. "Do you have a picture of her?" She glances to my pocket. "Just one so I can see her?"

She sounds so hopeful that I pull out my wallet and pull out the picture they took at daycare last year. I slide it over and the guard approaches.

"He's just showing me a picture." She holds up the photo with worn edges so he can see. "That's my daughter, Lily." Tears fill her eyes.

"She's very pretty." The huge guard looks at me when he says it.

"She has my hair. Do you have a girlfriend? Is that who does her hair?"

"I do her hair. I do everything for her," I say with a good dose of bitterness.

Because you couldn't stick around to handle it.

"Tell me what she likes. Is she funny or shy? Does she have a lot of friends?"

As she hammers me with questions, I think about what it would be like if I were the one who didn't know Lily. I'd be lost.

"She's funny and very outgoing, which she probably gets from you."

"She's not the controlled and silent type?" She smiles,

teasing me.

"I manage not to squeeze all the fun out of her. She meets friends everywhere she goes. She loves princesses, Rapunzel is her favorite. She's just...she's a loving, sweet little girl."

I slide the picture back into my wallet then clasp my hands together on top of the table.

Silence stretches out between us for a minute before I speak. "I'm sorry, Gretchen."

She looks up at me with tear stricken cheeks and red eyes. "You have nothing to be sorry for."

"I took you to Brent's. I didn't stop you from smoking that joint. I sure as hell didn't get you any help."

Her hand lands on top of mine and I resist the urge to pull back. I see that her once manicured nails are now short and brittle, her nail beds scabby as though she picks at them all day long.

"Marcus, you didn't put the needle in my arm. You sure as hell didn't keep going back to get me my fix. You mentioned rehab a few times, but even if you would've strapped me in the car, drove me there, I never would have stayed. I was so far gone." She shakes her head at herself and I can tell she's reliving some memory. "I robbed a store at gunpoint."

I nod, knowing how bad she got, but that hasn't stopped me from feeling like I was the one who struck the match in the first place.

"I can't believe you've held on to this guilt. I had no idea." She pushes her hands through her dull hair. "You have nothing to do with where I am now. I should've been around to help raise Lily beside you...that's the path I should have taken." She removes her hand from mine and wipes at the tears streaming down her face.

"I can't bring her here, Gretch." My voice cracks imagining my little girl being haunted by guards and metal detectors. "How about we start with the two of you exchanging letters?"

Her shoulders fall and she slumps down in her seat. "You have no idea how badly I want to hold her."

I do. I do because I feel the same way sometimes when she's only been away from me for a few hours.

"I'm not saying never. It's just—" I glance around the room again. "Not yet. She's too young to understand any of this."

A tear drops onto the grey plastic table and my own eyes squeeze shut. Somehow in all these years of pushing Gretchen away, it never seemed real. She didn't seem like the woman I once thought I could love. She was enemy number one the minute she walked out on Lily and it isn't until this very minute, that I've ever seen her as Lily's mom.

I reach out and cover her hands with my own and she looks over to me with bloodshot eyes. "I promise, if you write letters, she'll get every one of them. I'll send you pictures of her and if Lily wants, I'll forward any pictures she draws or anything else she asks me to."

"Okay," she says in a small voice.

"So, the attorney?"

"I'll call him off." She draws in a deep breath. "We'll do this together if you promise to work with me. I know this isn't stellar, but all I want is to be a part of her life somehow."

My hands tighten over hers. "We'll make it work...together."

A bell rings and one of the guards announces our time is up. We stand and I'm ready to say goodbye having a clear plan of what I need to do.

"I'll be in touch."

She rushes into my arms. "Thank you, Marcus."

I stand there, my arms at my sides until I catch the sight of the guard who Gretchen showed Lily's picture to and I lightly pat her back.

"Thank you, Gretchen. Thank you for doing what's best for Lily."

It's all I've ever tried to do myself and I'm starting to see that sometimes what's right might involve taking a risk that things don't turn out the way we want them to.

———

LILY and I walk into her favorite restaurant, Pho Shizzle.

"Can I have two kinds of noodles?" she asks, jumping into the booth.

Pho Shizzle is known for anything to do with noodles— from spaghetti to lo mein. All different kinds of noodles cooked on a flat top grill.

"You can get whatever you want."

"Even a shake?" Her eyes light up in excitement.

"Even a shake." She can have whatever she wants because I'm about to turn her world upside down.

Angela, the waitress, comes over.

"Lily!" she exclaims and Lily beams, loving the extra attention. "What are you getting today?"

"I want the white sauce noodles and the crispy ones."

Angela jots it down.

"And an Oreo shake," Lily adds and Angela glances over to me for permission.

I nod.

"And for you, Mr. Kent?"

"I'll have just the Korean with steak and a water, please."

"Comin' right up." She smiles and heads back to give our order to the kitchen.

As we wait for the food to come, I fiddle with the Parmesan cheese shaker wondering how to bring the subject of her mother up.

"Lily?"

She looks up from clinking the fork and spoon together.

"I wanted to talk to you about your mom."

The silverware drops to the table.

"Miss Cat?" The hopeful expression on her face guts me.

"No." I shake my head. "No. What do you mean Miss Cat?"

Lily tilts her head to the side. "Isn't she my mom? I told you I wanted her to be my mom."

Oh shit, I royally fucked this up.

"No, sweetie, she's not."

Her fingers brush the bracelet on her wrist and she sits back in the booth, too far for me to be able to reach her. "Oh."

"You have a mom who loves you very much, but she can't see you right now."

Her eyes light up a little. "Where is she?"

"She's away, but she wants to write to you. In fact, she's already written you some letters." I place two of them on the table and slide them over.

"Really?" She props up on her knees, her tiny hands grabbing at the envelopes.

"Would you like to see a picture of her?" I ask.

"Yeah." The smile on her face matches the one she normally has on Christmas morning.

I slide a picture of Gretchen and I from when we first started dating across the table.

"Is that you?" She points to a much younger and less groomed version of myself.

"That's your daddy."

She looks from me to the picture, her finger grazing over Gretchen. "She's pretty," she says.

"Just like you."

Her smile grows wider. "Thanks, Daddy."

She sits back in the booth, holding the picture in front of her, just staring at it.

Angela brings over our meals and I start eating while Lily processes the information.

"You okay, sweetie?" I ask, spooning some noodles into my mouth.

She nods and places the picture and envelopes on the table. "So, I'll meet her someday?"

"Yeah, someday."

She nods, her small brain trying to process the information. "Okay."

"Lil," I ask for her attention one more time.

She forks up a heaping pile of crispy noodles and looks up to me.

"I really like Miss Cat."

She smiles over her mouthful. "I know." She mumbles.

"I'd like Miss Cat to live with us."

Her eyes light up again and she swallows down the noodles in her mouth. "Really? Like she'd be my mommy?"

"Another mommy, yes." Her knees bounce up and down on the bench.

"I like Miss Cat, too." Her voice is giddy.

"So, you're okay if we make her part of our family?"

"Yeah!" She bounces up and down on her knees.

"Daddy made some mistakes and she's really mad at me right now. It might be a while before she forgives me."

"Daddy," she says in a voice that says I'm the silliest daddy in the world. "When I make a mistake you always tell me to say sorry to the person. That should work."

I smile at her innocence. "Will you help me win her over? We have to ask her really nice."

"Let's do it, Daddy!"

We devise a plan as we finish our meals.

I don't feel bad about suggesting Cat will be part of our family to my daughter without knowing the outcome because I do know how things will turn out. I'm not going to rest until that woman is mine again in every sense of the word.

35

CATERINA

For the last week, I've dreaded the drop-off and pick up from camp. Lucky for me, Marcus is a coward and has left Dane in charge of Lily's comings and goings. Not that I should expect more of him. I practically told him I wanted to stay in Climax Cove, have his babies and be a mommy to Lily, and he ran. Like I knew he would. The man trusts no one.

"My daddy isn't here yet." Lily comes up to me as I'm pinning up some of the art the kids have worked on all summer around the room for their big art show.

"Isn't your Uncle Dane getting you?" I stop the taping and stapling, seeing now that she's the only one still here.

"No, Daddy is coming." She sits in the chair and strokes her bracelet a few times. "Miss Cat?"

"Yeah, kiddo?"

"How come you never come over anymore? I miss you." She's frowning and looking down at her bracelet.

My heart shatters and this is a good reminder of why Marcus is so careful. After only being in their lives a short time, Lily's become confused.

"I miss you, too," I say.

"How come you don't come over then?" Her fingers rub the bracelet again.

"Your daddy and I have just been so busy." It's a lame excuse, but it's all I've got.

Marcus enters the cabin and I swear all oxygen leaves my lungs. He's in jeans and a t-shirt that stretches around his lean muscles looking as suave and sexy as he always does.

"Daddy!" Lily runs over and he scoops her up in his arms.

"Hey, sweetie." He gives her a big kiss.

I watch the exchange, admiring their relationship. The small, protected bubble they've created for themselves and the yearning to be a part of that has me clutching my chest.

"Hey, Uncle Dane is waiting outside with Toby. He has a surprise for you."

She wiggles until he drops her feet to the ground and then she jets off running out the door. "Bye, Miss Cat. See you tomorrow."

She's left me and Marcus to share the small amount of oxygen left in the room.

He walks closer and I step back. "Can we talk?" he says, with that deep rumble of his voice that resonates deep inside my bones.

"No." I place my hand in front of me.

"Please. I talked to Lily's mom a couple of days ago."

"That's good. I'm glad you got whatever you wanted out of it." The smirk on his lips says he did, but that's none of my concern.

"I'm sorry, Cat."

My back hits the wall and he stops his advance.

"Is this your piece?" He stops stalking toward me and

hovers over the metal tree sculpture I finished up earlier today.

"Yes." Having room to breathe, I step away, half tempted to take my piece and hide it from him because it feels so personal.

He and Lily were my inspiration.

"What's it called?" he asks.

"Blended."

Our eyes lock and I pray for the tears that are pricking my eyes to disappear. I don't want him to see my reaction.

"Why are the two tree trunks intertwined?" His fingers run along the metal branches with tiny leaves hanging off them.

"Two people coming together."

"And the big red apple?"

"Lily," I say in a soft whisper.

He turns around, his hand landing on my cheek and those tears I willed away run like a river down my cheeks.

"Please, Marcus, don't."

"Don't what? Tell you that I love you?"

I shake my head and squeeze my eyes shut, more tears spilling down my face.

"Tell you that I'm a jackass who should've seen what he had under his nose this entire time?"

He steps closer and my breath catches in my throat.

"Tell you that I don't want a minute to go by without you in my life?"

"You said it yourself, we're going in two different directions." I can barely get the words out past the painful lump in my throat.

"We're going to New York with you." He smiles.

I shake my head and he nods his.

"That's what you don't understand, I don't want to go to

New York. I can work anywhere, but Climax Cove is Lily's home. She's number one, remember?"

"Cat, I don't care. She'll be fine as long as she has us." He holds his hand up for me to take and I stare at it for a moment.

"You're sure?" I ask in a small voice, but I already know the answer, it's there in his eyes.

He nods.

"Well, then I think she'll be even better if she has the two of us in Climax Cove." I take his hand in mine and he pulls me into his arms.

"I love you, Cat. I'm sorry it took me so long to realize it." His arms wrap around my waist.

The rush of love from his words makes me feel euphoric. "Maybe older isn't always wiser."

He laughs, his one hand cupping my cheek.

"Ew, they're doing the kissy-kissy thing!" Lily screams.

"At least it's PG," Dane jokes.

We look toward the door to find we have an audience.

"I was half expecting to come in here and see Marcus' groin cleavage on display." Dane laughs at his own joke while Ava covers Lily's ears and shoots him a scathing look.

Marcus untangles himself from me, holding my hand as he bends down. "Come on, Lily."

She runs up and right into his arms. With her in his left, his right arm wraps around my waist pulling me into him. "She forgave you?" Lily asks and everyone laughs.

"She forgave me."

Lily opens her arms and I step in, her arm wrapping around my neck.

For the first time in forever, my heart feels like it's found home.

MARCUS

Later that night...

I LISTEN outside Lily's room as Cat says goodnight to Lily. They chat about the art show at camp and some of the other kids.

"Oh, Lily, I have your bracelet." Cat must pull it out of her pocket. I briefly remember Lily handing it to her when she was playing in the sandbox this evening.

"I don't need it anymore."

"You don't?" I hear the crack in Cat's voice.

"Nope. Miss Cat?"

"Yeah?"

"Thanks for forgiving my daddy."

I stifle a laugh since I was under strict instructions from Lily not to eavesdrop. Hey, sometimes you can't let your kids dictate the rules.

"You're welcome."

"Miss Cat?"

"Yeah?" I hear the enthusiasm in Cat's voice waning.

"Can I call you Cat?"

"You can call me anything you want, Lily."

"Mommy?"

"Yeah," Cat says and now there's a quiver in her voice.

"That's good?" Lily asks.

"That's perfect. Good night, Lily."

There's some rustling of bed sheets and I picture Cat bending over to kiss Lily on the forehead. She walks out of the room a minute later and swipes a tear from her cheek.

I take her hand and pull her into my bedroom.

"So, here are the rules. No flowers and no pink."

"Are you dictating how to decorate your bedroom?" Cat falls onto the bed and I join her, placing my arm around her waist.

"Our bedroom, baby, *our* bedroom."

It's funny how one tiny word can mean so much.

It isn't until later after we've made love and we're laying in bed, my eyes seconds from closing for the night, that Cat bolts up with the sheet pressed against her chest. "Oh, my God! Groin Cleavage." She stares over to me, her eyes wide with a realization I don't quite understand. "This has disaster written all over it."

EPILOGUE

MARCUS

Two years later…

"What's taking Mom so long?" Lily asks, sitting at the breakfast bar, sliding her eggs around her plate.

It's the first day of camp. Now that Cat and I are married, she no longer qualifies for Camp Tall Pines, but Vic opened another camp close to it that any kid can attend.

"She's in her studio, but she'll be out in a second."

After Cat moved in, I converted my office into a studio and built it out. The only remnant of my original office is the leather sofa she kept for the memories. It still gets a workout every now and then.

"I can't be late, Dad."

I hate this whole Mom and Dad thing and it wasn't until she stopped calling me Daddy that I missed hearing the word.

"You won't be late."

The doorbell rings and Lily jumps off the stool to answer it. Anything to dodge the breakfast on her plate.

Ava is outside the door with a box of her cupcakes. I open the door and she raises her hand up for Lily to high five.

"What's up, girl? You ready for camp?"

Lily follows Ava into the house.

"Why are you bringing us cupcakes?" I ask.

Ava places the box on the counter and turns her sassy self my way. "I'm bringing Lily cupcakes."

She bends down and smiles at Lily, whose hand reaches toward the pink box immediately.

"No, no. Eat your eggs." I point to the plate, grabbing her brush off the counter.

"Has anyone told you that you have horrible timing?" I cock my eyebrow at Ava and she laughs.

"There's always time for sweets. They warm the heart." Ava grabs a cup from the cupboard and fills it with coffee.

"Is that your slogan?" I chuckle.

She sits down on the breakfast stool next to Lily.

"You might not want to admit it but those cupcakes are about to make your day." She relaxes back. "Where's the lady of the house anyway?"

"Inspiration hit at three this morning." I shrug my shoulders. "Lily, turn around so I can do your hair."

Lily grabs the brush from my hands. "I got it. Jeez, Dad, I'm seven now."

I hold my hands up in the air, sharing a look with Ava, who's amused.

"Yeah, Marcus, she's seven, and that's nine years from driving a car and only eleven until she leaves us for college."

Cat appears in the kitchen and my heart skips a beat, which is normal whenever she's near me.

"Mom, I can't be late for camp." Lily directs all her attention on Cat as she joins us in the kitchen.

Cat's eyes flicker to the plate of eggs and she shakes her head. "Morning, Ava, you're the grand prize winner to witness the crazy Kent morning. First we argue about eating eggs and then we proceed to bicker until everyone goes their separate ways."

The wide smile on Cat's lips tells me she's being sarcastic. I wasn't ready for the drama to start so soon with Lily, but Cat constantly reminds me she's just growing older and with age comes independence. And dramatics apparently.

I hand my wife a cup of coffee and she places it on the counter, her eyes on the box.

"Two forkfuls and you get a cupcake before camp." She leans over the counter and whispers to Lily.

Lily hurriedly forks two small amounts into her mouth and chews, swallowing it with her orange juice.

"See what happens here, Ava?" I motion between the two women in my life.

She laughs. "I'm looking. Cat's like a kid herself." She sets down the cup on the counter. "I gotta get going, you know I have my own morning routine to get back to."

Cat rounds the counter and hugs her, whispering to her and they share a laugh.

"Enjoy those cupcakes," she says to Lily, kissing the top of her head.

"Bye, Aunt Ava." Lily sits antsy in her chair, staring at the box of cupcakes like Justin Bieber is about to pop out.

"Bye. And there's a special one in there for you, Marcus." She points to the box.

"I already had my kale smoothie and toast, but thanks."

Ava's laugh disappears as the front door clicks closed behind her.

"Can I open the box now?" Lily climbs onto her knees on the stool, leaning forward on the breakfast bar.

Cat comes back over to my side, her head falling on my chest. The smell of her coconut shampoo rousing the need I had for her when I woke up this morning, but I never bother her when she's working. Well, strike that, we've had our fair share of fun with clay, and paint, but I try to wait to be invited instead of interrupting.

"Go ahead." She nods at the box.

Lily is already familiar with Ava's packaging so she's able to manipulate the tape and insert in zero seconds flat. Then she stands there, frozen, looking down at the cupcakes. Her eyes peer over the open box, right to Cat.

"Mom?"

"Yes, sweetie."

She jumps off the stool and runs into the two of us, squeezing Cat around the waist. Cat's hand goes to her chaotic blonde hair, the sun glinting off the diamond ring that adorns Cat's left hand.

My family, nothing better.

Lily stares up to Cat with tears in her eyes and I clue in that they're sharing some type of moment I'm not a part of.

"All this over cupcakes?" I ask.

Lily wipes the tears and walks back to her stool, climbing up and turning the box around so I can see it.

Six cupcakes, three pink, three blue with a sign on the inside of the box congratulating Lily on being a big sister.

My eyes shift to Cat leaning against the counter. I place my hand on her flat stomach.

"Really?" I ask, my heart soaring to heights I didn't even know were possible.

We'd discussed a baby after we got married, but I told

Cat she needed to get her art career off the ground. That I wouldn't allow her to sacrifice the career she loves.

Her two hands land on my cheeks and she stares into my eyes. "Don't be mad. I went off the pill last month."

"How could I be mad?" I rub her belly and her own hand covers mine, both of us staring down at our joined hands.

"And I really wanted to surprise you."

"I'm surprised." My mind boggles with everything that I need to do to the house to have it ready for a baby.

"I love you," she says, placing a sweet kiss on my lips.

I swivel her around so her back is to the counter and I press a little firmer on her lips. "I think Jack can handle the shop today. How about we come back here after camp drop off?"

My eyes glance to the clock, seeing we're going to be late if we don't leave soon. "We have to go." I swipe my keys from the counter.

"Oh, Lily, let's get the frosting off your face. Does pink mean you want a baby sister?" Cat asks, wetting a paper towel and cleaning her face off.

Cat grabs the brush, trying to get it through Lily's blonde tangles, all while we shuffle to the door. A ponytail holder in her mouth, she finger combs Lily's hair into a neat ponytail. I guess seven doesn't count when it's your mom helping you out with your hair. Noted.

"Hey, Mom and Dad?" Lily asks as I hold her backpack out for her to put her arms through.

"Yeah?" we answer in unison.

"Where do babies come from?"

We both freeze and stare at one another over her head while she struggles to put on her backpack.

I point to Cat who holds up her hands in the air shaking her head frantically.

"Your turn," I say, holding the door open for the two women in my life, well, maybe three.

I smile to myself as they both climb in the truck. Life has never been sweeter.

Sometimes it pays to take chances, even if you're a control freak like me—some people are worth the risk.

The End

COCKAMAMIE UNICORN RAMBLINGS

Maybe you're wondering where the idea for the Single Dads Club series came from? No, well scroll down a paragraph or two. Yes? Okay, we're gonna give up the goods. Basically, Piper is a perv. LOL We're kidding. Sort-of.

Picture it...it's the summer of 2016. Piper is picking her kids up from day camp. All the children are sitting in groups with their camp counselors waiting for the parents to claim their rug rat. That's when Piper notices that there are A LOT of really good looking male camp counselors. We're not talking average, run of the mill good looks either. We're talking Abercrombie & Fitch models. For real.

So Piper's mind wanders as it often does. The first thing she thought? Damn if I was a college-aged girl I'D LOVE working here all summer. The second thought? I can only imagine the kind of shenanigans this group of counselors is going to get into over the summer. The third thought? I have to call Rayne and tell her we need to base a story around a summer camp and the hot guys that work there.

Clearly we massaged the idea a bit and instead of having

the guys work there, we had them be the parents dropping off the kids. Then we expanded some more and created the small town of Climax Cove in our minds and made sure all the action didn't just happen on campgrounds. Because really, who wants a twig poking you in the ass when you're trying to get it on?

After we had all the guys stories laid out in our mind we started thinking about covers. Pouring over picture after picture of hot guys and deciding which ones would be perfect to represent our character is a tough job, but we were happy to do it. 😊

But seriously, we've heard a bunch of you love Marcus' cover and we can't wait to unveil the other two. We're curious to see which of the three Single Dads Club covers are your favorite! Rayne is obsessed with the Real Deal cover and Piper's still drooling over the Sexy Beast cover. The handful of people we've shown all three covers to seem to favor Dirty Talker. We think it's the groin cleavage. It's ALL about the groin cleavage, unicorns.

We heard you when you said you wanted more of the Modern Love crew, and though we do have more planned for them in the future, we figured out a way to incorporate each of the couples from that series, into this new one. So keep your eyes peeled in future books for more of your favs.

As we write this we have NO idea how the Single Dads Club series will be received by readers. It's hard going from a series that most readers seemed to love into a new world. We're hopeful that we didn't disappoint and if you're on the fence please...keep reading! We love each story in this series more than the one before it. Dane lives up to his name in Dirty Talker and Garrett...our macho, brooding man has some secrets yet to be revealed.

We couldn't have pulled this off without the help of the

following people to whom we are grateful to have in our corner.

Letitia from RBA Designs for the amazing covers and for putting up with how nitpicky we can be.

Ellie from Love N Books for line editing when she was suffering from a bad back. Not a reason any girl wants to spend days on end lying on her back in bed. 😊

Shawna from Behind the Writer for her eagle eye proofreading skills and for comments like, "This sentence makes no sense."

Melissa Saneholtz for all her PR and KU wisdom.

Enticing Journey Book Promotions for working with us on this one.

All the bloggers who carved out time to promote us and/or read and review the book.

Michelle New for yet another set of killer graphics on a short timeline.

Our first readers of a really shitty, unedited copy—Heather and Angela.

Christine from Type A Formatting for such a pretty paperback.

All our early ARC readers, first for wanting to read our stuff early and for posting their reviews.

And last but in no way least, all our unicorns. <3 Your enthusiasm for our work knows no bounds. From sharing unicorn paraphernalia in our reader group and shouting from the rooftops to anyone who will listen that they should read our work. The best part of this new endeavor has been having you in our corner!

We can't wait for you to read Dane and Garrett's stories. They have SO much more to say!

xo,

Piper & Rayne

P.S. – If you're a unicorn and you thought you saw your name in between these pages, that wasn't an accident! And if you didn't see it this time, who knows? Maybe your name will make it into the next book. ❤

P.P.S. – Fun fact...the cover model's name is Marcus and though we tried and tried to give him another name we just could not seem to not call him anything other than Marcus when we were plotting the book out. And so, Marcus he remained.

ABOUT THE AUTHOR

Piper Rayne, or Piper and Rayne, whichever you prefer because we're not one author, we're two. Yep, you get two USA Today Bestselling authors for the price of one. Our goal is to bring you romance stories that have "Heart-warming Humor With a Side of Sizzle" (okay...you caught us, that's our tagline). A little about us... We both have kindle's full of one-clickable books. We're both married to husbands who drive us to drink. We're both chauffeurs to our kids. Most of all, we love hot heroes and quirky heroines that make us laugh, and we hope you do, too.

Goodreads
Facebook
Instagram
Pinterest
Bookbub
www.piperrayne.com

Join our newsletter and get 2 FREE BOOKS!
http://bit.ly/2tsNcpP

Be one of our UNICORNS and join our Facebook group!

ALSO BY PIPER RAYNE

The Modern Love World

Charmed by the Bartender

Hooked by the Boxer

Mad about the Banker

The Single Dad's Club

Real Deal

Dirty Talker

Sexy Beast

Hollywood Hearts

Mister Mom

Animal Attraction

Domestic Bliss

Bedroom Games

Cold as Ice

On Thin Ice

Break the Ice

Box Set

Charity Case

Manic Monday

Afternoon Delight

Happy Hour

Blue Collar Brothers

Flirting with Fire

Crushing on the Cop

Engaged to the EMT

The Baileys

Lessons from a One-Night Stand

Advice from a Jilted Bride

Birth of a Baby Daddy

Operation Bailey Wedding (Novella)

Falling for My Brother's Best Friend

Demise of a Self-Centered Playboy

Confessions of a Naughty Nanny

Operation Bailey Babies (Novella)

Secrets of the World's Worst Matchmaker

Winning My Best Friend's Girl

Rules for Dating your Ex

White Collar Brothers

Sexy Filthy Boss

Dirty Flirty Enemy

Wild Steamy Hook-up

The Rooftop Crew

My Bestie's Ex

A Royal Mistake

The Rival Roomies